# the heat seekers

Books by Zane

# the
# heat seekers

---

## zane

ATRIA BOOKS

New York London Toronto Sydney Singapore

Copyright © 2002 by Zane

All rights reserved, including the right to reproduce this book or portions thereof in any form whatsoever. For information address Atria Books, 1230 Avenue of the Americas, New York, NY 10020

ISBN: 0-7434-4289-X

ATRIA BOOKS is a trademark of Simon & Schuster, Inc.

*Designed by Jaime Putorti*

Printed in the U.S.A.

*This novel is dedicated to my parents, who I affectionately call LIB and JIM. You are the original heat seekers, because if you had not sought out the heat in one another nearly fifty years ago, my siblings and I never would have existed, God never would have blessed me with this talent, and not even a single word of this novel would have ever been written. This book truly belongs to you.*

# acknowledgments

First and foremost, I must thank the Lord for every single day that He grants me on this earth to rejuvenate and continue my thoughts from the previous day's journey. Secondly, I must thank my parents for their support, encouragement, and understanding when it comes to my sometimes confusing and always time-consuming goals. My deepest gratitude goes to my children for giving me a reason to breathe, a reason to struggle, and a reason to rejoice. I would like to express thanks and appreciation to my immediate and extended family: Charmaine, Carlita, David, Rick, Jazmin, Arianna, Ashley, Aunt Rose, Aunt Margaret, Percy, Ronita, Trey, Franklin, Renay, Bo, Alex, Alan, Brittany, Dee, Dana, Janet, Karen, Miss Maurice, Uncle Snook, Beverly, Fran, Aunt Cle, Aunt Jennie, Carl Jr., Phil, and everyone else in the enormous family tree. That includes my honorary family members in Kannapolis, North Carolina.

Sara Camilli, my literary agent, thank you as always for everything that you do to ensure that my career flourishes and for leading me down the correct paths. Thank you for the daily pep talks, even on the weekends, and for concerning yourself with my children when you have so many other things to do. Hopefully, my son will get that novel written in 2002 somewhere between skateboarding and his electric guitar, because his talent should not be wasted.

Pamela Crockett, Esq., thank you for the tremendous amount of effort you put into not only my business dealings but also our friendship. Thank you for sharing the frustration, for having my back through thick and thin, and for hanging in with me for the long haul. We share the same vision and the same ambition, and many times that keeps me moving, because failure has never been and will never be an option. Indira and Tislem have become my second set of children, and it is a delight to spend time with them. Also, a big shout-out to Tracy Crockett for hanging out with me when she comes down from NYC and for supporting my books.

Shonda Cheekes, your time is coming, and when you hit the ground running, even I will be in awe. Thank you for being there from day one and for the lengthy telephone calls to help stabilize the fifty million things that are always running through my head.

Tracy Sherrod, thanks for being such a wonderful editor and for believing in my work. I look forward to a long and prosperous future and appreciate the fact that you keep me informed about everything that involves my writing.

Thank you to the following African-American distributors for helping me become a self-published phenomenon seemingly overnight: Eric, Wendy, and Maxwell at A and B Books, Learie and Gail at Culture Plus Books, and Sam at Seaburn. Thank you to the dozens of African-American bookstores throughout the country that have lined their shelves with my titles and recommended my books to readers.

Thank you to *Black Expressions, Black Issues Book Review, Quarterly Black Review,* AALBC.com, Mosaicbooks.com, Timbooktu.com, NetNoir.com, BET.com, the RAW SISTAZ, the G.R.I.T.S., African-American Authors Helping Authors, the Nubian Chronicles, and all the other websites and book clubs both on- and off-line that have supported my books.

Thank you to the following authors for their support, whether it was something major or something you might not even remember doing: Carl Weber, Robert Fleming, Eric Jerome Dickey,

Franklin White, Marcus Majors, V. Anthony Rivers, Darrien Lee, Shonell Bacon, JDaniels, J. D. Mason, D. V. Bernard, Michelle Valentine, Delores Thorton, Karen E. Quinones Miller, Michael Presley, Laurinda Brown, Jamellah Ellis, LaJoyce Brookshire, Carol Taylor, Mark Crockett, Timmothy McCann, Alice Holman, Brandon Massey, Brian Egeston, Cydney Rax, Deirdre Savoy, Earl Sewell, Gayle Jackson Sloan, Gwynne Forster, Jacquelin Thomas, Marlon Green, Mary B. Morrison, Maxine Thompson, Pat G'Orge, Walker, Tracy Price-Thompson, Van Whitfield, Anthony Ri'chard, and William Fredrick Cooper. To all the other authors who have crossed my path, you are just as special to me, and I wish I could name every single one of you here, but I don't want my acknowledgments to be longer than my book.

Thank you to the sisterfriends who have all dealt with my eclectic personality throughout the years: Pamela Crockett and Shonda Cheekes, you get shout-outs again; Lisa Fox, Gail Kendrick, Sharon Johnson, Pamela Shannon, Cornelia Williams, Dawn Boswell, Tracy Jeter, Judy Phillips, Destiny Wood, Aliyah Bashir, and all the rest of you chicas.

Thank you to all the people who have worked so diligently to ensure that my words come to life onscreen during the past, present, and future: David "Money Train" Watts and FutureX, Keith Plummer and NI4Pics Productions, Mike Phifer, Mehki Phifer, Anthony Ri'chard and Phifer Media Management, Toya Watts and SEPIA, and everyone else that has expressed interest in my film projects.

Thank you to all the fantastic women that attend my networking/freakfest events at my home. It is such a pleasure to see dozens of women of all ages get along and compliment each other instead of engaging in the proverbial catfighting and jealous behavior. Our regular events will become legendary. Just wait and see.

Thank you to all of the book clubs, all of the bookstores, all of the vendors, all of the people on my mailing lists, all of the people that frequent my sites, and all of the people that support my efforts. Every e-mail means the world to me, whether it is two lines or two hundred. Every word is significant, and every thoughtful gesture is deeply appreciated. If I have forgotten anyone, please overlook my mistake, for I adore each and every one of you. If nobody has told you that you are loved and appreciated today, I am telling you now.

Last but definitely not least, thank you to my man, my boo, my soul mate, my baby, Wayne T. Stewart, for his loving support, encouragement, pampering, and understanding. While I realize that it is not easy dealing with an ambitious, workaholic sister like myself—on business calls after midnight, writing at three in the morning—you do it with ease. I have been in love with you since I was ten and I will be in love with you when I am a hundred. Thanks for being my heat seeker and allowing me to be yours.

A glance into a passing car.
A smile from a complete stranger.
A brief exchange in an elevator.
This is how it sometimes begins.

A seductive dance on a crowded dance floor.
A walk under the moonlight.
A phone conversation that lasts all night.
This is how it sometimes begins.

Everyone searches for it at some point in their
    lives.
The passion that will make them lose their senses.
The kisses that will entice and rejuvenate them.
They seek out the heat.

The only question is:
When they find it, can they handle it?

—Zane, 2001

# 1

## the seekers

### tempest

My hand hovered over the lighted dial pad of my cordless phone, debating about calling another sorry mofo. The first one wasn't home, and it was just as well. Giorgio was this brotha I met while I was in line at Starbucks waiting on a mocha cappuccino. He was attractive, nice and the perfect gentleman. We kicked it a few times together. Everything was kewl until I found out the nucca had six toes on his left foot. Yes, I said six damn toes. He had this miniature one hanging off the side. I discovered it one night when he treated me to a foot massage, and I decided to return the favor. Normally I would never venture to caress a man's feet, but I was being daring that night, and the shit will *never, ever, ever, ever* happen again. It freaked me out, that sixth toe, and it reminded me of that Stephen King flick, *The Dark Half.* I came to the conclusion that Giorgio had been genetically conceived as a twin but somehow swallowed his other half. For days after the gruesome discovery, I had nightmares about marrying him, waking up one morning, and seeing him standing there with a hatchet in his hand and grinning like Jack Nicholson in *The Shining*. No, that nucca had to go. I know it sounds shallow, but I would rather be safe than sorry.

I flipped through my version of the little black book, a tattered and worn four-by-six-inch plastic pink phone book with a black poodle on the cover. The only letters left from the word *address* were the *a,* the *r,* and the *e.* As I eyed the pages, a feeling of disgust overwhelmed me. So many names, so many sorry-ass mofos. And to think, I had allowed these nuccas inside my world, catered to their every desire and even performed on the parasites all the fellatio techniques I learned from that Monica chick's book, *The Complete Guide to Tongue and Jaw Maneuvering.*

Let me break it down for you.

Sorry mofo number one: Trent, a twenty-six-year-old systems analyst. Fondest memory: practicing tantric sex with him and basking in the afterglow of the numerous earth-shattering yoni (clit) massages he bestowed upon me. Most traumatic memory: walking in on him bestowing the lingam (dick) massage on his roommate Bill. I will never forget that day for as long as I live, mostly because I hurled up my partially digested lunch, kung pao chicken, all over the two of them and my favorite suit, a black wool number I snagged a great bargain on from a one-day sale at Macy's in Pentagon City Mall. I loved that suit. Damn them two homie-sexuals for ruining my shit.

There I was infatuated, with what I thought was a prime candidate for the Pussy Eater's Hall of Fame, when all along I was giving my sweet loving to a booty bandit, a rump wrangler, a sword swallower. No wonder he knew how to eat a pussy so damn good. Any man who can deep-throat nine to ten inches ought to be able to suck the lining and ovaries out of a pussy.

I shook my head in disbelief at the very thought of him, muttered an expletive, and then scratched his name out with a red Magic Marker. Goodness knows I would spread my thighs open for a three-legged baboon with one eye in the center of its forehead before I ration Trent another millimeter of puntang.

Sorry mofo number two: Hezekiel, a thirty-two-year-old produce manager at the friendly neighborhood supermarket. I know what you're thinking. What woman in her right mind would date a brotha named Hezekiel? *Sheeeeeeeiiiitttt,* every sistah I know wanted to break a piece off to his *fione* ass. As for you brothas, you shouldn't even fake the funk. If a sistah looked like Halle Berry but her name was Kizzy Kunte, you would be screaming out, "Work it, Kizzy! Work it!" in the bedroom.

Anyway, enough of defending myself. Back to the matter at hand. Fondest memory: the way he used to like to get freaky and suck on my fingers, toes, and everything in between. I don't know if it was due to his grassroots upbringing in the foothills of Kentucky or not, but the brotha was born with a platinum tongue. He told me once that he had a nipple fetish because it reminded him of milking his papa's prizewinning cow, Bessie. To hear him tell it, Bessie won the blue medal at every Kentucky State Fair for ten years in a row. Whatever it was, the brotha had mad skillz. Not skills, but *skillz.* He used to make me scream out his name in forty-two different languages. Most traumatic memory: letting him have $800 to get his BMW fixed. I gave him the money out of the goodness of my heart. It wasn't even a loan, mind you. It was a straight-up gift. Okay, I will confess. I was whipped. Tongue-whipped. At least until I found out the BMW was not even his but this beanpole anorexic bitch's. I saw the two of them cruising down at Haines Point in it while I was jogging.

The bastard had the nerve to almost run me over after his nerves got riled up from spotting me. I cussed his ass out, but all he did was haul ass and leave me in a cloud of exhaust. Even though the money was a gift, I contemplated taking his skank ass in front of Judge Judy and perjuring my ass off by claiming it was a loan so I could recoup my money. Trick ass!

Needless to say, the chances of me ever letting him suck on anything else, even my asshole, are slim to none, and Slim's scandalous ass is out of town kicking it with some hoochie at 135th and Fifth Avenue in Harlem. I put my Magic Marker to work again, and my phone book began to look like a toddler's drawing pad.

Sorry mofo number three: Scott, a twenty-nine-year-old graduate student. Fondest memory: having him recite his original poetry to me on our romantic five-day vacation at Hedonism II in Jamaica, making love in the sand under the island moon, erotic dancing to reggae music, and seeing if he could fuck me in every position known to modern man without breaking my back or putting himself in traction. Most traumatic memory: receiving my American Express bill and finding out the trifling-ass son of a Gila monster had charged the whole damn escapade on my card and neglected to mention it to me. That vacation cost me a grip, and if I ever see his venomous, hideous black behind again, I will unload my entire three-ounce can of pepper spray in his beady little eyes and finish him off with my stun gun. Twelve thousand volts to the head of his dick will set his ass straight but good. I scratched his name out so hard, I ripped the page.

Sorry mofo number four, and you are going to absolutely love this one: Kenny, a twenty-five-year-old bum extraordinaire who also happened to be my high school sweetheart and the one who busted my cherry bomb. Fondest memory: discovering the joy of sex together, sitting on the balcony of my aunt Geraldine's apartment after cramming some of her delicious soul food into our guts, and making plans for the future together. Most traumatic memory: finding out from my best friend Janessa that Aunt Geraldine and Kenny not only were knocking boots but had gotten hitched by the justice of the peace the day before he was supposed to take me to our senior prom. I figured Kenny must have been out of his fucking mind, so I asked him, "Are you out of your fucking mind?" You know what that stinking, malicious relative of Godzilla told me? He said the only reason he chose her over me was because she was on public assistance, and therefore food stamps would keep him from starving, and their rent would only be twenty dollars a month. The really sick part is that Kenny is three years younger than my cousin Marcus, Aunt Geraldine's son. I am *tooooooo* through with both of them, and I hope her old ass gets a leg cramp one night while they are fucking and ends up stuck in a pretzel shape from now until Armageddon. I ripped his old number out of my book and hers, stomped into the bathroom, and flushed them down the toilet.

I was still holding the cordless in my hand when I came back out into the living room. I tossed it on my black leather sectional and headed to the kitchen in search of the pint of double-chocolate-chip Häagen-Dazs ice cream I kept hidden in the back of my freezer especially for nights when the maggots invaded my thoughts. I don't know why I let them bother me. They were all out of my life, somewhere getting their freak on with another woman—or man, in Trent's case. Yet here I was working myself into a hissy fit over the fetid shit they did to me.

I found my ice cream, grabbed a spoon and a Pepsi, and headed to my bedroom to drown myself in sorrow. I flipped on *Jerry Springer,* got undressed, and threw on one of my home-alone nightgowns, a tee I picked up in New Carrolton Mall with *"I Just Can't Stand a Broke-Ass Man"* imprinted on both the front and back. I saved the good supply of nighties for when there was a man in the

house, a rare occurrence. I laughed at the women who were fighting over sorry-ass mofos on a talk show, but I am not sure whether
I pitied them or related to them and was really laughing at myself.
Whatever the case, I tore into my unhealthy snacks and settled in
for yet another boring Friday night.

## *janessa*

Friday night. *Millennium* night. There were only two shows I was
absolutely crazy about, other than *Jerry Springer* of course, 'cause
everyone loves *Jerry, Millennium,* and *The X-Files.* Something about
that supernatural, alien, not-of-this-world shit gets to me. It was
the season premiere, and I was as excited as a virgin teenage boy in
a whorehouse about to get some. I waited all week to see the show,
listening to plugs for it on WPGC 95.5 and catching a few of the
previews on Fox. I even stopped by Giant Food on my way home to
pick up some Pop Secret Movie Theater butter popcorn for the big
night. Don't you know someone in my family had to ruin it for me!
     Most of the time on Friday nights, my parents turned in early,
since Momma was the type who still got up at 5:00 A.M., even
though she had been retired for more than ten years. Pops preferred to pass the hell out after he got in from his maintenance job.
My lard-ass brother Fred pissed me off though. His ass is so big, he
could shut off a water main eruption with the crack of his anus
alone. There he was, laid out on the couch, snoring and sounding
like an off-key chorus of hyenas. He had his shoes and socks off,
and the au naturel odor emitting from them bad boys was stronger
than the butter flavoring on my popcorn. I turned the TV up
louder with the remote and held my nose with one hand while I
shoveled popcorn into my mouth with the other. I made a mental
note to definitely get a tube for my bedroom on my next payday,
'cause something had to give.

It was hot as hell up in the crib that night. Felt like Satan was breathing down the nape of my neck. I hated living in the projects. No central air. Roaches as big as rats, rats as big as dogs, and enough hoodlums to fill a state penitentiary. For months, I had considered asking Tempest if I could crash at her place. I knew she would say yes, but I also knew she would go into her mother-figure mode and get all in my grill about shit. I got enough of that from my real mother, so I didn't even go that route. I give props where props are due, though. If it wasn't for Tempest, I never would have gone through with night school and gotten my GED. If it wasn't for her, I never would have taken the postal exam and landed a job as a clerk at the local branch.

*Millennium* went off. The part I heard of it over Fred's snoring was pretty damn good. I was going to watch *Jerry Springer,* but the baked beans Fred had eaten for dinner kicked in, and the farts emitting from his ass could have been bottled as weed killer. I couldn't take the madness one more second.

I went up to my bedroom and tried to crash, but I had to leave the window open so I wouldn't suffocate. All hell had broken loose outside, and the noise was way past ridiculous. It was the first of the month, the busiest day of every month for the liquor stores and drug dealers because that's when all the junkies and addicts cash their welfare checks to pay for their habits instead of provid-ing for their children. The crack house across the street, the one run by that homeboy of Ripuoff's, Lewis, was jumping that night. I hear Ripuoff is doing twenty years to life in Lorton for manufac-turing that Niagra shit. Too bad I didn't get a couple of grape jelly jars full before he got sent up the river. I know some brothas who could use that shit for real.

I couldn't sleep, my nipples were harder than Ping-Pong balls and my beeper had not gone off all day. Where were all my dicks? Where was the beef? I knew the answer. They were out getting

their jollies off with some hoochie mommas or hitting the clubs
with their boys.

I needed a car bad. I was willing to settle for a hoopty if I had
to. I didn't care if the ride was held together by duct tape and
sounded like Chitty Chitty Bang Bang as long as it could get me
from point A to point B. I sat up in the bed and said, "Fuck it!" I
knew Tempest would be pissed if I called and threw her a guilt trip
about leaving me at home with Fred's stank ass, but I just had to
get out of there. I was bored, I was lonely, I was horny. I had gone
without getting my kitty kat stroked for more than four months,
and I was reasonably sure Tempest hadn't had sex since Kangol hats
were the bomb. We needed to get out and explore our horizons.
We needed to do the sistahgurl thing and hang out. We needed to
find some fione-ass men. I got up off the bed and headed back
down to the living room, which smelled like a natural gas explo-
sion, to find the phone.

## geren

I am still trying to figure out why I let Dvontè talk me into going
clubbing that night. Looking back at it now, I realize it must have
been fate. I was exhausted after a long day at the firm, and the last
thing I needed to do was deal with a smoke-filled room full of desperate women. That's all I seemed to run into, desperate women
in all shapes and sizes and from all walks of life.

Some of them were subtle in their endeavors, but most were
those kind who frequent churches and cabarets looking for Mr.
Right. The ones at nightclubs generally came right out with it and
held nothing back. Tits and ass busting out of dresses two sizes too
small, brushing up against me and sneaking a feel of my dick on
the dance floor, whispering nasty thoughts in my ear. Sure, I
slipped a few times and took advantage of the sexual favors they

were offering. The only problem was they would expect me to fall in love or lust with some imaginary bomb-ass pussy in the span of one roll in the hay and a hundred pumps, when all I'd ever wanted was a quick sexual release.

I decided there would definitely be no more of that. Times are hard, and penicillin no longer cures everything. Frankly, I preferred taking care of business myself somewhere between flipping through the pages of *Ebony Male* or *Sports Illustrated* on the toilet and hopping in the shower to get ready for work. It was safer, and my palm never expected me to propose to it afterward with a three-carat diamond.

Dvontè, on the other hand, was a hoochie-loving man. His philosophy was, the more punanny the better. I used to tell him he was going to run up on some lethal pussy one day and pay the piper, but he always replied, "We all have to go someday. I want to die laid up in the bed with my dick inside some hot, juicy pussy!"

Dvontè was my boy, but his playa behavior was getting old, and our outlooks on women and relationships were far from mutual.

All I ever really wanted was one woman who could satisfy all my needs, and not just my sexual ones. I am an avid believer that once there is an emotional bond and friendship, everything else falls smoothly into formation. Unfortunately, most of the sistahs I had dealings with were not on the same wavelength. I have never been anyone's fool, and my eyes were wide open to the fact that women were after me for two reasons: my looks were above average, and I had money. Lots of it.

There were a few sistahs who I honestly believed were genuine until they started asking me for things right and left. One even had the nerve to ask me to buy her a Lexus after the third date. She never heard from me again, and I suspect she is still catching the Metrobus unless she lucked out and hooked up with a so-called successful drug dealer who simply didn't give a fuck. Any self-righteous man who attained his wealth the honest way, through hard work and perseverance, wouldn't fall for an obvious gold digger like that—although I must admit that sports figures and entertainers do have a tendency to do that very thing. They are so overcome by the legions of pantiless groupies flinging themselves at them that they fall for the game. Fools, I tell you, because Geren Kincaid would never go out like that.

Looking around the club, I spotted all the various categories of women. First, there were the spandex queens. You know the type. Sistahs who have the nerve to squeeze into a size-six spandex outfit when they really wear a size twenty-six. More breast meat hanging outside of their tops than inside. Pants so tight that it makes a brotha want to break out an ink pen and play connect-the-dots on the rolls of cellulite protruding through the material. Sistahs who have to take a deep breath before they even attempt to sit down because the outfit is so tight they can't bend their legs. I am not saying I have anything against large women. I love *all* my black queens, but I prefer women who carry themselves with class. If a woman puts on high heels in the morning and they are flats by the afternoon, common sense should tell her she has no business sporting spandex. That's all I am saying.

Then there were the pedestal women, sistahs who think they are so damn fine a man better not even attempt to approach them. They come to the club early and take up all the good seats at the bar or at the tables by the dance floor so they can sit there and talk trash about other people all night, so worried about what other people are doing, what other people have on, how people are dancing, that they don't even want to take a potty break for fear of missing something. *They are not even fooling me!* Half of them sit there sipping on the same drink the whole damn night because they can only afford one and still make their rent payment. Often you only see these sistahs at clubs around the first and fifteenth of the month, after they've cashed their paychecks. Ninety-nine percent of them get paid on Friday and are pinching pennies by Monday morning.

Then there are the leeches, hitting up every brotha they can grab by the elbow for a drink. All the young hustlers love those kind of women, because they automatically think if they buy a couple of drinks, the sistah will give them an obligatory fuck. Most of them end up sitting in the bucket seat of their Ford Explorer or Chevy Blazer by the end of the night whacking off to Puff Daddy and the Family—mind you, with about fifty dollars less in their pockets.

Let us not forget the video queens—sistahs who have more fake stuff on them than real. Weaves, colored contacts, acrylic nails, gold caps on their teeth, silicone breasts, the whole works. Inside the club, under the dim lighting, some of them look fine as all hell. Wait till you get them outside, though. Some of them are straight up hurting. I mean hurt!

I stood there, leaning on the bar and sipping on a Hennessy and Coke, trying to keep myself from busting out laughing at Dvonte. Speaking of hurt, the sistah he was trying to mack looked like she could play the lead in *A Bug's Life*. He was sinking low, even for him. Brotha man must have wanted some bad to be talking to her. She had eyes that looked like they were about to burst out of her head and was so skinny, if she swallowed a marble you would have swore up and down she was nine months pregnant.

I saw him glance over at me, darting his eyes down at her breasts, trying to get me to size her up. The only problem was, there was nothing to size up. My twelve-year-old baby cousin Rhonda had a better-built body than the sistah he was trying to get up on. She was so skinny, her nipples were touching.

I pulled up the sleeve of my navy Hugo Boss suit and glanced at my watch. It wasn't even midnight yet. We'd gotten there about

eleven, and I was ready to go ten minutes later, but I promised
Dvontè we could hang out. If nothing else, I am always a man of
my word.

# *dvontè*

Geren was getting on my last damn nerve. Always trying to playa
hate. Like they say, "Don't hate the playa. Hate the game." He was
just mad because the only woman who had tried to step to him
looked old enough to have an autographed copy of the Bible. I
mean, she looked older than my grandmother. The sistah was
probably a waitress at the Last Supper. I chuckled because he had
some ugly woman eyeing his ass. I know he sensed her, but I don't
blame him for not looking her way. She was so ugly, it looked like
her neck threw up. Truth be known, though, if she could give good
head, I would have closed my eyes and let her suck me like a lol-
lipop.

I've never in my life used a woman. They use me. I just happen
to get a little ass in the process. Hell, if it were not for men like
me, there would be hundreds of thousands of lonely sistahs in the
world. I make a woman's life complete. Give her something to
look forward to after a long, stressful day at the office. Put a little
pep in her step.

Let's face it. Most women, and men for that matter, spend the
better part of every day doing something they hate to do: working.
The majority of people work to pay bills and make ends meet. The
only time they really get a chance to live it up is after work. I'm
there waiting for these ladies when they come home with wet lips
*and* a savory dick. What more could they ask for?

I'm a precious commodity these days—a black man with a job,
a place, and no secrets hiding in the closet. I'm heterosexual, drug
free, and I'm not a convicted felon. That alone makes me worth

my weight in gold. Add to that the fact that I work, have my own crib and car, and what you get is a man's man. That's me. Dvontè Richardson is a prince among men.

I have always been straight up with the sistahs. I want to get some ass and then roll out. I never fake the funk. If they don't want to play by my rules, then they can get to steppin' and tell their story walking. Sistahs always blame the man when something goes wrong, as if they weren't even present when the shit hit the fan. Like they were having an out-of-body experience, witnessing the whole sordid mess from afar. Who the hell are they trying to fool? *I know my rights!* I have the right to remain as freaky as I want to be for as long as I want to be. *Simple as that!* Looking back on things now, I should have kept my ass at home that night. Most of the sistahs were tore up from the floor up, and the one I ended up getting with almost ruined my whole damn life, even though she was fine. There is something to be said for making it a Blockbuster night. No doubt I would have been better off watching rented flicks.

# 2

## we be clubbin'

" 'Bout damn time you got here, Tempest!" Janessa took a deep breath so she could bend her midsection to get into the car. The red sheath she had on was too tight to maneuver in, and she barely managed to get into Tempest's Camry without ripping open a seam. "I was ready to bounce an hour ago."

"You have a lot of damn nerve," Tempest hissed back. "Consider yourself lucky I even showed. I had other plans for tonight, but I canceled them when you phoned me with that sob story of yours about being lonely and Fred farting in your face."

"Chile, please! You know you weren't doing a thing except sitting at home feeling sorry for yourself." Janessa reached over the gearshift to turn the radio down a few notches. "You think your music is loud enough? Sheesh!"

"No, not really," Tempest replied, turning it back up. "That's my cut!" she exclaimed, referring to "Nobody's Supposed to Be Here" by Deborah Cox.

"*Every* song is your damn cut," Janessa snapped back at her, searching through her tan leather handbag for a tube of ruby red lipstick.

"Yeah, but I can seriously relate to this one. I know exactly where the sistah is coming from when she sings about giving up on love."

"I bet you do," Janessa sneered sarcastically. "Anyone can look at you and tell your ass is celibate."

Tempest pulled off from the curb in front of Janessa's house with a jerk. "You are so damn silly! How in the world can someone look at me and tell I'm celibate? It's not like I'm wearing a sign on my ass or anything."

"No, there's no sign on your ass. It's just written all over your freakin' face." Janessa reached up to turn on the interior light, but Tempest stopped her. "Sistahs can tell when their homies aren't gettin' none. It's all in the eyes."

"No, use this." Tempest handed Janessa a lighted compact mirror, igging the analysis. "The glare from the overhead light impairs my driving."

"Thanks," Janessa said, opening it and expertly applying the lipstick, which matched her nails perfectly. She glanced over at Tempest. "You look like a nun in that black suit."

"Not a nun. A lady. Maybe you should try the conservative approach sometime." Tempest giggled, looking Janessa up and down and making no bones about her disapproval of the outfit.

"Hmph, yeah, right," Janessa smirked, brushing off the remark. "So what were you really doing when I called? Hmm? Watching television or doing those damn puzzle books again?"

Tempest didn't want to tell her the truth—that she'd been drowning her sorrow in ice cream and Pepsi. That she was hoping a man, just about any man, would call, but the only calls she got the whole evening were from her mother and a telemarketer wanting to know if she wanted home delivery of the *Washington Post*.

She sighed. "Why are you all up in my business, Janessa? It's not like you have a man!"

"I've had one since the last time you had one. That's for damn sure. If Howard hadn't gotten locked up on those bullshit charges, he and I would still be together."

"Bullshit charges?" Tempest chuckled, trying to rationalize Janessa's thought process. "His ass got caught red-handed pulling an armed robbery, and you keep trying to insist he was framed. You need to tell that nonsense to someone who isn't up on such *thangs* like me."

"Those charges *were* trumped up," Janessa stated defensively. "Howard was an innocent bystander. They just locked him up because he's a black man."

"Whatever, Janessa, but I saw that shit on the Fox ten-o'clock news, and he looked guilty as all hell to me. He came out good only getting ten to fifteen years. His ass could have gotten life."

"Howard is not going to do fifteen years. Not even ten. He told me when he called the other day that he would be out in about—"

"Called? You mean to tell me you're still letting his sorry ass call you collect from Lorton?"

Janessa rolled her eyes. "He only calls about once a week," she said, clucking her tongue. "It's not like he calls *every* day. Besides, I miss him, and I'm the only sunshine he has to brighten up his dreary situation. I bring him hope. He told me so himself."

"Sis, you have issues, but I love you just the same. Howard probably calls a different sistah collect every day of the week begging for something. Haven't you ever seen those women on talk shows who make a bunch of sacrifices for brothas who are locked up, only to get dumped with a quickness the second they get released?"

"Yeah, but you're overlooking one vital element."

"What element?"

"All those women on talk shows are old, white and lonely. They want a young stud, black or white, so bad that they are willing to make a fool of themselves like that."

"Hmph, if you say so. Let me ask you one more thing. Does Howard always call you on the same day of the week? If so, that's a dead giveaway. Maybe you are Miss Monday or Miss Tuesday or whatever."

"Shaddup, Tempest!" Janessa was boiling mad, mostly because Tempest was making sense. Now that she thought about it, Howard *did* always call on Thursdays. He always called between eight and nine at night, when the *Wayans Brothers* or *The Jamie Foxx Show* was on. Was she really Miss Thursday?

"I just hope you aren't giving him any of your hard-earned money?" Tempest interrupted Janessa's thought process.

"Of course not!" Janessa snapped, feeling guilty about the two hundred dollars she'd sent him the week before. Howard said he needed it to pay off this three-hundred-pound brotha who wanted to make him his bitch. Little did Janessa know that Tempest was well aware of it —Janessa's mother had called Tempest to throw a hissy fit about the money, which she felt could have been put to better use at the grocery store.

"Good! I was about to say," Tempest said, faking relief, "that's money you should be saving to get your own place. You're always complaining about Fred stinking up the house and all that. You need to plan your work and work your plan, sistahgurl."

"I know that's right, gurl," Janessa agreed, having flashbacks, or smellbacks rather, of Fred letting out gas on the couch earlier that night. "It is *seriously* time for me to make a move and get up out of there. I've outgrown the projects, if there is such a thing as outgrowing it. The only people I have to talk to around the way have given up on their dreams and aspirations. It's down right depressing sometimes. That's why I'm so glad I have you."

"You can always count on me, Janessa."

"I know gurl. Ditto over here, sis," Janessa said, holding up her hand for Tempest to slap her a high five.

They were silent for a few minutes, just listening to the jams on WPGC and looking at the lights as they headed downtown to DC Live.

"How are things at the post office?" Tempest asked.

"They're okay," Janessa replied. "Sometimes the supervisors rack on my nerves, though. They think they own me or some shit. I'm nobody's chattel."

"Amen to that!"

"Still, it feels damn good going to work every day and earning a living. For a while there, I was about to fall into that sitting-at-home-watching-soaps-all-day trap, but you pulled me back from the edge." Janessa reached over and patted Tempest on the hand. "If I've never said it, thank you."

Tempest glared over at her, trying to see if Janessa was getting teary-eyed, but couldn't tell because of the steady stream of streetlights flooding into the car. "No thanks necessary. You did it all by yourself, Janessa. I was just your cheering section, and I'm extremely proud of you."

"On the contrary, I didn't do it all by myself," Janessa objected. "If it weren't for you pushing me to make something out of myself, I would probably have no future. Even though I'm still living at home, I *do* have goals. I have a purpose in life, and I know in time, everything will pan out for me. I owe it all to you. You know you're my shero!"

Tempest grinned, trying to hold back her own tears. "Aww, shut the hell up before you make my ass cry. We're out here to go clubbin', remember? Not that I even know what to do in a club anymore. This should prove to be interesting."

"I've been meaning to ask you. What *exactly* do you have against clubs?"

"It's not that I have anything against clubs. I've just outgrown them, like you've outgrown the projects. Clubs are nothing but meat markets. Always have been, always will be. I don't even need to school you on that one."

"True! I'm looking for some grade A, prime, FDA-approved dang-a-lang myself." They both fell out laughing. "And a big, juicy tongue to go with it wouldn't hurt."

"You are too damn funny!" Tempest slowed the car down, glancing up and down the street. "Well, we're here. Let's start looking for a parking space."

Janessa pointed to their left. "There's one over there, sis."

"Naw." Tempest sighed disappointedly. "That's in front of a hydrant."

"Gurl, no one is going to bother your ass over there. You better go ahead and grab that spot before someone else gets it."

"Uh-uh, no way. I'm not about to get towed trying to get up in a club. You know D.C. is on the brink of bankruptcy. Hell, they probably support half the city government employees by collecting parking ticket and towing money."

Janessa sucked her tongue, ready to go check out the men. "Aiight, let's try the next street over then."

"Cool!" Tempest made a right at the corner, still looking for a spot. "By the way, whatever happened with that blind date Cynda hooked you up with?"

"Tempest, I should slap you for even bringing that skank man up," Janessa hissed.

"Damn, was he that bad?"

"Gurl, when I say skank, I do mean that shit literally," Janessa turned up her nose, like something foul was trying to invade her nostrils. "He looked aiight but when we got to his place, I almost fell the fuck out."

"How come?"

"First of all, I don't believe the brotha had a habit of bathing on a regular basis. Now you know that's pathetic, because a bar of soap is about the cheapest damn thing you can buy in the store."

"Eww, damn," Tempest chuckled. "He had that au naturel thing going on, huh?"

"Au naturel and then some." Janessa giggled. "That brotha could make a skunk haul ass in fear."

"Dizammmm!"

"Not only that. His place was so damn filthy, you could barely see his nasty-ass carpet. He told me to get comfortable and take off my shoes, but there was no freakin' way. Even the cockroaches were sporting slippers up in that bitch."

Tempest fell out laughing and slapped Janessa on the knee. "You're hilarious, gurl!"

"I'm just telling you like it is!" Janessa straightened suddenly in her seat, pointing up ahead. "There's someone about to pull out over there."

"Great! Let's get this over with," Tempest replied. "Let's go in here and find you a man, so I can take my ass home and go to sleep."

"I have a feeling this is going to be your lucky night, Tempest!"

"Hmph. I seriously doubt all that, but you never know!"

# 3

## let the games begin

Janessa and Tempest walked into the club. It was jam-packed. True to form, within a couple of minutes Janessa headed straight to the dance floor, while Tempest aimed for the bar. It wasn't that she was an alcoholic or anything, far from it; she only drank an average of four or five times a year. She just wanted to bum-rush a stool so she would have somewhere to sit for the remainder of the night—she had absolutely no intention of dancing. Go out there, shake her ass and get all funktified for what? To pick up a man? She didn't *even* think so!

Tempest hopped on a stool at the end of the bar nearest to the dance floor as soon as some brotha in a purple suit jumped up to grab a passing hoochie by the elbow and ask her to dance. The girl in the skintight black dress glanced his way, laughed and said, "Hell naw, you must be kidding! Asking me to dance with that bama suit on!"

Tempest felt sorry for him—being called a bama is enough to hurt any brotha—but she laughed at his Barney-looking ass anyway. When he swung around to retrieve his seat, she turned away and ordered a gin and tonic with a twist of lime. *Hmph, that's what he gets! Coming up in here trying to get some ass! Move your feet, lose your seat!*

Once she got her drink, which was seriously weak, she positioned herself so she had an eagle's-eye view of the entire room and started checking out the brothas. Just like she figured, they all had issues, and it was *tooooooo* damn obvious.

First, she spotted a no-cash, no-ass brotha. Yes, she had developed names for all them bad boys. He had on a fly suit, but his face was messed da hell up. He had zits—no, make that craters—in his face, and his eyes were bloodshot. Not from drugs or alcohol—just one of those brothas who couldn't benefit from eye drops if his life depended on it. She knew for a fact that a brotha like that either had to pay for pussy or jack off to an issue of *Black Tail* or *Hustler,* depending on whether or not he was suffering from jungle fever. Judging from his stance, he'd obviously studied pimpology, so she took him to be a switch hitter. He would probably fuck anything.

Then, she spotted a momma's boy, and not the kind you are probably thinking of. A momma's boy is a man who has only been inside of one pussy in his entire life; his momma's. In other words, a man who hasn't had puddy since puddy had he. He appeared to be about twenty-five and was quivering in a dimly lit corner like he was afraid to approach a sistah. He was one of the brothas who comes to clubs to admire women from afar so he can go home and experience a wet dream about them later. Tempest figured he was probably cruising around D.C. in a 1972 Pinto with hydraulics, red stuffed dice hanging from the rearview mirror, and a kit.

Of course, the club scene wouldn't have been complete without a Mr. I Know I'm All That. There were plenty of those fools there that night—Tempest spotted at least a dozen in a matter of seconds, profiling throughout the club. Men who think they are the salt of the earth, the cream of the crop, the bomb-diggity but are scrounging to put some ends together to buy a drink for themselves, much less anyone else. Tempest's Mr. I Know I'm All That category had various subdivisions. There were the JEEP brothas—*Just Enough Education to Pass,* the kind who make about twenty typos when they try to write a sistah a love letter. There were the I-had brothas, who always brag about the flashy cars and other material things they used to have that somehow evaporated into thin air. Then, there were the I-was-the-shit-back-in-high-school brothas, who still dwell on the fact they were sports stars back in 1978 but never went pro because of an injury, which really meant they were cut when it came to college ball. Let's not forget the loan-me-a-dollar brothas who attempt to hit sistahs up for cash promising to pay them back when they get their check from Mickey D's or, even worse, a generic burger joint. At least if a man works at Mickey D's, he can bring you a decent junk meal home every now and then.

Last but definitely not least, there were what Tempest affectionately called the questionable brothas representing. Ever since she caught her prize pussy eater Trent deep-throating a dick, she recognized a little feminity in quite a few brothas. She always had her homie-sexual radar in full effect. She might have left home without her American Express card, but she never left the radar at home. She tried to avoid them at all costs because to each his own, but no man was sticking his dick in her coochie after it had been in the dark hole of a 250-pound brotha nicknamed Precious who wore a pink tutu and size 16EEE ballet slippers to bed.

Tempest took small sips of her drink, wishing she were anyplace else, even home alone, as much as she dreaded the scenario. She zoomed in on Janessa, who was having a helluva time dancing with some handsome brotha off *Loungin'* by LL Cool J—cute, but not Tempest's type. She would always rate men, even if one of her gurls was talking to them, and especially when they were knocking boots; she liked to gauge whether her gurls were wasting their time or not. Just a habit of hers, albeit a bad one.

Tempest firmly believed she could tell whether a man was a good lover at first sight, and she pegged the one Janessa was dancing with to be mediocre at best. He probably thought he was the second coming of Valentino. Ironically, she found out later, she was right—her intuition had never steered her wrong. All of her previous men had been good lovers, some of them damn good. It was just that they all had other nasty, raunchy, trifling shit going on in their lives.

She contemplated making a mad dash for the bathroom to tinkle, but debated about leaving her jacket on the stool to save her spot. She had picked it up at *Ross for Less* for $9.99, so if it sprouted wings and flew away it was all good. However, she knew good and damn well her seat would be gone when she returned, anyway. Contrary to popular belief, she thought to herself, chivalry is definitely dead.

She contemplated calling Barney-bama over and asking him to save it, but thought better of it. He was still standing there looking pitiful and getting turned down by fifty-eleven hoochies. He very well might have saved the seat, but Tempest knew he would try to get some play afterward, and she didn't even want to be bothered.

Tempest crossed her legs to hold it in, trying to get Janessa's attention by waving her arms. Janessa knew the routine. Arm-waving meant, Get your ass off the dance floor long enough for me to go tinkle.

"Doing bar-stool aerobics?"

Tempest glanced to her left to see what stupid-ass fool had made the statement. She was pleasantly surprised. The brotha was fine. Scratch that, he was F-I-O-N-E. Tall, dark and handsome with a navy Hugo Boss double-breasted suit on. Tempest could spot good taste a mile away. On top of that, he smelled downright lickable. She recognized the scent but couldn't quite place its name. It was expensive, though.

She managed to swallow the smart-aleck remark before it escaped her lips and blushed instead, finding it hard to believe she was still capable of blushing. "No, just trying to flag my girl down," Tempest replied. "She's on the dance floor."

"The sistah in the red dress, right?"

Hmm, he had that Barry White voice going on also. An added bonus, Tempest thought to herself. She eyed him up and down, trying to find something, *anything,* retarded looking about the man, but simply put, he looked like the words *F-U-C-K M-E* spelled out to her. "Yes, the one in the red dress," she replied cautiously, wondering how he knew that and if he was really playing a role to get to Janessa through her. She knew some men preferred hoochiness over the conservative type. "How do you know that we're together?"

"Because I've been watching you since you sashayed in here," he said. "I witnessed the two of you make an entrance. Two beautifully stunning women are hard to miss. Especially in a place like this."

Tempest began to warm up to him a little. She could feel the icicles falling off her face and evaporating into thin air. That *sashayed* and *stunningly beautiful* kind of got to her. "A place like this? What do you mean by that?"

He laughed again. Was he laughing at her? It was beginning to irritate her slightly, but not enough for her to get up and walk away from his fine ass.

"No offense to the sistahs in here, but a lot of them have issues."

Tempest couldn't help but break a grin. The brotha was stealing her word. "What do you know about issues?"

"I know an issue is what an emotional defect becomes when it graduates from being a problem."

"That's real deep," Tempest replied, in awe of his wording again. She longed to hear more, wondering if it *was* possible to meet a decent man in a meat market. To think, he was standing beside her the whole time she was checking out the rest of the dog pound. Shame on it all! "So what's your name? Darius?"

"No," he snapped, seemingly offended. "Why on earth would you suggest my name is Darius?"

"I don't know! You just look like a Darius to me. It's not like I asked if your name was Doreen or Dorothy or something. Get a grip!"

He smirked while Tempest tried to play it off by taking another sip of her drink. She didn't mean to offend the brotha. It was just that she'd always envisioned marrying a man named Darius, but she had yet to meet one. Janessa always said she had more of a chance of meeting a man named Rogaine than Darius, but you couldn't tell Tempest anything once she was convinced. Maybe the fine specimen of a man standing beside her wasn't the one after all.

"Well, do you care to know my real name?"

Tempest giggled, realizing she was being a bit too obvious about slightly losing interest since his name wasn't Darius. "Umm sure, what's your name?"

He reached out to shake her hand. She gave it to him. What the hell? "My name is Geren, and yours?"

"Tempest," she answered, waiting for him to ask her a stupid question. *Does that mean you have a temper? Does that mean you're like a storm in the bedroom?* If she had a dollar for every nucca that asked her one or the other, she would have been sitting on top of the world like Brandy and Mase. "It's nice to meet you, Geren."

"Same here." He didn't ask her a stupid question. What a

shock! His eyes darted toward the dance floor just as "I'll Be Dat" by Redman came on. "Care to dance?"

As much as Tempest wanted to, since that happened to be her cut of the month—well, at least *one* of her cuts—she was more concerned with needing a Depends. "I would love to dance, but can you give me a minute to run to the little girl's room?"

"No problem. I'll be right here waiting when you return."

Tempest almost lost control of her bladder for real when he flashed his cinematic smile. Now she was battling two things—having to go potty and being horny. Since it was physically impossible to cum and pee at the same time, Tempest was hoping for the orgasm. Lawd knows she could have used one.

"I'll be right back!" Tempest leaned over and yelled in his ear, practically shouting. Damn, even his ears looked delicious! She could picture herself sucking on his earlobes all night. Maybe not all night, but a good fifteen minutes before heading farther south.

Geren watched Tempest barge her way through the crowded club to the rest room. He had no idea why he even approached her. He had noticed her when she came in, though—that was no lie. She was so modestly dressed compared to the hot momma she came with. He appreciated a woman who didn't feel she had to advertise her goods. From where he was sitting, she had a lot of goods to offer. Even in that homely black suit, he could tell she was hauling a lot of junk in her trunk. Nothing like a big booty and a smile. She had both, and he could hardly wait to see what she had in her mind.

Tempest managed to make it to the rest room somehow, and not a moment too soon. As usual, the ladies' room was standing room only. As soon as Tempest squatted, at least a two-liter came flowing out of her bladder. She came out of the stall and found Janessa in the mirror straightening her dress—what there was of it.

"Uh-huh," Janessa started in on her. "I saw your fresh behind out there flirting, Tempest."

Tempest laughed, pushing her out of the way so she could wash her hands. The rest of the vanity area had women adjusting everything from lipstick to bra straps in the mirror. One sistah was trying to fit a pair of 44DDDs into a 36A. Maybe she thinks four breastesses are better than two, Tempest thought.

"I wasn't even flirting, Janessa," Tempest said, halfway convinced the statement was true. "He just told me his name."

"Geren."

Tempest diverted her eyes to Janessa's reflection in the mirror, wondering how she could have known that. Janessa had hit the dance floor with a quickness so there was no way Geren could have tried to talk to her before Tempest met him at the bar. "How'd you know that? Do you know him from someplace?" she asked brazenly.

"Nope, never met him." Janessa giggled. "The dude I've been dancing with for the past ten songs is his best friend. Dvontè told me Geren's name."

"Dvontè, huh?"

Janessa started grinning from ear to ear, and Tempest knew it meant trouble. She sensed the beginnings of a one-night stand developing. "You really like him, don't you?"

"He's aiight," Janessa replied. "He asked me for the digits, but I'm making him sweat it out."

"So that means you're going to give them to him?"

"Damn skippy! Did you see how fine that man is?"

They started out the door to make room for the next group of hoochie mommas. "Not really," Tempest lied so Janessa wouldn't know she'd thoroughly checked him out. "It's too dark to see clearly up in here, and you were all the way on the dance floor."

"Well, I'll have to introduce you two, then." Janessa knew

Tempest was frontin'. She knew the heifer had bionic vision when it came to checking out the brothas.

Once they got back to the bar, introductions were made all around. Tempest was not even impressed. Dvontè was beside Geren, sitting on her stool *and* her $9.99 jacket. She wanted to pimp-slap his ass.

Dvontè didn't particularly care for Tempest either. He figured she was one of those celibate sistahs, sitting on her pussy like she's collecting dividends on the shit. Then again, she might be one of those undercover freakazoids, he thought.

After they'd exchanged pleasantries, Geren reminded Tempest that she owed him a dance. No sooner had she taken his hand so he could lead the way when the DJ switched up on them and put on a slow jam, "Beauty" by Dru Hill.

That threw Tempest for a loop. For some reason, whenever she finally got ready to make a spectacle of herself on the dance floor because she still did all the old dances like the Bus Stop and the Robot, the DJ would put on a slow I-wanna-smoke-your-boots-off song.

Tempest decided to go for it anyway. Besides, she wanted to see if Geren really was all that. There was only one way to find out without demanding he drop his drawers. She knew once he started grinding up against her, one of four things was bound to happen. He would either have a pelvic area flatter than hers, she would feel a pencil pricking her skin, she would feel a soft banana that had some potential or he would make her eyes bulge. When a man had an elephantine dick, she couldn't help but visualize it in her mind. They hit the dance floor, and if Tempest hadn't immediately closed her eyelids, her eyes would have popped slap out of her head.

# 4

## to date or not to date

Janessa and Tempest stayed at the club until it closed at 3:00 A.M., which was a first. Normally, Tempest would give Janessa two hours max to get her groove on before she started motioning toward the exit.

Not that night though. Tempest danced the night away with Geren and even drank a couple of hurricanes. When the two of them weren't freaking all over each other on the dance floor, they were off somewhere lingering in a dark corner.

The entire ride home, Janessa tried to get the lowdown from her. Tempest just kept belting out, "I don't see nothing wrong with a little bump and grind," the chorus from that old R. Kelly slow jam. A far cry from "Nobody's Supposed to Be Here," which was *sooooooo* indicative of her feelings on the way to the club.

Tempest practically skipped up the sidewalk to her building, taking the steps two at a time up to her third-floor condo, but she finally cut the singing once they got inside. Not a second too soon for Janessa—she loved Tempest, but wished she would leave singing da hell alone.

"I'm about to hop in the shower," Tempest blurted out, a far-away, glassy look in her eyes. She seemed distracted as she spoke, her mind obviously still on Geren. "I can't stand smelling like cig-arette smoke, so I'm going to wash my hair right quick."

"Damn, Tempest! How many times a week do you wash your freakin' hair?" For all the years Janessa had known her, Tempest had had this mad obsession about her hair.

"I only wash it a couple of times a week," Tempest replied, smacking her lips. "I just like to smell fresh, is all. If it weren't for you dragging my ass to that nicotine-infested club, I wouldn't feel so dirty in the first place."

"Hmph, well from the looks of it, you didn't make out too bad tonight, homie." Janessa plopped down on the sofa and flicked on the tube. She could finally watch some TV without Fred's skank ass sitting across from her. *What's Happening Now* was on. Janessa used to love her some Rog, ReRun, and Dwayne when she was a kid. She thought Dee was the bomb and used to lick her lips fantasizing about what one of Shirley's cheeseburgers would taste like. "So spill it, Tempest. Are you and Geren going to hook up again, or what?"

"Maybe, maybe not," Tempest smirked. "He seems trustwor-thy enough. Then again, they *all* do in the beginning. I agreed to take his number, but I need to think long and hard before I call him. I'm sick and tired of putting my heart and soul into a rela-tionship only to end up being hurt."

Tempest took off the blazer of her suit and went to get some fresh towels and sheets, along with a blanket and pillow, for Janessa from the linen closet. After she came back in the living room and placed them down beside her, Janessa decided to sweat the issue. "So, are you gonna call?"

"I don't know, geesh," Tempest hissed, giving her a flustered glance. "Like I said, I need to give this whole thing some *serious* consideration."

"Tempest, you have to learn to leave the past in the past. Granted, a lot of nuccas in D.C. are up to no damn good, but Geren seems like he has it going on," Janessa stated convincingly. "He's attractive, successful, and currently unattached. You're attractive, successful, and currently unattached. You would be doing yourself a serious injustice not to at least give the brotha a chance."

"How do you know so much about Geren?" Tempest asked with mild but amused irritation, the corners of her mouth clearly fighting back a smile.

"I quizzed Dvontè about him, of course. He and I both agree. You and Geren look mad cute together."

Tempest giggled and turned her back to Janessa, trying to hide the fact she was blushing. "Speaking of Dvontè, I'm extremely proud of you for not leaving the club with him tonight."

How dare she? "Oh, so now I'm a hoe, huh?"

Tempest came over and gave Janessa a love-slap on her shoulder. "Of course not. That's not how I meant it."

"How many different ways are there for you to mean it, heifer?" Janessa was pissed, and not even trying to fake the funk about it. Tempest gave her a blank stare, trying to think of an answer. They both knew she couldn't. "My one-night stand days are over, Tempest! They have been for a long-ass time! I thought you, of all people, understood that! You're supposed to be my gurl and shit!"

"I am your gurl, you silly goose," Tempest chuckled, pinching Janessa's left cheek before heading to the bathroom. "Don't even get loud up in here with me, sistahgurl. I might have to open a can of whup-ass and beat you down with that pillow."

"Yeah, right tramp." Janessa laughed, feeling the tension breaking. "I know you think you're my second mother, but I can handle my bizness. You just handle yours."

Tempest poked her head back around the corner. "Just be careful with Dvontè. He has playa written all over him." Janessa didn't reply. She just wanted the whole thing to be squashed. "I'll be out in a few. Make yourself at home, but you know that drill already. Want me to help you pull out the sofa bed?"

"Naw, I got it!" Once Janessa heard the showerhead come on, she searched Tempest's computer desk for a notepad and pen. By the time Tempest finished doing whatever da hell it was she did to her freakin' hair three or four times a week, Janessa was ass out.

Some things never change, Tempest thought to herself. When she came out of the bathroom, feeling fresh and rejuvenated, Janessa was sprawled out on the sofa bed, and the covers were on the floor.

When they were in junior high, they would have sleepovers and share Tempest's twin bed. Janessa used to sleep so damn wild, Tempest nicknamed her Scissorlegs. Janessa would spread her legs wide like a pair of scissors and knock her off the bed onto the floor half the night. Tempest couldn't count the number of times she had woken up with a backache and bruised thighs, not to mention Janessa's toe prints all over her.

The ability to do splits in bed probably comes in handy with the brothas, but not in my bed, Tempest thought. That's why she bought a sofa bed in the first place; when Janessa stayed over, Tempest would still be able to walk in the morning.

Tempest covered her up—an exercise in futility, since everything was destined to hit the floor again five minutes later—and went back in the bathroom to wrap her damp hair up in a silk scarf. She left the television on; Janessa was used to sleeping with noise. There was a crack house right across the street from her parents, with people running in and out every two minutes.

Tempest's neighbors were extremely quiet, so cable had to suffice.

By the time Tempest set her digital alarm clock for ten and threw her I Just Can't Stand a Broke-Ass Man tee back on, it was damn near 5 A.M. She was exhausted and couldn't wait to call the hogs. She pulled the comforter back on her queen-size canopy bed and laughed when she spotted a note on her pillow.

She snuggled into her warm bed, propped herself up, and read it:

*Tempest,*

*I know you think this shit is funny because I always write you letters whenever I'm scared to tell you something face-to-face.Well, here goes!*

*I kind of, sort of, did something tonight that will more than likely piss you off.*

*You know Marquita is getting married next weekend? I thought it would be a good thing if we took some dates, so . . . Geren and Dvontè will be here to pick us up at three.*

*It's time for you to start living again. I'm worried sick about you, and I owe you everything that I am. Let me repay you.*

*So make sure you get the bomb-ass outfit, preferably something low-cut that shows a lot of leg, and get that freakin' hair straight. You have a date next week, whether you like it or not!*

*Love and Kisses,*
*Janessa*

*P.S. Don't even think about waking my ass up for your dumb aerobics class tomorrow! That's a sorry substitution for fucking, and you know it!*

Tempest fell out laughing. She had every intention of waking her ass up. So she made me a date behind my back? The nerve of the huzzy! Little did Janessa know, she had made Tempest's night.

She dozed off with a grin, dreaming about Geren Kincaid. She couldn't wait to lay her eyes on his fine ass again.

"I can't believe I let you talk me into this!" Janessa exclaimed, limping into the locker room of the Sports & Health Club. She flung herself down on a wooden bench by a set of lockers and rubbed the small of her back. "I hope you're happy. Thanks to you, I won't be able to stand up straight for three days."

"Aw, squash it, Janessa," Tempest lashed back at her. "Cardio-karate is the bomb. You need to start doing the class three times a week like I do." She turned around, positioned her spandex-clad ass in Janessa's face, and slapped it for her benefit. "See this tight ass? I'm telling you, this shit pays off, gurl!"

"Hmm, quick question. What's the point of having a slamming body if you're holding out on your pussy like it's a golden ticket from a Willy Wonka Chocolate Bar?" The eagle's-eye view of Tempest's ass was beginning to lose its appeal, so she added, "Kindly remove your buffalo butt from my face, please!"

"Buffalo butt?" Tempest took the towel from around her neck and slapped Janessa upside the head with it. "I look damn good, and you know it."

"It's all good, Tempest," Janessa replied, giving credit where credit was due. Tempest was the bomb, and not just because she was her homie. "Just don't ask me to come to any more of these classes, because my back can't handle it. I'm celibate, so my joints are kind of stiff. Wait till I start getting my freak on again on a regular basis, I'll show your buffalo-butt ass up in class. Like I always say, this is a sorry-ass substitute for fucking."

Tempest straddled the bench and faced her. "Aiight, time for a heart-to-heart."

Janessa played dumb. "About?"

Tempest punched her on the arm. Hurt like all hell, too. "About your little note from last night, Miss Thang!"

"Oh, that!" Janessa rolled her eyes and diverted them to the floor, waiting for her tongue-lashing. "Listen, Tempest, before you jump down my throat, I'm convinced I did the right thing. If I'd left it up to you, another good man would've slipped right through your fingers."

There was an uncomfortable silence. Janessa could feel Tempest staring a hole through her. She couldn't take it anymore. She jumped up and leaned against the lockers, crossing her arms in front of her. "Say something, dammit!"

Tempest glanced up at her. "What do you expect me to say, Janessa?"

"I dunno. Sheesh! Cuss me out, call me a trifling bitch, tell me I'm on your shit list, or sumptin!"

"Okay, I'll say something." Tempest stood up and got all up in her grill. Janessa felt a pimp-slap coming on. Instead Tempest kissed her gently on the cheek. "Thank you, sis!"

"Thank you?" Janessa was lost like a whore in church. "Am I hearing things up in here?"

"No, you're not hearing things." Tempest chuckled, grinning from ear to ear. "Thanks for hooking me up with Geren. I'm really looking forward to it."

"Say what?" Janessa sat back down on the bench before she keeled the fuck over. "You mean you're actually happy about all of this?"

"Very happy!" Tempest opened her locker and got out her gym bag. "Come on, let's hit the showers so we can go shopping for that bomb-ass dress you demanded I get for the wedding."

"Damn, damn, damn! Do miracles never cease?"

"Don't look so shocked. Like you said, he is attractive, success-ful and unattached. Why not go for it?"

"Exactly my point." Janessa got up to get her bag out of her locker. "I just knew you were going to open a can of whup-ass on me. What a relief!"

They both fell out laughing. "Normally, I would. Most of your notes do piss my ass off. This one was a far cry from the last one, though. Remember?"

Janessa played dumb again. "Nope, sure don't."

"Yeah, right, trick." Tempest chuckled. "Last year about this time, you wrote me a note telling me that you *accidentally* let Everett, that dude I was interested in, ram his dick up in you."

Janessa turned her back to Tempest, ashamed. "That was an accident! I swear!"

"It doesn't matter." Tempest giggled. "As it turned out, he was a two-minute brotha, and you ended up having to go through hell to get rid of his ass. That's what you get. Better you than me!"

It was Janessa's turn to hit Tempest with a towel. "You're so mean!"

"Then there was the first note you ever wrote me. Way back in elementary school, about Steven Miller, the first boy I ever had a crush on. You kissed him on the playground, and you were afraid to tell me."

"You did kick my ass for real then!" Just the mention of the ass-whupping made Janessa's butt start to ache. "You wouldn't speak to me for weeks."

"You've always had a thing for my men."

"Not all of them," Janessa objected. "Just a couple of them."

"Hmph, well, you keep your grubby little hands off Geren."

"Sheit, I would never! He's fine and all, but I want to get jiggy with Dvontè. Besides, we're grown women now, and I would never do anything to you like that now." Tempest rolled her eyes and headed to the showers. Janessa called after her, "I mean it, too!"

# 5

## the bachelorette party

Tempest walked into the kitchen at Janessa's grandmother's house and attempted to turn around before she was spotted.

"Hey there, Tempest! What's up with you, gurl?" Janessa's cousin Chiquita inquired.

Tempest let the swinging door close behind her and walked farther into the old-fashioned, overcrowded kitchen. "How are you doing, Chiquita?"

"Same ole, same ole," Chiquita replied, turning around from the sink where she was washing greens for her sister's wedding reception the next day so she could look Tempest up and down. "You're looking good, Tempest, gurl."

"So are you. I love what you did with your hair," Tempest lied, staring at Chiquita's hairstyle and wondering what was up with it.

There were finger waves on the left side, crimps on the right side, and a gigantic fake roll of hair on the back that was two shades darker than her natural hair. Tempest always found Marquita and Chiquita amusing. They were the most hoochified sistahs that she knew. The fact that they were Janessa's first cousins wasn't much of a surprise because Janessa was running a close third in the hoochie-of-the-decade contest.

"Thanks." Chiquita blushed, running wet fingers through the roll on the back with pride. She was convinced she had it going on. "Conchita Dina Alonzo Morales over at Weave Central hooked my ass up."

"She did a bangin' job," Tempest lied again, searching through the lower cabinets for the gallon of potato wine Mrs. Porter had sent her upstairs to fetch. Tempest found the dusty bottle and wondered how many decades it had been crammed down there.

They were all over Mrs. Porter's Northeast row house for Marquita's bachelorette party. Tempest had no idea how she'd even ended up there. She'd agreed to go to the wedding rehearsal with Janessa. She'd even agreed to stand in for the bride, which was a trip in itself—half the wedding party had been smoking weed and could barely manage to walk down the aisle without giggling or munching on potato chips. She definitely hadn't planned on the bachelorette party, though. Janessa *claimed* she needed a ride from the rehearsal dinner over there, so Tempest complied, even though there were dozens of other women headed that way.

Tempest turned around and became enthralled in Chiquita's fucked-da-hell-up hairstyle again. "Yeah, she really worked your hair over gurlfriend," Tempest said, trying to suppress a smile.

"Didn't she though?" Chiquita grabbed another handful of fresh greens out of the produce bag and ran them under the running faucet. "You ever been there?"

"Naw, I can't say I've had the pleasure." Tempest chuckled,

knowing there was no way in the world she would share the same stylist with Chiquita, Marquita, or Janessa, for that matter. "I do my own hair most of the time."

"Well, you should definitely check Conchita out," Chiquita persisted. "Her shop is at the corner of Extension Avenue and Tracks Lane in Fakehair."

"Fakehair?" Tempest giggled. *Figures!*

"Yeah, Fakehair, Maryland. Right off the beltway." Chiquita turned off the faucet and dried her hands on a dish towel. She went over to the opposite counter and started rummaging through her fake Louis Vuitton handbag. "Hold up. I've got a card somewhere."

Tempest watched her pull out everything from a twelve-pack of condoms to some Monistat 7. "That's okay, Chiquita. You can just give me her number later."

Chiquita shoved all of the stuff back into her purse. "Okay, but make sure you try some of the Jamaican bean pies they sell in the back of the salon when you go."

Tempest couldn't hold her laughter in any longer. "I'll be sure to do that," she cackled. "Listen, I'm going to go back downstairs. Your grandmother's waiting for me to bring the wine."

"I'll grab the cups," Chiquita offered, getting a package of plastic cups off the top of the fridge and holding the door open for Tempest, who was trying to carry the wine without getting dust all over her black pantsuit.

"Thanks!"

"So how'd you like the wedding rehearsal?" Chiquita asked while they walked through the dining room to the basement steps off the hall.

"It was cool," Tempest answered, not wanting to give her real opinion. The wedding rehearsal had been a mess. She was just glad she hadn't gotten a weed contact from the groomsmen who were getting high on the back pew.

"Thanks for standing in for Marquita. My sister's a nervous freakin' wreck about the wedding tomorrow."

"It was no problem, really," Tempest said, thinking she would be a nervous wreck too if she was getting ready to marry a man who looked like Marquita's fiancé.

"I can't wait till tomorrow myself!" Chiquita exclaimed. "The wedding's going to be the bomb-diggity!"

"Sure seems like it." Tempest smirked, following Chiquita down the basement steps.

There were about forty sistahs crammed into a ten-by-twelve-foot room without a drop of air circulating. Tempest was trippin' out—the women in the room ranged from eighteen to eighty. Some were even senile. Hell, Janessa's grandmother Mrs. Porter was half blind in one eye and couldn't see a damn thing out of the other one. One thing she could do was bake up some mean sweet potato pie. Tempest quickly downed two slices, even though she'd managed not to get a weed contact.

The male strippers were running late, and all of the women were anxiously awaiting their arrival. Janessa and her cousin Chiquita had ventured out a couple of nights before to catch the Wednesday-night male revue at the Black Screw, where they found the strippers they hired.

Tempest was looking forward to the show. Through the big-dick-alert grapevine of the D.C. Society of Sistahs in Pursuit of Good Men, Tempest had heard some very intriguing rumors about the Black Screw. She'd never been there personally, and frankly, her ass was half scared to go. Sistahs claimed the place was sportin' wall-to-wall naked men with Mandingo dicks. Legend had it that there was even a brotha in there who was sportin' such a gargantuan dang-a-lang that he sucked it onstage. Tempest wondered who on earth would fuck a man like that. Big can be a good thing, but too damn big can be hazardous to your pelvic muscles.

Tempest briefly dated a brotha originally from Bermuda, who was raised in London. Nevel's accent turned her on big-time. She loved it when he called her "luv." Everything was cool between them until they ended up in a compromising position one night in his Adam's Morgan flat. Nevel took it out of his pants; Tempest took it in with her eyes and immediately faked a muscle cramp in her leg.

She toyed with the idea of saying she was on her period, or even faking nausea. She knew no man wanted some so bad that he would willingly risk a sistah hurling all over his back or, worse yet, his dick.

Nevel tried to massage the cramp out so he could get some, but there was no way in the hell he was sticking that thing up in her. Tempest considered herself adventurous, but she was not about to venture there. She ran the worst-case scenario through her head, pondering whether or not her health insurance would cover surgical dick removal from a vagina.

She was tempted to give his dick a test drive but decided to keep her leg cramp and hobble on out to her car. She ran home to call Janessa to spill the beans, and that huzzy had the nerve to ask for his digits. Even though Tempest had no intention of ever seeing Nevel again, sistahgurl wasn't getting anything from her—all she needed was Janessa bragging on getting the bottom knocked out of her pussy.

"Listen up, everybody," Janessa announced. "The strippers just called and said they would be here in about an hour, so we're gonna play a couple of games while we're waiting."

"What kind of games?" Janessa's Aunt Mabel asked. "I hope they're not boring."

"Oh, I doubt you will be bored, Aunt Mabel," Janessa replied, winking at her. Her aunt sat up on the edge of her seat after registering that comment. She knew how wild Janessa could be, and it suddenly seemed like the night was getting interesting. "First, we're going to play Pin the Dick on the Mandingo," Janessa continued. "And then we're going to play a quick round of Ghetto Jeopardy. By that time, the dancers should be here."

"Oooh, I just love Ghetto Jeopardy!" Tracy, one of the bridesmaids, said excitedly. "Ya'll ever played that joint before?"

Most of the women shook their heads and answered no, but another bridesmaid, Yvonne, yelled out, "I have! We played at my family reunion last year. My peeps came to blows over it, though, because we were betting quarters. It was almost as bad as Acey Ducey. We had to ban that game from our reunions after my Uncle Jack ended up with a broken nose."

"Umm, Yvonne, thanks for the family history lesson," Janessa said, smacking her lips. "But we'd like to get started some time today. Damn!"

Yvonne rolled her eyes at Janessa and went to sulk in a corner. It was common knowledge that the two of them hated each other. They even got into a fistfight one Saturday night at a Junkyard Band go-go when they were teenagers, and the police had to break it up.

Everyone's eyes almost popped out of their sockets when Janessa went to the laundry room and returned with a life-size poster of a brotha with a huge, elephantine dick down to his ankles.

"Who in the hell is that?" Marquita asked, sipping a cup of potato wine. "Dang, I thought my boo had a big one!"

"That's Mandingo," Chiquita replied. "I told you about him. He's one of the headliners at the Black Screw."

"Dizammmmmmm, I hope he's the one you've got coming here tonight!" Marquita exclaimed, looking like she was ready to feel herself up just thinking about him.

"Naw, he's not," Janessa said, dejected. "He already had another party to do tonight, so we missed out. He was definitely my first choice, though."

"Mine, too," Chiquita agreed, giving Janessa a high five. "He had me creaming all over myself at the club when he was performing."

Tempest cleared her throat, hoping to remind Janessa, Marquita, and Chiquita that there were older women in the room who probably hadn't seen a dick in decades.

Janessa caught her drift and hung the picture up with some tape on the wall by the fireplace.

"Okay, this is pretty simple," Janessa began. "It has the same rules as Pin the Tail on the Donkey, except you have to pin the dick on the Mandingo."

She handed each of the women a cutout photocopy of a dick, much shorter than the one on the wall, and gave them a piece of tape to use to stick it on. They each took turns being blindfolded and trying to hit the right spot. Tempest passed on her turn because she thought the whole thing was damn ridiculous, not to mention inappropriate to do around senior citizens.

Ironically, the senior citizens were the ones who had the most fun playing. In fact, Janessa's grandmother, half blind and all, won the game by pinning it on the exact spot.

"Dizammmmmm, Grandma, you won," Marquita exclaimed. "You didn't forget where it is, did you?"

"You go on with your bad self," Aunt Mabel guffawed. "You did better than me. Mine is the one all the way up there under his armpit."

Mrs. Porter flashed her dentures. "It's like riding a bike, young ladies. Just like riding a bike. You never forget!"

They all fell out laughing. Janessa asked Tempest to go get the red gift bag from under the steps while she took the picture down off the wall.

"Grandma, Tempest is getting your prize," Janessa informed her. "I hope it's not too much for you to handle."

When Tempest heard that comment, she decided to sneak a peek in the bag. She knew how sick Janessa could be, but still, she couldn't believe her eyes. "Janessa, you know you need to take this back and get her something else!" she snapped.

"Tempest, bring the present on over here," Mrs. Porter ordered. "I've been around a long time. There's nothing in that bag I haven't seen before."

Tempest slowly walked over to the sofa and handed her the bag. "I want you all to know I have absolutely nothing to do with what's in there." Tempest rolled her eyes and clucked her tongue in Janessa's direction and then mouthed the words, "Sick ass!"

Mrs. Porter pulled the fourteen-inch dark brown dildo out of the bag and hollered, "Oh *myyyyyyy* goodness!"

Everyone snickered, and some of the older women stared at it, trying to figure out what it was.

"Grandma, do you even know what that is?" Marquita probed.

Mrs. Porter gave Marquita a love-slap on the leg. "Of course I know what it is! Everyone knows what a vibrator looks like!"

Chiquita chuckled. "Ahem, actually that's a dildo, Grandma."

Mrs. Porter gazed over at Chiquita, who was standing up beside Janessa and Tempest. "What's the difference? Dildo. Vibrator. They both serve the same purpose."

Aunt Mabel decided to educate them all. "A vibrator you just stick in, and it moves all by itself. It runs off batteries. With a dildo, you have to manually stimulate yourself with it."

Janessa's mouth fell open. "Dang, Aunt Mabel, how do you know so much about them?"

"She sounds like an expert," Marquita concluded, wondering if the freakiness she tended to exude herself was genealogical.

"Maybe I am an expert," Aunt Mabel said, blushing. "I wasn't born yesterday, you know."

Janessa took a long look at her grandmother sitting on the couch with the gigantic, elephantine dildo in her fragile hand and envisioned having to call an ambulance if she tried to actually use it. She could never forgive herself if her grandmother ended up in traction or something. "Grandma, Tempest is probably right." Janessa walked over to the couch and tried to take the dildo from her. "I'll take it back and get you something more appropriate."

Mrs. Porter yanked it away and pushed it down between the cushions on the couch. "Reach for it again and pull back a stub, missy!"

Janessa wasn't sure whether her grandmother was joking about the violence or not. She knew how horny she'd been during her current dick drought and figured her grandmother had probably gone about thirty years without any action. She decided to get the party moving along. "Aiight, let's get ready to play Ghetto Jeopardy," she announced to the room.

Janessa went to the laundry room to get the game off the dryer, and Tempest followed her, grabbed her by the elbow, and seethed, "No more raunchy gifts, Janessa, or we're steppin' out back so I can open a can of whup-ass. I can't believe you just gave your grandmother a damn dildo!"

Janessa freed herself from Tempest's grasp. "Dang, I'm just trying to keep the party interesting." She pouted. "Besides, technically, you gave it to her, not me."

Janessa giggled, but Tempest didn't see anything amusing. "I hope these strippers you and Chiquita have coming over here aren't planning on getting buck wild, because if they do, I'm leaving. I'm not about to sit up in here watching a bunch of senior citizens cream all over themselves."

"Tempest, quit the mothering! Damn!"

"Speaking of mothers, where in the world is yours?" Tempest inquired. "Why didn't she come to the party?"

"She claimed she was going home to get some rest after the rehearsal dinner." Janessa grimaced. "Besides, the last thing we need here is my mother. She would make us all sit around and give Marquita tips on being a good and proper wife and all the other bullshit she's always talking."

They went back out into the main room, and Tempest helped Janessa set up the game and get people organized into two teams.

"Okay," Janessa began, pulling a card from the deck once they were all settled. "The category is Eighties Television. For two hundred points, the name of the character on *The Jeffersons* who played George and Louise's son."

Aunt Mabel jumped up off her chair. "Who is Lionel?"

"Correct," Janessa said. "Next question, the name of—"

Aunt Mabel was still excited over the first question. "Lionel had the biggest, juiciest ass. Brotha looked like he was hung like a horse, too!"

Everyone busted out laughing, and bunches of high fives were passed about. Tempest decided to try some of the potato wine. It was apparent it was going to be a long-ass night.

"Aunt Mabel, can we move on now?" Janessa asked, rolling her eyes.

Aunt Mabel sat back down and started whispering to the woman beside her, probably still talking about Lionel's ass.

"Ya'll ready for the next question?" Janessa inquired of the rowdy group. They all yelled out yes, so she continued. "For six hundred points in the category Prison Movies. Name the movie that Leon Isaac Kennedy and his wife starred in."

Everyone yelled out *"Penitentiary"* in unison, and one woman asked, "What ever happened to those two anyway?"

A few people shrugged because they didn't have a clue.

"Next question," Janessa began. "Name the actor who won the Playa of the Year in the movie *The Mack*."

Marquita beat everyone to the punch. "Who is Max Julien?"

"Correct, Marquita," Janessa said, smiling at her. "Oops, sorry, that was for four hundred points, by the way, and the category was Pimp Movies."

"Dang, were there that many pimp movies back in the day?" Chiquita asked.

"Hell, yeah!" Aunt Mabel exclaimed. "Pimping was a big profession years ago. These days, most women are packing heat and work the corners on their own." She shut up when she realized all eyes were glued on her, though. She wasn't quite ready to reveal her "other" profession.

Janessa was just about to get in her grill and ask her how she knew so damn much about it when the doorbell rang.

Saved by the mofo bell, Aunt Mabel thought to herself.

Janessa and Chiquita went upstairs to get the door. Tempest said a silent prayer to herself that things weren't about to get more out of hand than they already were. When she spotted not one but two sets of muscular legs coming down the steps, she knew they were in for it.

Janessa proudly introduced them to the room. "This tall, muscular man over here with the sexy bedroom eyes and sleek, firm physique goes by the name of the Lone Banger." She squeezed the muscles in the arm of an extremely tall, about six-foot-seven, dark-skin brotha who Tempest had to admit was fine. If she ran into him in a dark alley, she would tear his dick up.

Janessa moved over to the other dancer, who was considerably shorter, about five-foot-nine, but undeniably fine as well. He was light-skinned with hazel eyes and a body that seemed to exude sex out of every pore. "This here is Cum Daddy. Apparently he likes to go at it five or six times a night."

"That's just an appetizer, baby. Just an appetizer," he said with a smile, flexing his muscles for everyone to get a better look. They both had on tank tops with "The Black Screw" silk-screened on them and skintight black pants.

Tempest wanted to get up and leave; she just didn't feel it was appropriate to get freaky in front of her elders. As fine as they were, though, she wasn't about to budge until she saw a little sumptin' sumptin'.

The Lone Banger handed Chiquita a cassette tape to put on for their performance, surveyed the room, and announced, "Ladies, by the time this night is over, there won't be a dry pair of panties in the house."

Then the freakiness began.

# 6

## the wedding

"Hold up one sec! I'll be right back!"

Tempest left Janessa in a stupor at the front door of her apartment and rushed into her bedroom.

"Where are you going?" Janessa asked. "We have to hurry up and get dressed."

"I am dressed!" Tempest yelled from the bedroom.

"Not in this, you aren't!" Janessa yelled back at her, holding up a black garment bag in her right hand.

"I'll be back out there in a minute."

Janessa grew impatient and went into Tempest's bedroom. She was shocked to find Tempest lying up in the bed with the covers up to her chin. "What the hell are you doing, sis?"

"Going back to bed so I can wake up all over again." Tempest pulled the comforter over her head completely and turned over on her side, facing away from Janessa. "It's obvious I'm having a freakin' nightmare."

"Ha! Ha! Ha! Very funny!" Janessa threw the garment bag on Tempest's dresser and then yanked the comforter off Tempest and completely off the bed, tossing it on the floor. "Now get up, take off the outfit you have on, and put on the bridesmaid gown. Hurry up so we won't be late."

"Janessa, *pleassssssse* tell me you're kidding," Tempest pleaded. "This is some sort of sick joke, right?"

"No, it's not," Janessa replied, smacking her lips in disgust. "I already told you, Chiquita fractured her leg last night trying to do some freaky, acrobatic sex shit with her boyfriend. Those strippers at the party must have seriously put her in the mood, because she's laid up in the hospital with her leg elevated in a cast."

Tempest rolled her eyes, no more swayed by the second rendition of the story than by the first one Janessa had thrown at her when she answered the door. "Well, that's unfortunate," she said, trying to show an ounce of compassion. "I feel sorry for Chiquita, I really do. However, there is no way in the hell I'm taking her place in Marquita's wedding. That shit is just simply out of the question."

"What's wrong with you?" Janessa threw the garment bag on the foot of the bed and starting unzipping it. "I ask you for one damn favor, for my family, mind you, and you start trippin' on me."

"Janessa, I love you. You know that." Tempest propped herself up on her elbows so she could see the monstrosity Janessa was pulling out of the bag. "But I don't love you enough to wear that raunchy, tasteless, ridiculous-looking dress."

"Come on, shit!" Janessa squealed. "I have to wear one just like it. Mine is out in the living room, on the couch."

"That's all good," Tempest said, glaring at the red flame satin dress with ruffles, which looked more like a hooker's street-corner outfit than a bridesmaid gown. "I'm happy for you, and I'll cheer you on from the front pew, but I'm not——"

"You will not be cheering me on from the pew, because your ass is going to be standing right beside me."

"You must be on crack!"

"I'm not on crack, but I bet I'll slap the living shit out of you if you don't put this dress on, Tempest!"

"Just try it." Tempest chuckled, knowing good and damn well Janessa would never have the guts to lay a finger on her.

Realizing that her idle threats were falling on deaf ears, Janessa resorted to her next tactic, a guilt trip. "Tempest, you just don't know," she began, sitting on the bed beside her and rubbing away nonexistent tears. "Marquita had me on the phone all morning. She's so upset about all of this. She just doesn't want her wedding day to be ruined. Can't you understand that? Can't you *feeeeeel* her pain?"

Oh brother, Tempest thought to herself. Gurlfriend is really laying it on thick.

"Why can't she just have three bridesmaids instead of four?"

"Because Curtis has four groomsmen, and they need to keep it even. Come on, now. You know it wouldn't look right for him to have more attendants than her, and it would be dead wrong for him to kick one of them out the wedding at the last minute."

"Well, why me?" Tempest asked. She and Marquita knew each other through Janessa, but they were never tight like that. "Doesn't she have anyone else she can ask?"

"Not anyone else who can fit this dress." Janessa held the dress up by the hanger to emphasize the point. "All of her other friends wear size twenty and above. They can't get their asses in this dress, even if we let it out as far as it will go."

"Hmph, I might not be able to get in it either. Chiquita has itty-bitty titties. In case you haven't noticed, mine are about three times bigger." Tempest grabbed her breasts and held them up. "What am I supposed to do? Let all my stuff hang out?"

Janessa grinned mischievously. The mere fact that Tempest was making titty comparisons meant she was at least considering it.

"We'll work it out." Janessa stood up and started rummaging through the top drawer of Tempest's dresser for a needle and thread. "If not for Marquita, do it for me. You know you're my shero."

"Damn," Tempest muttered under her breath. She got up off the bed and starting taking off the bomb-ass outfit she had on. "I can't believe this. My first date with Geren, my first date, *period,* in ages, and I have to look like a cheap hooker."

Janessa gave her a huge hug and kiss on the cheek. "No, neither one of us are going to look like hookers. We're going to look fly as all hell, like we always do. Remember this is a first-date situation for me, too."

Tempest wanted to make a comment about Dvontè but held it in. He gave her the impression he didn't care what a woman wore when she went out with him as long as it had easy access to the nana. Geren was different, though—at least, she hoped so.

Tempest was lost in a trance, wondering what it would be like to go out on a date with Geren, aka Mr. Fine Ass. After all, he did look like the words *F-U-C-K  M-E* spelled out.

"You want me to do your hair for you, gurl?" Janessa asked, breaking Tempest's concentration.

"My hair?" Tempest panicked, almost knocking Janessa down to get to the mirror. After inspecting it and realizing there wasn't a hair out of place, she confronted Janessa. "My hair's already done. I spent almost three hours on it this morning after I got home from the bachelorette party. So what are you trying to say?"

"Nothing," Janessa responded quickly. "Your hair's all that and a

bag of chips, as usual. I was just trying to show you my appreciation for agreeing to do it. That's all."

"Oh." Tempest giggled. "In that case, you can come over here
every weekend for the next month and clean my crib, wash my
laundry, and cook my meals."

"Now you must be the one on crack," Janessa hissed, slapping
Tempest gently on the shoulder. "You know the kid doesn't even
clean up after herself, so you know I'm not cleaning up after your
ass."

"Okay, fine. I'll settle for you just cleaning the toilets."

"Oh, hells naw! It's bad enough I have to deal with Fred's
stankin' craps. I adore you. I love you. You're my shero, but—"

"But what?"

"But your shit does stink!"

"And so does yours!" Tempest exclaimed, coming right back
at her. "Hell, whenever you stay over, I have to make sure I buy two
extra cans of air freshener and air out the joint after you leave."

"Whatever, heifer!"

"Whatever, tramp!"

"Oh, damn!" Janessa ran into the living room to get her dress.
"It's almost time for them fine-ass nuccas to get here. We better
hurry up."

"Yeah," Tempest said, picking up her own dress. "Hurry up and
put on these ugly-ass dresses so we can look like tramps."

Janessa came running out of the bathroom when she heard the
knock on Tempest's door. She smoothed out the bottom of her
dress and flung the door open, expecting to see both Dvontè and
Geren standing there.

"Good afternoon, Janessa," Geren said, cracking a smile at her.
"You look stunning, as usual."

Janessa's eyes immediately drifted to the beautiful bouquet of
white roses in Geren's hands.

"Are those for me?" she asked jokingly.

Geren cleared his throat, wondering if she was serious. "No, actually, these are for Tempest."

"Oh," Janessa replied sarcastically. She peeked around the corner of the door out into the hallway, assuming Dvontè was lurking out there somewhere, waiting for his turn to speak. He was nowhere in sight. "Where's Dvontè?"

"He's down in the car. It's so hot outside, he thought it would be a good idea to keep the air-conditioning running."

"Hmph, I see!"

Geren hated lying for Dvontè. The truth of the matter was that Dvontè didn't believe in catering to females by coming to their door. He was the when-I-blow-my-horn-you-need-to-hightail-it-outside type of brotha, while Geren was the complete opposite: a perfect gentleman.

"We wouldn't want you ladies to feel uncomfortable or sweat out your hair or anything. The TV stations have been scrolling a heat advisory across the screen all morning. The heat index is close to one hundred fifteen degrees."

"*Danggggggg,* that is hot! No wonder I felt like my insides were boiling when I caught a cab over here."

Geren let out a sigh of relief. Janessa apparently bought his explanation.

"Come on in," Janessa said, moving to the side so he could come inside. "I forgot my manners for a second."

"Thank you." Geren walked into the entry foyer and glanced down at his watch. They had less than thirty minutes to get to the church on time. "Is Tempest ready?"

"Almost. I must warn you, though." Janessa frowned and shook her head. "She's not a happy camper."

"Really?"

"Word up!"

Geren immediately started to panic. All week he'd hoped Tempest wouldn't change her mind. After all, he hadn't even discussed the date with her, only with Janessa. He hated being dissed, and all of a sudden, he felt a diss coming on.

Janessa started walking down the hallway toward the kitchen. "I'm going to go find something to put these in. Make yourself at home."

"Thanks!"

Geren walked into the living room and was stunned to see how meticulously clean the place was. Most women he dated left everything from shoes to magazines to clipped toenails strewn all over their living room floors, but not Tempest. He always kept his place clean, too, so things were looking up as far as compatibility. He wondered if the rest of her place was as clean, or if she was one of those who just perpetrated by keeping the highly visible rooms in order.

He walked over to her leather sectional sofa and lifted up a seat cushion, expecting to find a bunch of food wrappings and hair curlers stuffed underneath it. Nothing. He was bent over to replace the cushion when he felt someone's eyes on his ass.

"Hello, Geren."

"Hey, Tempest!" He pushed the cushion back into place and turned around to look at her. The first thing he noticed were her breasts about to bust out of the dress she had on. "You look great!"

"You don't have to lie." Tempest rolled her eyes and came farther into the living room.

"I'm not lying," Geren replied, hoping the eye rolling didn't pertain to him messing through her sofa. "I think you're gorgeous."

"Not in this dress, I'm not." Tempest sat down on the arm of the sofa and put her right hand on her hip. "I look like a hooker."

Geren cleared his throat, trying to think of an appropriate response and keep his eyes off her breasts at the same time. He wasn't an expert on streetwalkers, but she didn't look like one to him. The dress wasn't the most tasteful, but it was the same one Janessa had on when she greeted him at the door. Janessa's boobs were fully covered, though.

"I didn't realize both you and Janessa were in the wedding party. Dvontè mentioned that Janessa was, but—"

"Yeah, well, I didn't realize it either until a couple of hours ago," Tempest muttered, clucking her tongue in disgust. "Believe me, if I had seen this coming, I would have left town for the weekend."

Geren could tell Tempest was really disturbed by the recent turn of events and didn't know quite what to say, so he fell silent.

"Janessa's cousin Chiquita had a freak accident last night, so I'm her last-minute substitute."

"I see." Geren was curious to know what "a freak accident" entailed, and was about to ask when Tempest preempted his question.

"Where's Dvontè?" she inquired, an edge of suspicion in her voice.

"He's down in the car."

"Oh." *He is so trifling,* Tempest thought to herself. She wasn't surprised Dvontè had waited in the car. She knew his type and just hoped Janessa wouldn't fall for his playa ass too hard.

Geren debated about whether or not to try to feed Tempest the same fabricated explanation he gave Janessa. He decided against it. "By the way, I bought you some—"

"Bomb-ass roses!" Janessa exclaimed as she came bouncing back into the room holding a cobalt-blue glass vase with the flowers inside.

Tempest got up off the arm of the sofa, took the vase, and

smelled the fragrant roses. "They're lovely," she said, trying to hold back a blush. "Thanks!"

Geren grinned at her, glad to finally see her mood improving. "You're more than welcome."

Tempest kind of felt bad for Janessa, since she knew Dvontè hadn't bought her any flowers.

Janessa seemed to read Tempest's mind. "Ya'll ready to bounce, sis?"

Tempest placed the roses on her glass coffee table and then intertwined her arm with Geren's. He placed his hand over hers and realized she was trembling slightly. She surely couldn't have been cold, so an "uh-oh" started running track through his mind.

The "uh-oh" turned to an "oh-hell-no" when Tempest made her next statement.

"Janessa, do you mind going on ahead? I'd like to talk to Geren alone for a second."

"Cool with me, but don't take too long." Janessa smacked her lips, pushed the strap of her small handbag farther up on her shoulder, and headed for the door. "If we're late, Marquita will throw another hissy fit and start in with that crying madness."

"We'll be right down," Tempest assured her, pulling away from Geren and practically pushing Janessa out of the door. She closed it behind her and just stood there, staring at the door frame.

"Is there something wrong, Tempest?"

"Not exactly." Tempest turned around to face him. He was so close to her, she could feel his minty-fresh breath on her cheek. "I just feel the need to clarify something."

"And what might that be?" Geren asked, with obvious concern in his voice.

"My appearance," Tempest blurted out with obvious embarrassment. "Normally, I wouldn't be caught dead in a get-up like this."

Geren fought to suppress a laugh. He thought she was so cute, standing there trying to justify the outfit.

"I'm the conservative type," she added. "I realize my breasts are hanging out, but that's not my fault. This was the best Janessa and I could do in the time frame we had to work with."

Geren reached down and retook her hand. "Tempest, don't worry your pretty little head over it. I knew the moment I laid eyes on you that you were conservative, as you put it."

Tempest sighed in relief. "So you understand where I'm coming from, then?"

"Absolutely!" Geren had to catch himself and clear his head; he was about to salivate over her hardened nipples. He could make them out through the material of the form-fitting dress. He forced himself to look in her eyes and ignore her breasts. "I'm just glad that's all you wanted to talk to me about. It's no big deal."

"Well, it's a very big deal to me."

Geren had to let the laugh out. She was really trippin' over the dress. Her humility intrigued him.

Tempest yanked her hand away and headed back into the living room. "See, you're laughing at me."

"No, I'm not," Geren insisted, trailing her. "I'm simply relieved. For a minute, I thought you were going to back out of our date and tell me to beat it. Since I didn't have the liberty of actually calling you to confirm, I've been on pins and needles all week. Janessa set this up, but I thought surely you would call at some point to finalize things. When I didn't hear from you, I got nervous."

"Geren, I have to be honest. I'm a bit reluctant to go back out on the dating scene. We had a wonderful time at the club last week. I usually hate clubs but you helped me relax and enjoy myself."

Geren raised his eyebrows. "Oh, yeah?"

"Yes, but I've been dragged through the mud by so many men that I trusted. It makes me wonder how many times a mouse has to get caught on a glue pad before it realizes it needs to walk around it."

Geren claimed Tempest's hand for yet a third time and kissed her gently on her knuckles. He knew there was no use in trying to explain that he was different. In time, he would just have to prove it to her.

Tempest felt her cheeks become flushed. "With that said, I've been looking forward to seeing you again."

"Really?" Geren asked, kissing her hand again with tender, full lips.

"Yes. I had certain reservations at first. Mainly, I wondered if you were only doing this so Dvontè and Janessa could still hook up."

Geren pulled her to him and boldly put his arm around her waist. He gazed deeply into her eyes. "I'll put it this way. If we didn't have plans for today and you didn't use my number, I would have waited about a month, maybe not even that long, before I tracked you down."

"Get real!" Tempest tried to pull away from him, but he tightened his grip.

"I am for real. I have no clue where this is going or where it even can go, but I would like for us to find out. Is that cool with you?"

Tempest was at a lost for words. So many times she had been fooled. Might he really be the needle in the haystack?

She glanced at the door. "Shall we go?"

Geren released her and held his arm out so she could walk past him. "Conservative ladies first."

Tempest giggled. So what if she looked like a hoochie? She was still the same person inside, and that's all that mattered.

Geren and Dvontè both sat on the fifth pew of the Brightwood Baptist Church with their mouths hanging wide open. They couldn't believe their eyes. The groom-to-be and his best man were waiting patiently at the altar for the processional to begin. Together, they totaled one man of normal height.

"Do you see this shit, man?" Dvontè asked, jabbing Geren in the rib.

"Shhhhhhh!" Geren leaned closer in to him on the hard wooden pew so he could whisper in his ear. "Dvontè, you know better than to curse in church. If nothing else, I know your mother taught you that much."

Dvontè looked at Geren with disdain. "Okay, fine. Do you see this *crap*, man?"

Geren chuckled. "How can I not see it?" He sat back in the pew once the ventilation system let him get a good whiff of Dvontè's sour breath. "Dang, man, a Tic Tac wouldn't hurt you right about now."

Dvontè rolled his eyes and blew into his own hand. The heat almost drilled a hole through it, and he realized his breath was stankin' for some reason. It had to be the pastrami sandwich he'd had for lunch.

"She's marrying a midget. A fuckin', I mean freakin' Lilliputian."

Geren laughed again. "I didn't realize you knew such big words. You must have learned them to impress the honies."

Someone behind them cleared her throat, and Geren turned around to see an older woman with gray hair and a huge red fancy hat glaring at them. From her expression, he knew she must have overheard Dvontè's foul language. He glared over at Dvontè. "Could you lower your voice? You're embarrassing me."

"Embarrassing you? We both need to be shot for sitting up in here." Dvontè noticed a young woman in her early twenties staring at him seductively from a few rows in front of them. He flashed her one of his cinematic smiles and almost hurled when she flashed an entire upper row of gold teeth in return.

He looked down at his wedding program, hoping the woman would find someone else to try to flirt with. He noticed the paper the program was printed on was standard white copy paper instead of the parchment paper normally used for weddings. He hadn't been to many weddings, but he knew that was tacky.

Suddenly he felt someone's hand on his thigh. He almost jumped out of his seat when he realized that a woman who looked old enough to be his great-great-grandmother was trying to feel him up.

Dvontè jabbed Geren in the ribs again. "Move down a little, man, or trade places with me."

Geren moved down a couple of feet on the pew but he was not about to play musical seats with Dvontè. "I thought you liked all women?" he asked teasingly. "Aren't you the one always saying eight to eighty, blind, crippled, or crazy?"

"That's just a figure of speech, man."

Geren sat up a few inches so he could wink at the older woman. She winked back at him and then started looking Dvontè up and down.

Dvontè felt sick to his stomach. "See, this is exactly why I don't do weddings. These people are certifiable. When I went to the bathroom, this midget turned around, giggling and shit, and tried to take a leak on my shoe. He was high or sumptin'. He's lucky I moved my foot just in time, or else my ankle would still be lodged in his pygmy ass."

The woman behind them cleared her throat again, lodging her complaint against the language. Geren punched Dvontè on the leg. "Just calm down, Dvontè. We're on dates, remember?"

"Hmph, some kind of date. They're both in the wedding, and we're sitting out here in a sea of desperate, ugly hoes." Dvontè loosened up the band of his wristwatch and stared at the dial. "When is this thing going to start, anyway? They're running mad late."

"How should I know?" Geren responded, looking at his own watch and realizing five o'clock had long come and gone. "At least we'll get to spend some time with the ladies at the reception."

Dvontè fidgeted with his necktie. He hated wearing them. When he went to clubs, he didn't have to deal with them, and his office was casual and laid-back.

"All I know is that I expect, no I *demand,* some ass after all of this."

"Watch your mouth, man," Geren hissed at him.

Dvontè lowered his voice a few notches before continuing. "I'm banging the hell out of Janessa till sunrise. I can tell you that much right now."

"There you go assuming again. You always think sistahs are going to be down on the first date."

"That's because they always are." Dvontè wanted to school Geren, tell him the after-wedding sex had already been discussed and confirmed between him and Janessa, but he knew Geren wouldn't approve. "When you're smooth like me, you can get it whenever and however you want it."

"Whatever, man," Geren said, having heard enough. He stood

up and started inching his way out of the pew. "I'm about to run to the restroom before they march down the aisle."

"Watch out for pygmies in there smokin' crack," Dvontè whispered after him. "You might get squirted."

Once Geren was gone, Dvontè surveyed the church and noticed a bunch of tore-up-from-the-floor-up women eyeing him. He pulled his suit jacket tighter around him and crossed his arms. He had never felt so violated.

Tempest was propped on top of the vanity in the crowded ladies' lounge, staring at the lead paint peeling off the ceiling of the old church. For the past hour, she had listened to Marquita wail over her impending marriage to a runt. She could only imagine what Geren must have been thinking. It was bad enough she had to wear the hoochie dress, but she hadn't warned Geren that there would be midgets running all around. Actually, she thought she would leave that part as a surprise, but now the thrill was over.

"Look, Marquita," Tempest said, getting down off the vanity and pushing her way through the circle of women surrounding the bride-to-be. "Far be it from me to cop an attitude up in here, but are you going to do this thing or not?"

"Heck, yeah, she's doing it," one of Janessa and Marquita's aunts yelled out. Aunt Blanche was the oldest sister of both Janessa and Marquita's mother. She had driven all the way up from her farm in North Carolina and it was obvious she wasn't even having the drama. "I spent all yesterday morning slaughtering hogs and cleaning more than two hundred pounds of chitterlings. Not to mention driving up here in the heat with those things in my trunk. There is going to be a wedding here today, or *else*."

Janessa looked up at Tempest from her position beside Marquita on the single tattered sofa in the lounge. She had her arm around Marquita, trying to console her, but the chitterlings comment made her want to run to a stall and vomit. Tempest rolled her eyes at her, and Janessa knew she was going to get it good once they were alone.

"Ya'll move back some and let the chile breathe," Grandma Porter demanded, pushing them all away from Marquita. "What seems to be the problem, baby? You can tell Grandma anything."

Tempest couldn't help but notice the wide grin on Grandma Porter's face. Not only that, but her whole body seemed relaxed. Obviously, the dildo had been put to good use after they cleared out from the bachelorette party.

"It's just that—that—that—" Marquita stuttered with tear-drenched eyes.

"What, baby?" Grandma Porter asked, gently rubbing Marquita's shoulder.

"I'm not sure I'm good enough for Curtis. I'm not sure I can satisfy him, if you know what I mean."

Everyone stared at each other, all wondering the same exact thing. Was Marquita marrying a man she had never slept with?

"Chile, please!" the aunt from North Carolina squealed. "How much effort does it take to sexually satisfy a troll."

"No, she didn't call him a troll," Tempest said, trying to suppress a laugh. "That's foul."

"Okay—short, then. The man is short. Anyone can see he's only about what? Four-one? Four-two? My seven-year-old is taller than that Curtis fella she's marrying. Last night when we got to the rehearsal dinner, I started to ask him if he wanted to go play horse-shoes with my son until I realized he was the groom."

Everyone fell out laughing—everyone except Marquita and Grandma Porter.

"Don't make fun of my man, Aunt Blanche," Marquita warned,

standing up and about to break bad. "He may be short but he's from Raoul's Midget-Breeding Farm, so he is all that!"

"Raoul's what?" Aunt Blanche asked.

Janessa launched into an explanation. "Raoul has this farm out on Route 29 where he breeds well-hung midgets and hires them out as escorts."

"Say what?" Aunt Blanche took Tempest's spot on the vanity and started fanning herself with one of the Acme Funeral Home fans she'd picked up off a pew earlier. "Well-hung midgets?"

"Raoul is the best man today," Tempest added, confirming Janessa's earlier statement. "You'll get to meet him and some of the others."

"Well, since Curtis is your man, as you call him," Janessa stated with sarcasm, "how about you go out there and marry him, so I can take these shoes off? They are killing my feet."

"I second the motion," Tempest agreed. Her feet were a size smaller than Chiquita's, but the cheap Payless satin pumps were still causing her feet to ache.

"Ya'll are right!" Marquita exclaimed. "Curtis is my man! Just because I have to limp to work sometimes after we have sex doesn't mean I can't handle him. I mean, if he didn't like it, he wouldn't be marrying me. Right?"

"Right!" Tempest shouted out, hoping it would all soon be over.

Grandma Porter frowned. "In all my years, I've never had a man make me limp anywhere. Those midgets must really be something."

"Grandma, you want me to hook you up with one of them?"

"Naw, not necessary. Now that I have my dildo, that's about all this old woman can handle."

Everyone started cackling except Aunt Blanche, who had missed out on the bachelorette party and grew concerned.

"Momma, what are you doing with one of those battery-operated gadgets?"

"That's a vibrator!" all the rest of the women shouted out in unison.

Before Aunt Blanche could ask another question, Marquita wiped her eyes with the sleeve of her J.C. Penney catalog wedding dress and swung open the door to the lounge. "Let's get this here show on the road!"

"Whew, we finally get a chance to sit down and chat for a few!" Geren exclaimed, throwing his left leg over the bench of one of the picnic tables in Janessa's grandmother's backyard.

Tempest giggled as she sat down beside him. "Yeah, I know." She looked around the yard at the various people doing everything from frying up croakers in the black pots over an open flame to tossing horseshoes to playing spades. "Marquita and Curtis are talking about having a water-balloon fight, but I'm not even down with that."

"Water-balloon fight?" Geren asked with disbelief.

Tempest nodded her head after taking a sip of her grape Kool-Aid. "Yup! You have to admit it fits right in with the rest of today's festivities."

Geren sighed heavily and took a swig of his Miller Light. "I guess."

Tempest swatted a sugar-hunting fly away from her cup. "So how did you like the wedding? Honestly?"

Geren lowered his eyes to the table trying to think of something appropriate to say. "It was . . . was . . . was—"

"Yes?"

"Let's just say it was different," he finally uttered.

Tempest laughed. "You're being kind. This whole day has been like a bad B movie."

Geren started laughing with her.

"My favorite part," Tempest continued through her cackles, "was when Curtis had to climb up on the step stool to kiss the bride."

Geren started laughing so hard then that he had to hold his stomach. "That was wild, but the really off-the-hook part was when people threw black-eyed peas at them when they left the church."

Tempest gave him a light slap on the arm. "Ha, ha! How about the hoopty they rolled out in?"

"Aw man, who could forget the yellow Charger with empty beer cans tied to the bumper."

"Did you notice that the *t* was left out of 'Just Married' on the trunk?" Tempest asked through tear-drenched eyes.

"Naw, I missed that one," Geren replied, trying to bring his amusement under control. He felt bad making fun of people, especially on their wedding day. But in that situation, it really couldn't be helped. "What I want to know is how brotha man can even drive a car as short as he is. I bet Gary Coleman and Webster both have at least a foot on him."

"*Ooooooohhh,* you so crazy!"

Tempest reached for an empty paper plate farther down on the table and started trying to pulverize the fly that was continuing to get on her nerves.

"I know how he drives it, though," she added. "I got nosy last night at the rehearsal and peeked inside."

"And?" Geren asked anxiously. For the life of him, he thought it was not humanly possible for a person that short to operate an automobile.

"He has these extension pedals for the gas and brake, and he sits on top of two Power Rangers pillows so he can see over the dash," Tempest answered, trying to keep a straight face.

"*Damnnnnnnn!*"

"I know. That's deep, isn't it?"

"Deep and then some. I have seen it . . ."

"Excuse me. I don't mean to interrupt you, but can I ask you a question?"

Geren and Tempest both looked around to see who said this. They even looked under the table, and then Tempest finally noticed some pudgy short legs standing at the north end. She leaned over so she could look over the tabletop and spotted the best man, Raoul.

"Who, me?" Tempest asked, not wanting to be bothered. She was trying to get to know Geren with his fine ass.

"Yes, you," Raoul replied snidely.

Tempest smirked at him. She was well aware of his reputation and thought it was ridiculous. "I'm not in the market for a well-endowed midget, if that's what you want."

"Very funny!" Raoul hissed back at her. "I would never discuss business today. My boy just tied the knot. What type of man do you think I am?"

"Hmph, I take you to be about half of a man, from where I'm sitting."

Raoul shook his stubby finger up at her. "See, I knew it!"

"Knew what?" Geren asked, finally coming out of his shock-induced trance. All of these midgets were tripping him out, but the well-endowed comment threw him for a loop.

"I knew she was related to those triflin' Whitfields as soon as I saw her standing in for Marquita last night at the rehearsal!" Raoul replied, crossing his arms in front of him and rolling his eyes.

"My last name is not Whitfield," Tempest stated with obvious disdain. "In fact, I don't even know any Whitfields."

"Hmmmmmmmm, I don't blame you for lying about it. I wouldn't admit to being kin to that nasty, ill-bred covenant of witches turned bitches either."

Geren fell out laughing, but Tempest failed to see the humor. "I have no idea what you're talking about but would you mind if I talked with my date?" She waited patiently for a few seconds for Raoul to waddle away. When he didn't budge, she added, "Alone!"

"Fine, just be like that," Raoul said, on the verge of throwing a hissy fit. "I need to get going soon anyway. I'm handling the night shift at my motel."

"You have a motel, too?" Tempest asked.

"Yeah, it's right across the street from my midget breeding farm and next door to my burger joint."

"You have a business card, little man?" Geren inquired, halfway impressed by Raoul. "I like your entrepreneurial spirit."

"I'm not a little man." Raoul placed his left hand over his chest. "I have a big heart, among other things, and that's what counts." He reached into his pocket with his free hand and pulled out a business card, handing it to Geren.

"Thanks!"

"No problemo. Come by one weekend and give a brotha some business. If you bring your woman here with you, I'll let ya'll have ten percent off our Oompa Loompa Deluxe Honeymoon Suite."

Tempest and Geren both started guffawing. Then Tempest's smile turned to a frown. "I don't know how to tell you this Raoul, but that French poodle over there has been eyeing you like she's hungry for the past few minutes."

Raoul swung his half-neck around and spotted the white predator standing by a tree. "Shit! I'm 'bout to go!" He pulled the collar of his tuxedo up around his half-neck as if that would protect his Adam's apple in case of an attack. "Nice meeting you, ummmmmmm—"

"Tempest."

"Geren."

"Tempest and Geren. Unique names. You make a cute couple, too."

"Thanks," Geren said, noticing that Tempest was blushing.

"Catch you later," Raoul said, waving as he walked off.

"Peace," Tempest shouted out after him. "I hope he makes it to his remote control car before that poodle makes him the catch of the day."

Geren gawked at her. "Did you say remote control?"

Tempest flung her hand at him and held up her palm. "Pleassssssse don't ask!"

Geren chuckled but didn't press any further. He had witnessed enough unbelievable stuff for one day.

"Where did Janessa and Dvontè run off to?" Tempest inquired, realizing she hadn't seen hide nor hair of them for about an hour.

"They're probably out in my car, chillin' and waiting on us. Dvontè got sick and tired of dodging all the women."

Tempest smacked her lips. "I thought he relished being the object of affection?"

"Normally he does, but not today." Geren held his hands up over his face, trying to hide the smile on his face. "These sistahs are out there. One woman flashed her sagging breasts at him in the parking lot at the church."

"Realllllly?"

"Absolutely!" Geren had a quick flashback of the woman's breasts. They were touching her belly button, and it almost made him hurl.

"What about you?" Tempest raised her eyebrow. "No woman exposed herself to you?"

Geren put his hands back down and reached over to rub his

thumb across Tempest's right cheek. "Not yet, but the night is still young. Anything's possible."

Tempest pulled back from him. She was nervous as hell. She started looking around the yard in an effort to divert her eyes away from Geren's stare. "Well, it looks like the party is dying down. Why don't we extend our well wishes to the bride and groom and go find Janessa and Dvontè?"

"Sounds like a winner."

"Lawd knows I'm ready to take this dress off and toss it in the trash compactor."

Geren laughed. He couldn't believe Tempest was still trippin' off the dress. "You really do look nice Tempest. I mean that."

"Why, thank you, Mr. Kincaid," Tempest replied, finally looking back at him. Damn, he was fine! "You're rather dapper yourself."

She was getting up from the table when she heard a boom box start blaring from the back porch. She looked that way and noticed a bunch of drunk people, spread out in two lines. "Flashlight" by Parliament Funkadelic was cranking from the speakers.

"Oh, no, a Soul Train line!" Tempest exclaimed.

"I haven't seen one of those in years," Geren said, getting up from the table and standing behind her.

Tempest swung around and looked at him excitedly, like she'd just won the Powerball. "Come on, let's go down the line!"

Geren took a long look at the couple presently going down the line. The man was doing the Freeze, and the woman was doing the Happy Feet. "You can't be serious?"

"Just one time," Tempest responded, pulling him toward the porch by the elbow. *"Pleasssssse!!!!!* You need to loosen up a little."

Geren let out a heavy sigh. "Okay, okay," he said, giving in. "If it means that much to you, but don't expect me to do the Robot, the Moonwalk or jumping splits."

Tempest giggled. "I'm going to do the jumping splits!"

Geren let that sink in for a second and asked, "You want my jacket. We wouldn't want any accidental indecent exposure."

Tempest stopped dead in her tracks and punched him gently in the ribs. "Stop teasing me!"

Geren chuckled, gazing at her protruding breasts. "Sorry, I couldn't help it. I just had to throw that one in there."

Tempest reached her arms inside his jacket and started tickling him. "Are you ticklish? I bet you are."

"Tempest, quit!" Geren quickly pulled away, not wanting to confess that he was indeed ticklish. It just didn't seem *manly*. He took her hand and started toward the porch again. "Let's hurry up before the song ends!"

# 7

## the aftermath

"Boy, oh boy, that was some wedding!" Geren exclaimed, following Tempest up the stairwell to her third-floor apartment and admiring the view of her ass in the process.

"Yes, it was," Tempest replied. "I don't know when I've had so much fun. I know I said just one turn in the Soul Train line, but—"

"But we ended up going down the line fifty-eleven times," Geren said, preempting the rest of her statement.

They both laughed until they got to her apartment door. Geren couldn't help but notice how long and thick Tempest's eyelashes were while she rumbled through her purse for her set of keys. Even after dancing out there in that heat for more than an hour, Tempest still looked fresh and appealing to him.

"If you think today was wild, you should have seen the bachelorette party last night. It was *quite* an experience."

"Really? What happened last night?" Geren inquired, his curiosity instantly piqued. "Did she have strippers?"

"Of course," Tempest replied. "But not just any ordinary strippers. They were buck wild."

"Word? Were they midgets?"

Tempest chuckled as she slid her key into the lock. "No, these brothas were definitely not midgets."

"Buck wild in what way then?"

"Trust me, you *definitely* don't want to know all of that!"

Geren decided to drop the matter. Apparently, it was one of those sistahgurl secrets women take to their graves. Just like men kept bachelor party happenings top secret. He was more interested in getting to know more about Tempest anyway. The bachelorette party was insignificant.

Tempest went inside but Geren hesitated in the doorway, awaiting a formal invitation. Even though he had been inside earlier, Janessa had been there, and it was the middle of the afternoon, not the middle of the night. He didn't want to assume too much too soon.

After flinging her purse on the sofa, Tempest swung around to face him. She couldn't help but wonder what it would be like to kiss him when she saw him standing there with his hands buried in his pockets. He was a handsome brotha, there was no denying that.

"Aren't you going to come in?"

"Sure!" Geren didn't even try to mask his excitement. He came inside and closed the door behind him. "I didn't want you to think I was being pushy or anything like that."

"Not at all," Tempest replied, suddenly realizing she was alone in her place *at night* with a fine-ass man for the first time in quite a while. "Would you like something to drink?"

"What do you have?"

"Hmm, the usual. Soda, orange juice, spring water." Tempest cracked a grin and then added, "Cherry-flavored Kool-Aid."

Geren licked his lips, and Tempest had the urge to lick them for him. He wanted to go for the Kool-Aid but didn't want to risk a sugar rush so late at night. "I'll take some orange juice, if you don't mind."

Tempest motioned toward the sofa on her way to the kitchen. "Please have a seat, make yourself comfortable. I'll be right back."

Geren plopped down on the sofa and instantly felt relaxed. He had no doubt he could easily fall asleep on the soft, thick cushions, especially as worn out as he was after dancing his ass off in the Soul Train line.

He took a more detailed survey of Tempest's apartment than he had earlier and was impressed with her African-American framed prints. The apartment was a mixture of dark furniture with lighter fixtures. He still couldn't get over the fact that she was such a meticulous housekeeper.

Drawn to a huge cabinet attached to one of the walls, he got up to make a closer inspection. There were six rows of alphabetized original copies of African-American videotapes. He spotted several he had heard about all of his life but never viewed, such as *Mandingo, Imitation of Life, The Mack, Dolemite, Foxy Brown,* and *Shaft.*

"I've been collecting them since I was in high school," Tempest whispered into Geren's ear, startling him. He hadn't heard her come back into the room. She was so close to him, he could smell the Lifesaver she had in her mouth—the mouth he was aching to explore with his tongue.

He turned to face her and had to struggle to resist the urge to kiss her thick, juicy lips. He took the glass of orange juice she was holding out to him. "Thanks!"

"Welcome," Tempest replied, getting lost in his eyes. "So, do you like movies?"

"Yeah, I love them! Obviously not as much as you, though." Geren walked around her and went to sit down on the sofa. He didn't want her to bear witness to the erection growing in his pants. "You have quite an extensive collection."

"Would you like to watch one? I know it's getting rather late, but I'm a night owl anyway. I can hang if you can."

"Sure!"

"Which one?"

"How about *The Mack?*" Geren didn't really care about watching a movie. He just wasn't ready to leave Tempest just yet.

"That's cool with me." Tempest giggled. She grabbed the video off the shelf, took it out of the case, and slid it into the VCR. Then she joined him on the sofa and sat extremely close to him. She shocked herself with that move. The old Tempest would have been pressed into the opposite corner with a toss pillow held up to her chest for added protection. For some reason, she felt comfortable around Geren. Any way she looked at it, that had to be a definite plus.

The tape started, but Geren was too distracted by Tempest's beauty to give a damn what Max Julien was doing on the thirty-two-inch screen. He was drawn in by her hair, her full, sensuous lips, the tiny dimple in her left cheek, but most of all, he loved the way she smelled.

"So, Tempest, tell me a little about yourself."

"Like?" she inquired, batting her long eyelashes at him.

"Anything and everything. I'd like to know it all."

Tempest put her knee up on the sofa so she could face him. "Well, let's see. I was born on a cold October night in nineteen—"

Geren chuckled and held up his palm. "Well, maybe not *every-thing.*"

Tempest blushed. "You did say you wanted to know it all."

"Let's narrow it down a bit. How about the abbreviated version?"

"In that case, ask me a particular question, and I will give you a specific answer." She rubbed him gently on the knee and then snatched her hand back before he could swipe it up into his. If he had succeeded in taking her hand right that second, she would have jumped his bones. "As long as it isn't *too* personal."

Geren placed his hands firmly on his lap, straightened his back, and sighed. "Okay then, let's start with your occupation."

"I'm a social worker and counselor at a crisis center for unwed teenage mothers."

"That's great!" Geren shouted so loudly that Tempest was taken aback. "I'm truly impressed. I thought you were probably into something else."

"Something else like what?" Tempest blared, bordering on being offended by his comment. She opted to hold off judgment until she heard his reply.

"I don't know," Geren stated hesitantly, wondering if he was about to put his foot in his mouth. "Maybe a beautician or a retail manager or something like that."

"How in the world did you narrow it down to those two?"

"I didn't," Geren said in defense of himself. "Those are just a couple of examples. It's just that you're so fly, with the pretty hair and fresh clothes."

"Chile, please!" Tempest got up off the sofa. "Speaking of clothes, I'll be back in a couple of minutes. I've got to get out of this ugnoramous dress before the dye in the material rubs off on my skin."

"Okay, I'll be here."

Tempest paused in the doorway of her bedroom. "Let me ask you a question. What do you do for a living?"

"I'm an investment banker."

"Oh, I see," Tempest said snidely. "I figured you were probably a maître d' or electronics salesman."

Geren laughed as she disappeared in the bedroom. "Touché!"

Janessa pulled the fluffy pillow up tighter around her ears. Between Dvontè's snoring and the ticking of the alarm clock on his nightstand, she couldn't fall asleep if her life depended on it. There was more to it than that, though. She was straight-up ashamed. Agreeing in advance to give Dvontè some pussy if he went with her to the wedding was a huge mistake.

She looked over at him, sprawled beside her on the brass king-size bed, and wondered how many other sistahs had occupied the side she was on over the years. It mattered, and it didn't matter. She realized that at her age, any man she might possibly hook up with would have had numerous, maybe even dozens of, women in his past. That's what makes a man a seasoned lover, and she needed that in her life. Hell, she needed a lover, period.

Yet and still, she'd been disappointed when Dvontè put in a less-than-stellar performance once Geren and Tempest dropped them off at his place. She was expecting the earth-shattering, toe-curling sexual experience he'd promised her repetitively during their phone conversations of the previous week.

Dvontè did eat her pussy, but only briefly. His oral fixation was hardly a match for her own. She'd sucked his dick but good, and received a weak tongue-lashing in return. His dick was a nice size, but he came too fast. She wouldn't venture to call him a two-minute brotha, but he definitely wasn't a ten-minute one.

Dvontè turned over on his side, facing Janessa, and his pussy breath almost made her turn away. She couldn't get used to smelling her essence emanating from a brotha's mouth or tasting it on his tongue. Nothing turned her off more than a man that would go down on her and expect her to tongue the shit out of him immediately afterward. That just wasn't her thing, and at least Dvontè didn't even go there. Not that he even had time to. He came and then passed out less than three minutes later.

It became painfully obvious that sleep wasn't going to come anytime soon, so Janessa got up and went out into Dvontè's kitchen to look for something to drink. She got a wine cooler out of the fridge and then sat down on his couch in the living room and flicked on his television. Chris Rock's *Bigger and Blacker* special was on HBO.

Even though Chris was a hilarious mofo, Janessa's thoughts drifted to Howard. Damn shame all that good loving was locked up in the penitentiary. No other man had hit it like him. She derived so much pleasure from his sex.

The comedy special went off, and Janessa debated whether or not to go back in the bedroom. So what if Dvontè wasn't the bomb after all? He was a man, and she needed some regular sex. She got up to go back into the bedroom, determined to get Dvontè to rise to the occasion. After all, most men last longer after they bust the first nut.

As she pulled the covers off him so she could grasp his limp dick in her right hand, she wondered if Tempest and Geren were getting their freak on. Tempest liked to play that role, but when it came right down to it, she needed some sexual release from time to time just like everybody else.

Janessa took one last swig of her wine cooler, sat it on the nightstand beside the annoying clock, and leaned over so she could suck Dvontè's dick into her mouth.

Tempest stood out on her balcony, watching the sun rise over the horizon and enjoying the morning breeze as it tingled against her skin. She glanced inside to see if Geren was still sleeping soundly on her sofa. Yes, he was still there, covered with her Dallas Cowboys throw. A fully clothed gentleman who managed to get through the entire night without trying to get in her panties. It wasn't a dream.

They'd stayed up talking all night, about everything—their childhood, their families, their past relationships. Tempest couldn't believe all the skeletons she'd revealed to him. She told him about all the maggots of her past, and he listened. He actually listened. He didn't call it male bashing, like a typical man would. After all, how can it be male bashing when she was simply stating facts about her own experiences? Indisputable facts.

From the sound of it, Geren had run across a lot of triflin' sistahs himself. He hadn't had an easy way in the romance department. Maybe they could find what they needed in each other. Just maybe.

One thing was for sure. Tempest definitely wanted to see Geren again. She planned to tell him that the moment he woke up. She inhaled deeply, taking in some of the fresh air, and then went inside to get some clean towels and a new toothbrush out of her linen closet for him. It had been a long time since she had to do that, and just the thought of the simple task made her grin.

As she tiptoed past him, she wondered what she had in her kitchen so she could throw together a halfway decent breakfast. She froze when she heard him whisper her name. She turned, expecting to find him awake and looking at her, but he was still fast asleep. Damn, he'd said her name in his sleep. Could he really be the one?

# 8

## the morning after

"How's it going, Fred?" Tempest inquired, though she couldn't have cared less.

"Tempest!" Fred exclaimed, licking his lips. "Long time, no see, gurl!"

Tempest sucked in a deep breath and rolled her eyes waiting for Fred to get finished with his regular routine. Every time she came over there, he would eye her from head to toe.

Tempest lost her patience after a few seconds. "Fred, are you going to move out of my way and let me in sometime today, or what?"

"Dang, my bad!" Fred said, moving to the side of the doorway so she could come in. "Where are my manners?"

"Good question," Tempest replied. "Is Janessa here?"

"Yeah, she's upstairs sleeping." He followed Tempest into the living room. "She must have pulled an all nighter with one of her mack daddies. She came falling up in here after seven, and Momma almost went upside her head."

Tempest shook her head in disbelief. Janessa was a grown woman, and Mrs. Carter still treated her like a teenage virgin. "Is that right?"

"Yup! It was mad funny, too. I love to see Janessa and Momma go at it. They're like two peas in a pod. Both determined as hell to get their way."

"Hmph, I heard that!" Tempest looked around the room. It had been a while since she'd been inside. She always picked Janessa up curbside because they were in a hurry to go this place or that place. Janessa hated being in the house, so she would always be waiting anxiously on the front porch for Tempest to come get her. Tempest could smell bacon grease and freshly baked bread coming from the kitchen. "Where are your parents? In the kitchen?"

"Nope, they went to church as usual."

"Nothing wrong with that. I need to start back going myself. I've been lax since my parents moved to Florida."

"How are they anyway?"

"Just fine," Tempest answered, wondering if there were any actual leftovers from breakfast or just the scent circulating in the air. "They love the weather. My mother always hated snow anyway. She's originally from the Dirty South."

"Oh, yeah? What part?"

"Hotlanta!"

"Cool, I never knew that. I always thought both of your folks were from D.C."

"My dad was born here. My mother didn't move up this way until the ninth grade."

Tempest caught Fred staring at her breasts again and decided it was time to cut the small talk. "Well, I'm about to go up and holla at Janessa. Nice seeing you, Fred."

He pounced and quickly threw himself between Tempest and the flight of stairs. "Hold up a second!"

Tempest rolled her eyes. "What is it?"

"I was just wondering when you and I are gonna hook up and slap some skins? You've been frontin' on giving up that punanny for years now!"

"You seriously need to leave that crack alone," Tempest lashed out at him.

"Gurl, I don't do that shit! I'm just trying to see what's up with you."

"You *really* want to know?"

"Hell yeah! Let a brotha know what's up!"

"You *really, really* want to know?"

"Yeah, gurl! Tell me sumptin, damn! Anytime, anyplace! It's on you. This is your world. I'm just a squirrel trying to get a nut." He smiled his goofy grin and added, "Get it? I'm trying to get a nut? Or bust a nut rather."

Tempest inspected Fred over for the first time in years. He was even more unappealing than when they were younger. "Aiight, we can do this!"

"Word?"

"Most definitely!"

"So when is the big event?" Fred asked, licking his lips in antic-ipation. "I want to make sure I'm buff for your ass!"

Tempest laughed at him. She couldn't manage to keep a straight face for one more millisecond. "When the dinosaurs rein-habit the earth." Fred looked like someone had just slapped him. "Now get da hell out of my way!"

Tempest shoved Fred out of her path and took the stairs two at a time. She rapped lightly on Janessa's bedroom door but got no answer. She tried the knob, and was surprised it budged. Ever since puberty set in, Janessa had been avid about locking her door to keep out roving eyes. Fred would always have his homies over, and all of their trifling asses would try to sneak a peek.

Janessa was sprawled across the double bed in her usual Scissorlegs position, calling the hogs big-time. Tempest was about to rouse her by shaking her shoulder, but a lightbulb went off in her head.

She eased herself up on the bed beside Janessa and gently squeezed her nostrils together. Janessa started making a disgusting noise that sounded like an anaconda regurgitating a boar. Tempest had to cover her mouth with her free hand to prevent herself from giggling.

Janessa started swatting at her nose, still lost in dreamland somewhere. Tempest couldn't keep it in any longer and burst out laughing.

Janessa jerked her eyes open and pushed Tempest's hand away.

"Wake up, sleepyhead!" Tempest ordered. "We need to have another heart-to-heart."

Janessa slowly made it up onto her elbows, diverting her eyes to the clock radio on her nightstand. "Damn, what time is it?"

"Time for you to be up and about." Tempest got up off the bed and went to the window to open the mini-blinds. "You want me to go down to the kitchen and make you some coffee?"

"Absolutely not! You know I don't mess with that stuff," Janessa barked, blinded by the sunlight. "If it's not Kool-Aid or Pepsi, I don't drink it."

Tempest cackled. "All that dye is going to make you psychotic one of these days."

"I just realized something."

"What?"

"That you're in my house," Janessa replied. "This is the first time you've been in here since way back in the day."

"That's your fault," Tempest said, quickly shifting the blame. "You're always in such a big hurry to get out of here. By the time I pull up, you're making a mad dash for the car."

Janessa laughed. "You got me there."

"I was hoping to see your parents, but they're still at church. I'll be sure to stop by later this week and visit. Other than talking to your mother on the phone, we've lost contact."

The mother-on-the-phone line hit home with Janessa. "What did you and my mother talk about?"

Tempest realized her error. The last thing she needed was Janessa discovering that her mother was calling Tempest, reporting on Janessa's dealings with Howard the jailbird. "Nothing. I'm referring to the casual greetings we give each other when I call looking for you."

"Oh, I see!" Janessa wasn't even buying into it. She could always tell when Tempest was lying. She smelled a conspiracy but decided to temporarily drop the subject. "So, to what do we owe this honor?"

"What honor?"

"Having Miss Tempest, Miss Thang herself, up in the crib."

Tempest picked up a pillow and flung it at Janessa's head. "You're so silly!"

Janessa's face lit up as she ventured a guess. "This is about Geren, right?"

"Kind of," Tempest reluctantly admitted. "I need your help with something."

"Don't tell me you forgot how to ride a dick or something like that, because if you need lessons, I might have to charge a sistah fifty bucks an hour."

Tempest retrieved the pillow and banged Janessa on the head

with it repeatedly. "Hellified sex isn't a problem. I have that covered."

Janessa hopped up and started jumping up and down on the bed like she'd won the lotto. "I knew it! You gave it up last night! You go, gurl!"

Tempest sat on the bed and noticed Janessa's new television, in the corner by the closet. "You finally got a TV, huh? Now you can watch all your favorite shows without smelling Fred's prostate."

They both doubled over in laughter.

"Don't even try to change the subject." Janessa chuckled. "I just want to know one thing."

"What's that?"

"Did you make him licky-licky before you let him sticky-sticky?"

"The only thing Geren licked at my place last night were stamps. He helped me get the flyers for the community day at the center ready to mail on Monday."

"Hold up! You mean to tell me you had that fine-ass nucca in your apartment *alone,* and you two were stuffing envelopes all night?"

"Stuffing envelopes, watching movies, and talking about life in general."

"What movies?"

"*The Mack* and *Foxy Brown.* Can you believe he'd never seen either one of those?"

"Damn, where is bro man from? Alaska?"

Tempest giggled. "No, he grew up in the Metro area. He's originally from Potomac."

"That explains it then. He's one of those uppity, bourgeois negroes from the suburbs."

"Not hardly," Tempest disagreed. "Geren is extremely down to earth. He made me feel so comfortable. I felt like I could tell him anything and everything. In fact, I practically told him my life story."

Janessa couldn't help but notice the sparkle in Tempest's eyes, a gleam that hadn't been there in a long time. "Tempest, you really like the dude, huh?"

"Yeah, I do." Tempest blushed. "We're hooking up next weekend."

"Good for you!" Janessa put her arm around Tempest's shoulder and gave her a big squeeze. "I have a feeling Dvontè and I will be seeing a lot more of each other also."

Tempest was reluctant to ask, since she already knew the answer. "You slept with him, didn't you?"

Janessa turned her head in the other direction to hide her disgrace and let go of Tempest. "I didn't mean for it to happen, sis. He's just so sexy and romantic, and one thing led to another."

Tempest fell silent. Any comment she had to make would have been negative in nature.

"He threw on some slow jams, I still had a buzz from the cheap champagne at the wedding reception, and he started sucking my fingers. That did my ass in! You know how I get when a man sucks my fingers and toes."

Tempest still refused to put her two cents in, and Janessa was tired of trying to justify her actions. "Look, I'm grown, so let's just drop it."

"Fine with me," Tempest said. "I have nothing to say about it. It's your life, Janessa."

The tension in the room was thick. Janessa tried to break the ice. "If you didn't come over here for sex tips, what do you need my help with?"

Tempest grinned. *"Well,* I told Geren a little fib. He asked me to go Rollerblading with him next Saturday, and I kinda sorta told him I was an expert."

"How much of an expert?" Janessa asked, knowing Tempest had two left feet and could barely walk straight without tripping over something.

"Damn near a pro!"

They both fell back on the bed, crying laughing.

"So, what are you going to do?"

"Learn how to skate or fake a leg cramp or something."

"You and your damn leg cramps." Janessa giggled, staring up at the ceiling and targeting the remains of a swatted fly from a few years back. "By the way, I used that line on a brotha when he tried to get some. It worked like a mofo charm."

Tempest laughed. "I told you it would."

"Damn sure did!" Janessa slapped Tempest on the thigh. "Now what the hell do I have to do with you learning how to skate?"

"Don't you know how?"

"Hell, naw, I can't skate!"

"I thought you used to go down to the ice-skating rink on the mall in Northwest."

"That was to check out men; not to skate."

"Great! Looks like I'm busted, then. I'll figure out some way to get out of it. Maybe I'll say I have the flu and ask him to come over and bring me some chicken soup."

"The flu? In the summertime? Chile, please!"

"Good point," Tempest agreed. "I wonder if he would really bring me some, though. He seems like the type." Tempest got up off the bed. "I'm going to go get the yellow pages. Maybe I can take some skating lessons at Wheaton Regional Park or something like that."

"Sounds like a winner."

Tempest yanked the bedroom door open, and Fred tumbled in onto the floor. She glared down at him. "It's a damn shame you're still lurking around here eavesdropping. Get a life, why don't you!"

"Uh, uh, I was ju-ju-just coming up here to put the antennae on Janessa's new TV," he stuttered, lying his ass off. He looked at Janessa. "You asked me to do it. Remember?"

"That was three days ago," Janessa hissed. "Like Tempest said, you're just a nosy mofo. *Now get out!*"

Tempest started down the hallway so she could go downstairs to get the book.

"Tempest, hold up," Fred said, coming after her.

"What is it?" Tempest asked, obviously irritated. "I already told you we could get busy the first time you spot a T-Rex walking down Pennsylvania Avenue."

"No, that's not it. I was just playing with you about the sex, gurl." Fred chuckled, trying to save face.

"What is it then?"

"I know how to skate. I could teach you."

"You know how to Rollerblade?"

"Real good, too," Fred boasted. "My boys and I go blading all the time in Rock Creek Park over by the Carter Baron."

Tempest stood at the top of the stairs, contemplating her next move. Beggars can't be choosers, she thought to herself. "Okay, Fred, desperate times call for desperate measures. I refuse to let Geren find out I can't skate, so put on your teacher's hat. It's going to be a long day!"

Dvontè strolled into one of the racquetball courts in Gold's Gym in Wheaton, Maryland, at four-thirty that afternoon. Geren was hitting a ball up against the wall, working up a sweat.

Dvontè threw his gym bag down on the bench. He took off his Wilson Athletic jogging pants and Champion sweatshirt, stripping down to shorts and a tee like Geren.

Geren hit the ball one last time, then walked over to the bench to join Dvontè, pulling his goggles up to the top of his head and glancing down at his watch. "You're late, man! We only have the court reserved for another thirty minutes."

"Relax, it's all good," Dvontè replied indignantly. "There's no one waiting for a court, so we can play for an hour as usual."

"That's cool!"

"I started not to even show. But I figured your ass would be here, and I didn't want to leave you hanging."

"Why wouldn't I be here, Dvontè?" Geren asked. "We play racquetball every Sunday afternoon."

"Unless it's football season."

"True that!" They gave each other a high five. "Nothing comes before football!"

"Well, I'm not going to say *all* that. I can name one thing that does."

"What?" Geren inquired. He knew Dvontè was a serious football fan.

"Pussy, of course!"

Geren picked up his towel and slapped Dvontè on the arm before using it to wipe his brow. "I should've known. You have a one-track mind."

"Speaking of which," Dvontè said, bending over and warming up with some stretches. "I know you didn't get any last night."

Geren chuckled. "You're unbelievable. Who said I was trying to get any last night?"

Dvontè grinned, realizing he had hit the nail on the head. "Like I said, I know you didn't. Anyone can look at Tempest and tell she is one of those holdouts."

Geren threw his right leg up on the bench to do some calf stretches. "It was just our first date, Dvontè. Sheesh! Not all sistahs give it up on the first date."

"Hmph, all the women I deal with do, or there won't be a second one," Dvontè proclaimed.

Geren hated to let his male ego get the best of him, but he needed to size up the competition. "So, I take it you and Janessa got busy last night?"

Dvontè glared at him like he had the Bubonic Plague. "Surely you jest! Of course we got busy. That was predetermined."

"Predetermined?"

"Yeah, I told her the other night on the phone I expected some ass after the wedding."

"And she agreed?"

"We got freaky all night long." Dvontè reached into his bag for his goggles. "That gurl is something else in the sack. I figured she would be down, but she let me do whatever the hell I wanted."

"Good for you!" Geren couldn't believe that some sistahs still set themselves up like that. He only hoped that nothing Dvontè did to Janessa ended up casting a negative light on him with Tempest.

"It was even better for her," Dvontè continued, embellishing what actually happened. "I worked her body over big-time. She's probably sitting by the phone willing me to make a midday booty call."

"Are you going to call her again?" Geren asked, part of him wishing the answer would be no.

"All in good time," Dvontè answered. "I have other bitches riding this dick, too. I have to spread the loving around."

Something about the B-word always set Geren off. "Dvontè, what did I tell you about calling sistahs out of their name? A bitch is a female dog."

"Exactly!" Dvontè exclaimed, satisfied with the definition. "Women always talk about men being dogs, but they're no better. They all have their own agenda, just like we do."

"Maybe all they want is a real relationship."

"Man, you're living on Fantasy Island." Dvontè rolled his eyes. "What type of real relationship starts out with a woman sucking a damn dick on the first date? If she'll blow me, she'll blow any man who comes along."

"That's not even true!" Geren couldn't believe Dvontè and his immature mentality. "See, it's brothas like you that give good men like me a bad name."

"You may be a good man, but you're also a pussyless man. That's why you're trying to work off some of that sexual tension on the court. You're here because you couldn't get any sexin' last night."

Geren was on the brink of getting irate. "I really like Tempest! I enjoy her company, and I've already made plans to see her again next weekend."

"Whoopty-do! Maybe she'll even let you cop a feel or two, if you're lucky."

"I'm not concerned about that. Tempest and I will be together when the time is right for both of us, and not a second before. Sure, I wanted to be with her last night intimately, but she's been hurt by too many brothas. I'm determined to show her what real men act like."

Dvontè pulled the goggles down over his eyes, trying to mask the anger in them. "So you're saying I'm not a real man?"

Geren adjusted his own goggles. "If the shoe fits."

Dvontè took his racquet out of the casing. "Just because I don't believe in kissing a woman's feet and shit doesn't make me any less of a man than you."

"Maybe not, but the fact I can whup your ass on this racquet-ball court does." Geren smirked, as he issued the challenge.

"We'll just see about that!"

# 9

## rollerblading hell

Geren picked Tempest up at noon, and it took every ounce of self-control he had not to fall out laughing when she opened up the door. She looked more like she was going to battle than Rollerblading. She was wearing a silver bike helmet with arm, elbow, shoulder and knee pads. The black spandex crop top and bike shorts looked mighty appealing to him though. He got an instant rise in his shorts.

"You sure you have enough protection on?" he asked her jokingly, after they were settled in his car and headed out.

She eyed him up and down before putting on her black Oakleys. "I don't know. I might need something else to protect me from you."

"Hmm, I see." Geren wanted to reach over and rub her knee but was afraid he would draw back a stub. "So you go Rollerblading all the time, huh?"

"I never said I go *all* the time," Tempest answered, smacking her lips. "Maybe a couple of times a month or so."

"I see."

"Is that all you can say? I see?"

"Well, I do have one other question," Geren stated, glancing over his shoulder while they waited at a stoplight. He took a good, long look at the Rollerblades Tempest tossed on the back floor when she got in. "Those skates look brand-new. Are you sure you've been blading before?"

"Geren, are you accusing me of fabrication?" Tempest took her glasses back off, looking like she wanted to go upside his head. "Because if that is what you're insinuating, you might as well turn this car around and take my ass back home right now." She realized she was busted as far as the skates, so she added, "As a matter of fact, those are a new pair. My old ones are too worn so I decided to get some new ones. Is that a crime?"

"No, not at all. I was just won——"

"It's not like I asked you to pay for them or anything," she continued. "I can spend my money on anything I like."

"I never said you couldn't." Geren was getting pissed. She was carrying the drama a bit too far. "Look, I'm sorry aiight?"

Tempest sucked her gums, rolled her eyes, and replaced her glasses. "Well, okay then."

They were both speechless, so Geren threw in a Jerrold Dameon CD. He was quickly realizing that there were two Tempests; the nice one and the bitchy one. Heaven help him, but he was still intrigued and wanted to get to know her better, regardless of her evil twin.

"So, Geren, where are we going *blading* anyway?" Tempest stressed the word *blading,* trying to prove she was an expert on the subject. "Haines Point? Rock Creek Park?"

Geren had originally planned to take her to Rock Creek Park, near the back entrance to the National Zoo, but quickly ditched the idea. One, he didn't want her to think she was regulating, and two, he was determined to make her admit she didn't know hide nor hair about Rollerblading. "Actually, I thought we would head over to the brokerage firm and blade through the indoor parking garage. I know the attendant, and it will be practically empty today except for the new associates still trying to prove they are worthy enough to be there."

"The brokerage firm parking garage?" Geren could hear the nervousness in Tempest's voice.

"Yes." He chuckled. "I figure we can kill two birds with one stone. I can show you my office and then we can do some serious blading, like they do on the ESPN Extreme Games. You ever check those out on cable?"

"No, I can't say that I have," Tempest replied cautiously. "What are the Extreme Games?"

"Oh, that's when they do all kinds of wild and crazy things, like laying down on skateboards and racing through the streets, sky-diving, and other cool stuff. The Rollerbladers really get down. I bet you could show them a thing or two, since you're such an expert."

Tempest let out a hideous laugh. "Yeah, I bet I could." She tightened up one of her knee pads and then added, "You know, it's such a beautiful day, and I really had my heart set on skating in the park. Who wants to go inside some dim, exhaust-filled parking garage on a day like this? That's sadomasochistic."

She was looking for a way out, but Geren was not even having it. "Okay, I'll tell you what. We'll swing by the office. I need to pick up a file I need for a breakfast meeting on Monday anyway. Then we'll do a couple of speed-skating laps down the ramps. After that, we can head on over to Rock Creek Park, do some more skating, maybe tour the zoo, and then have a late lunch or early dinner on Connecticut Avenue."

"Sounds like heaven," Tempest said, lying her ass off.

"Cool," Geren replied. "We're almost there. Just a couple more lights."

Tempest let out that hideous laugh again. Geren laughed too, real loud. He couldn't wait to see her make a fool of herself.

Okay, so I bit off a little bit more than I could chew, Tempest thought to herself. I don't know a damn thing about Roller-blading, roller-skating, or any other kind of rolling except for rolling my hair.

Her Aunt Geraldine, the one who ended up shacking with her high school sweetheart, took Tempest to the roller rink once when she was about nine. Tempest had never forgotten the humiliation.

There she was, sitting on the front stoop in a new pair of Jordache jeans, a white knit sweater, and a gold chain belt, thinking Aunt Geraldine was picking her up to go to the mall. That was their usual Saturday routine. She would scoop Tempest up on her way to Iverson Mall or Capital Plaza, and they would go spend the money Aunt Geraldine's man of the week had given her.

But, *noooooooo,* not that day. Aunt Geraldine had this ingenious idea about going skating so Tempest could meet some new friends. Tempest couldn't care less about meeting new friends. She had a best friend: Janessa.

Tempest fell on her ass so much that day, she had to sleep on top of a pile of pillows for two weeks. Thoughts of the ordeal flashed through her mind while Geren bopped his head to the jazz music coming from his car's stereo system.

"Everything's going to be just fine," Tempest whispered to herself.

Geren turned the radio down. "What was that? I couldn't hear you."

"Nothing. I was just thinking about something."

Geren started snickering and turned the radio back up.

When they pulled up to his office building, Tempest was floored by the fancy fountain out front and the sparkling glass windows of the main tower. "This whole building belongs to the firm?"

"Every square inch of it," Geren replied, pulling into the parking garage and waving at the attendant. "We're one of the largest brokerage firms in the country, second only to one in New York."

"Cool," Tempest replied, definitely impressed.

Tempest was in awe from the second she stepped into Geren's office building. Marble floors throughout the first floor, plush carpeting on the tenth floor where his office was located, and brass nameplates on all the office doors.

She almost fell out when she entered his spacious office. His desk and bookcases were ebony wood, and his chairs were all tan leather. There were six computers with flat monitors lined up on a large table on the far left wall.

He had an armoire with a thirty-five-inch television, VCR and DVD player as well as the bomb-ass stereo system. All the equipment was made by the Phoenix Corporation. Tempest wondered how Geren even managed to get any work done in such a plush atmosphere.

"Nice office!" Tempest exclaimed. "Very, very nice!"

"Why, thank you." Geren walked over and hit the enter button on one of the computers, waking it up from its sleep mode. Numbers started flashing across the screen as he sat down in a high-backed chair to read them. "I won't be long. Have a seat wherever you like."

Tempest walked around the office, checking out every nook and cranny. "When you said you were an investment banker, I didn't realize you had it like *this*. Sure, you drive a fancy car and wear nice suits, but lots of brothas do that when they're just big-time perpetrators."

"I hold my own." Geren swiveled around in his chair so he could admire her beauty while she admired his office. "You know, if I didn't know any better, I would think you were a gold digger."

Tempest snapped at him. "And you would be thinking wrong!"

"Hold up! No need to get feisty." Geren sensed their date was heading down the wrong path. "I said, if I didn't know any better. You don't strike me as the materialistic type. Not in the least."

"That's because I'm not. Everything I have, I obtained through my own sweat and tears. I've never come out of my mouth and asked a man for money. In fact, I've halfway supported most of the brothas I've had dealings with."

"Why are you getting so defensive all of a sudden?" Geren asked, becoming increasingly irritated. "I was just joking, Tempest. Damn!"

Tempest sat down in one of the wing chairs facing his desk. "Well, you have a sick sense of humor. I'm tired of men always assuming sistahs are after their money. This is nineteen-ninety-nine. Sistahs are doing it for themselves."

Geren chuckled. "I couldn't agree with you more." Geren got up and walked over to Tempest, sitting in the chair beside her and rubbing her on the knee. "Now I see where you get your name from. You have quite a temper on you, gurl."

That really agitated Tempest. "I got my name from my momma! A baby can't be born with a nasty attitude, dufus!"

"Oh, so now I'm a dufus?"

Tempest rolled her eyes in his direction again, but he still held on to her knee because it felt good to him.

"At least you admit you have a nasty attitude. I guess I should be grateful for that."

Tempest slapped Geren's hand away and then crossed her arms in front of her. "I'm ready to go home."

Geren couldn't believe his ears. "You've got to be kidding. What about the rest of our date?"

Tempest got up and picked up the handset of the phone on his desk. "Do you mind driving me, or should I call a cab?"

"Uh-uh-uh, now I get it!" Geren waved his index finger in front of her face. "This is your useless attempt to lure me into a full-blown altercation so you won't have to go blading."

"Don't be ridiculous! I'm just not in the mood to do anything now. At least, not with you. Your gold-digger comment spoiled it for me."

"What about lunch?"

"We can still do that, I suppose. As long as we go dutch. Better yet, lunch is on me."

"Just admit it, Tempest."

"Admit what?"

"That you don't know nada about in-line skating. You're afraid I'm going to show you up."

"This is ludicrous."

"I tell you what. I promise to take it easy on you. Scout's honor."

"Geren, the topic of this conversation has gone way past some freakin' skating."

"Okay, fine. Why don't you tell me where the conversation has gone? Clarify it for me, please."

"You want to know what my real problem is?"

"Most definitely!"

"Men who always come out of their mouths with derogatory comments about sistahs."

"For the tenth time, I was just joking."

"Okay, whatever. Can we just leave now?"

"Let me just send some data files to my home computer, and we can head on out." Geren grew tired of trying to reason with Tempest. "I still say you're trying to get out of blading."

Tempest rolled her eyes at him. "You're a trip."

"No, you're a trip," Geren came right back at her.

"Fine. You want to see some serious blading." Tempest took off to the door, huffing and puffing along the way. "I'll show you some serious blading."

Once they got out in the parking garage, Tempest was determined to prove Geren wrong. After all, Fred had given her a lesson, and she only fell a few times. Nothing major.

They had their skates strapped on and were standing on the top of one of the ramps of the garage on the third level.

"You ready?" Geren glanced over at her standing beside him and giggled. She looked scared shitless.

"Not only am I ready," Tempest responded, elbowing him. "I'm going first."

"Umm, maybe we should go together, Tempest. I wouldn't want you to get hurt."

"Hurt?" Tempest hissed at him. "Nucca, please. Watch my smoke."

Geren reluctantly let her go ahead of him, even though he had a bad feeling. He realized he was right by the time Tempest got to the first turn. Her legs started wobbling and shaking.

Geren took off as fast as he could to try to catch up to her, but she'd gained speed and was temporarily out of his sight. The next thing he heard was Tempest screaming, "Oh, shit!"

Geren got to the bottom of the garage and didn't see Tempest anywhere. "Tempest!" he yelled out. "Where are you?"

"I'm over here."

"Over where?" Geren asked in a panic, looking around for her among the few parked cars that were scattered around.

"Over here, dammit!"

Geren finally realized where her voice was coming from and rushed over to the Dumpster on the rear wall. He climbed up on one of the metal handles and looked over the top. It was all he could do not to double over in laughter when he spotted Tempest sitting there, surrounded by garbage.

"How in the hell did you get in there?" he inquired, absolutely amazed at her predicament.

"I came down the ramp too fast and flipped in here," Tempest confessed, ashamed and embarrassed. "Could you please help me get out? My back hurts, and I don't think I can get up by myself."

"Awwwwwww, poor baby," Geren said, mocking her. "Give me your hand, Miss Rollerblade Queen, and I'll pull you out."

Tempest managed to reach up to him, and he pulled her up and over the side.

Before Geren could get a word in edgewise, Tempest snapped at him. "Don't say one word! Not one damn word!"

Geren snickered while Tempest half-walked and half-skated to his car, holding her back with one hand and pulling trash out of her hair with the other.


"If you say one smart thing, I swear I will go upside your head." Tempest was holding on to Geren's neck tightly while he carried her into his house.

"I'm not saying a thing."

"Good."

Geren placed her down on the sofa in his living room. Once again, Tempest was in awe of his taste. His house was laid.

"Let me get you a pillow to prop your legs up."

Geren grabbed a toss pillow and elevated Tempest's legs.

"Thanks, Geren."

"You're welcome," he replied, looking genuinely concerned. "You want something to drink?"

"No, thanks."

Geren sat down beside Tempest on the sofa and picked up one of several remotes. "Want the TV on? I don't have a huge movie collection like you do, but I have cable and a few tapes I forgot to take back to Blockbuster about six months ago."

"Six months?" Tempest giggled. "I'm surprised they haven't sent 5-0 out to look for you."

Geren shrugged. "Naw, they just charged the full price out to my credit card when I didn't return them."

"Shame on it all!"

"Instead of TV, how about some music?"

"That's cool with me. This is your place, after all."

Geren got up and walked over to a stereo cabinet. Tempest was shocked when he opened the doors. It was packed full of the latest audio equipment, everything from an MP3 player to a rewritable CD player. She noticed they were all manufactured by the Phoenix Corporation, just like the computers in his office.

"You really have a thing for Phoenix stuff, huh?"

Geren pretended like he didn't hear her and plopped in Prince's *1999* CD. "You remember this song?" he asked as "International Lover" started pumping through the speakers situated throughout the room.

"Boy, do I!" Tempest giggled like a teenager. "Janessa and I were in the sixth grade, and you couldn't tell us we weren't the shit."

Geren laughed. "Yeah, I remember those days. Seems like yesterday, doesn't it?"

"Indeed."

"You look tense." Geren walked up behind Tempest, sat on the arm of the sofa, and started massaging her shoulders. "Let me help you relax."

Tempest was getting into the music and the massage, which was banging, until Geren's hands slipped from the nape of her neck down to her breasts. "Ummmmmmmm, I don't need to relax that much!" she exclaimed, pushing his hands away.

"Sorry, nothing beats a fail but a try." Geren looked embarrassed and pulled Tempest back toward him. "I'll just stick to your shoulders."

Tempest shut her eyes and let him work the tension out of her. "You have nice hands," she commented. "Soft for a man."

"Shhhhh, don't tell anyone. They might think I'm gay."

They both laughed. "Naw, no way," Tempest replied. "I can spot a homie-sexual a mile off. My radar would have gone off the moment I laid eyes on you in the club."

"Funny you should mention that," Geren replied. "I was reading this article the other day about men doing other men on the down-low."

"Hmph, sounds like interesting reading material." Tempest smirked, glad that someone finally just put the shit on out there. Brothas had always been on the down-low, fakin' the funk and cheatin' on the sistahs with other men. In her book, those men were right up there next to the men who deserted their children in the shitty-ass section.

"It was wild."

Geren started going for the tits again, and Tempest sat up. "I feel so dirty."

"Why?"

Tempest turned around and eyed him suspiciously. How on earth could he not know why she felt dirty? "Well, maybe it has something to do with all that garbage tumbling down on my head," she said sarcastically.

Geren fought to suppress a smile. "I see."

"I know I smell stank. You don't have to pretend otherwise." Tempest lifted the front of her shirt up to her nose so she could take a whiff. "Dizammmmmmm!"

"How about a shower?"

"Alone or with you?" Tempest asked, pondering over whether it was too soon to get jiggy with him. She craved him in the worst way.

"Whichever you prefer."

Damn, no, he didn't go there, Tempest thought to herself. Leaving it up to me, so I can be the one who looks like a straight-up hoe. "I don't have any other clothes."

"You can wear my bathrobe or one of my big T-shirts while I wash yours right quick." Geren bit his bottom lip, hoping Tempest would invite him to join her but not holding his breath. She just didn't seem the type, which was good and bad. Good because it meant she wasn't giving it up easily to any Jamal, Raymond, or Mohammed. Bad because he really wanted to lick her all over and feel her from the inside.

"I dunno about all this."

"What's wrong? You don't trust me?" Geren asked innocently.

"Should I?"

"Undoubtedly."

Tempest scrutinized her recycled virginhood a little while longer before stating, "Well, okay then. I would like to take a shower, alone."

"Cool!" Geren replied, highly disappointed. He watched her get up off the sofa and head to the bathroom down the hall. Damn, how did she get all of that junk in her trunk? She's finer than frog's hair. "I'll order some food to be delivered, since we never had that lunch."

"Wanna go dutch?" Tempest asked sarcastically, recalling their earlier conversation in his office.

"Gurl, get on in there," Geren chided, picking up the handset of his phone to call the soul food restaurant down the street. "There are plenty towels in the linen closet, and my robe is hanging on the back of the door."

"That feels absolutely fantastic!" Tempest squealed at the top of her lungs.

They were sitting out on Geren's sun deck. It had a fantastic view of the Potomac River, and the lights were just coming on throughout the city at early dusk. Tempest still had on Geren's thick, cotton robe and was stuffed to the brim with baby back ribs, collard greens, and potato salad. Geren was stunned by how much food Tempest had put away. He was just glad he'd ordered extra. He had planned on saving it for his Sunday dinner, but Tempest emptied all of the Styrofoam containers.

"That's it! That's the spot!" Tempest exclaimed.

Geren was washing her hair for her on his deck. He had her leaning back, and he was giving her a sensual shampoo with honeysuckle-scented shampoo and a pitcher of lukewarm water. Tempest had often dreamed of a man washing her hair, but it never happened. She also wanted a man to wash her feet in a river, like Allen Payne did to Jada Pinkett Smith in *Jason's Lyric*. Geren was scoring mad brownie points.

"I'm glad you're enjoying it," Geren said, as he tenderly caressed her scalp. This was a new one for him, too, but he was enjoying every minute of it.

"Oh, yeah! Harder! Harder!" Tempest yelled, blushing when she realized how sexual it sounded.

Geren got a hard-on that could split bricks, wondering if she yelled out like that in the bed.

He worked on her hair for a good hour, going back and forth into the house to get more water. On his fifty-eleventh trip, he returned to find Tempest fast asleep and snoring lightly in the deck chair. He picked her up and carried her inside, placing her gently on his bed. He sat down beside her and stared at her while she took sporadic breaths. He had never been so infatuated with a woman before in his entire life. Maybe she was the one.

He debated about opening up the robe and taking a peek but decided against it. When and if Tempest wanted him to see her body, he wanted her to willingly show him everything.

He got up off the bed and walked out into the hall, leaving the door slightly ajar. He went to go check on the clothes in the dryer and fell asleep on the sofa while listening to "International Lover" on repeat and fantasizing about Tempest.

"Good morning, sleepyhead." Tempest awoke the next morning to find Geren standing over her.

She was totally embarrassed for falling asleep like that while he was washing her hair. Then again, if his fingertips were so powerful, she could only imagine the potency of his dick.

She glanced over on his dresser and spotted a tray packed full of goodies: croissants with butter, scrambled eggs, and smoked sausage. It smelled delightful. "Oh, my, you cook, too? You're just full of surprises."

Geren laughed. He had felt compelled to cook after the way she tore up the food the night before. He didn't want her to wake up starving. "The best are yet to come," he replied, rubbing his fingers through her slightly damp hair. "You want me to blow it dry for you?"

Tempest blushed. "You keep this up, and I might just fall helplessly in love with you."

Geren kissed her seductively on her forehead, allowing his lips to linger for a few seconds so he could take in her aroma. *Forget the food!* "That's my game plan."

# 10

## a night out on the town

Tempest and Geren met Dvontè and Janessa at the Samurai Restaurant in the Georgetown Park Mall the next Friday. Janessa and Tempest snickered and blushed like schoolgirls who hadn't seen each other in a decade. Tempest was dying to fill Janessa in on the Rollerblading fiasco that had turned into a sensual shampoo and massage session, and Janessa was anxious to tell Tempest about the oral ecstasy Dvontè had been lavishing on her. He'd seriously improved since their first night together. He must've gotten used to her taste.

They took off to the ladies' room almost before everyone could speak casual greetings, leaving Geren and Dvontè in the entry area to wait for their table.

"Gurl!" Tempest exclaimed as soon as the bathroom door swung closed behind them. "It's time for a meeting in the ladies' room! I've always wondered what that song meant, but now I see! I have so much to tell you!"

"Tempest, you are not going to believe this!"

"Hold up! Let me go first," Tempest pleaded.

"Aiight, go ahead but make it snappy," Janessa demanded, wanting to spill her own gossip.

"Well, for starters, Geren and I did go Rollerblading," Tempest began.

"Are you crazy? I thought you were going to fake a leg cramp or something."

"I couldn't back down. Besides, Fred taught me a little bit."

"Fred is a dufus," Janessa said brazenly, clucking her tongue. "I can't believe your ass tried to perpetrate like that. What happened? Did you fall?"

"Hell, yeah, I fell, and it hurt something horrible." Janessa started laughing, and Tempest plucked her on the arm. "It's not funny!"

"Okay, sorry, sis," Janessa said, trying to straighten up her face. "Go ahead."

"Anyway, I fell on my ass, and for the first time in my life, I wished I did have that buffalo butt you keep claiming I have. I could have used the padding."

Janessa fell out laughing again.

"I thought I told you not to laugh."

"How can you expect me to stand here and listen to the crazy shit you say and not laugh?" Janessa looked in the mirror and toyed with the shoulder pads of the hunter green dress she had on. "I mean, come on, Tempest. Get real. You are so damn funny."

"N E Way," Tempest continued, rolling her eyes. "Geren took me back to his place, and it's the shit by the way. I'll describe it to you later. He took me over there and gave me the bomb-ass massage."

"On your shoulders or your busted-up ass?"

Tempest registered that thought, wondering why he didn't offer to massage her ass. Maybe she should have asked, but that would have been hoochified. "Just my shoulders."

"Oh," Janessa said, the disappointment apparent in her voice. "Is that it? I want to tell you what happened with Dvontè and me."

"No, that's not it," Tempest said mockingly. "Guess what? Geren washed my hair for me. Right there on his patio. He went and got a basin full of warm water and gave me the most sensual shampoo I have ever experienced. I wanted to jump his bones so bad."

"Did you? Jump his bones?" Tempest diverted her eyes to the mirror, grabbed a tissue out of the box on the counter, and started messing with her lipstick. "I take that as a no," Janessa said. "You better come up off of that puddy before some other sistah does. As fine as Geren is, I'm sure he has mad women after him."

"If it is meant to be, it will be," Tempest replied in a stony voice. She wanted to include some additional information but discarded the option. It was obvious Janessa was only intrigued by actual fuck tales, so she just settled for messing with the dramatic dolman sleeves of the white silk blouse she was sporting with black dress slacks. "So what's up with Mr. Dvontè, or should I call him Mr. Playa?"

"That comment was totally uncalled for!"

"I'm sorry," Tempest quickly and genuinely apologized. She didn't know enough about Dvontè to cast judgment, so she had made an unsubstantiated comment about the brotha. "Tell me what happened."

Before Janessa could blurt out the first sentence, they heard the toilet flush in one of the stalls. They hadn't realized that someone else was in there, and Tempest suddenly blushed with embarrassment about their overheard conversation.

They both started primping in the wall-length mirror, trying to busy themselves until the other woman left so they could get back to gossiping. Both of their mouths flew open when they saw a six-foot-five man come out of the handicapped stall—with a floral dress on.

Janessa looked at Tempest's reflection in the mirror and saw her eyes bulge. Tempest started rifling through her purse, searching for her wide-toothed comb, and Janessa pretended to straighten up her bra. She looked down at the man's feet when he came over to wash his hands and figured he had to be sporting at least a size-thirteen dress sandal.

He was white with blue eyes and wore a blond, curly wig under a straw hat. Tempest almost busted out laughing when he pulled out his own tube of lipstick and expertly applied it in the mirror. He was standing in between them and startled them both when he spoke.

"How you ladies doin' tonight?" he drawled in a heavy Southern accent.

Tempest was speechless.

"We're fine, and you?" Janessa replied.

"Just fine. However, I'm ready to get my eat on," he said coyly. "I'm starvin'!" Tempest and Janessa both fell silent, hoping he would get the hell out. He adjusted his bra, which was obviously stuffed with something, and headed toward the door. "Well, you ladies have a good one."

"You, too," Tempest sputtered out.

He was halfway out the door when he turned around and added, "By the way, that sensual massage/shampoo thing sounds like it's the bomb, girl! You have a good man like that, you better keep him. I agree with your girlfriend. You need to give it up before he steps out on you. Hell, if I wasn't already in love, I might go after him myself. He sounds like a winner."

Once he was gone, Janessa fell up against one of the stall doors, bent over in laughter. "Oh, my goodness, did you see that shit?"

Tempest chuckled, "How could I miss it? Did you hear what he said to me?"

"Hell, yeah, that was too damn funny!"

"See, that's why I always keep my homie-sexual radar activated." Tempest cackled. "That dude probably wears suits to work every day and then does his freaky shit at night. I wouldn't be surprised if he's married with two or three kids."

"Shame on it!" Janessa exclaimed. "I can't even talk about Dvontè right now. I'm just *too* through after this shit!"

Tempest was glad; she didn't feel like hearing about Dvontè any damn way. "Let's go on out, then. Maybe our table is ready by now."

"Cool with me," Janessa replied, and they headed out the door.

Geren was growing impatient with the service at the restaurant. He'd called ahead to make reservations, and the delay in being seated was unacceptable.

"I'll be back," he said, glancing at Dvontè. "I'm going to see what's up with the table."

Dvontè grabbed him by the elbow. "What's the big hurry? The women are still in the bathroom anyway. Probably talking about us."

Geren chuckled. "You're probably right. Women are a trip."

"I can't believe I let you drag me out here, man," Dvontè complained, loosening up his tie.

"I didn't drag you anywhere," Geren countered. "I simply suggested we take the ladies out on a double date, since they're best friends and so are we. It makes sense for all of us to hang out together on occasion."

"Hang out? Man, the only hanging out I'm trying to do with Janessa is in the bedroom. I did that wedding gig, but that was to get the drawers. Now that I have them, I shouldn't have to pay to play."

"You're one sick cookie, Dvontè," Geren proclaimed, trying to figure him out. "You mean to tell me you weren't planning on taking Janessa out *anywhere?*"

"That's exactly what I'm saying. Janessa is just a booty service, pure and simple. I'm not even trying to do that relationship thing."

"Does she know that?"

Dvontè waved Geren off with his hand when he saw the women approaching. "Whatever, man. I'm here tonight, aren't I?"

With that said, they both threw on strained smiles and joined in casual conversation with the ladies until their table was ready.

During dinner, Tempest and Janessa filled the men in on what happened in the bathroom. They searched the restaurant for the Amazon man so they could point him out, but couldn't find him among the crowd. They were dying to see who or what he was having dinner with.

The Japanese chef prepared their meals for them on the steamer table, and Janessa was mesmerized with the way he threw the knives in the air and chopped up everything with such precision. Geren and Dvontè both had steak with vegetables, and the women had shrimp with vegetables.

Dvontè almost got sick to his stomach watching Geren cater to Tempest's every whim like she was the Queen of Sheba. Geren even fed her and wiped the corners of her mouth when some of the green tea trickled out the corners. How disgusting, Dvontè said to himself. Another good brotha bites the dust. He's already whipped, and she probably hasn't even given up the ass yet!

They left the restaurant and decided to walk around Georgetown for a little while. Janessa tried to cuddle up with Dvontè by looping her arm through his like Tempest had done with Geren, but Dvontè wasn't even having it. He didn't want to risk one of his other honies spotting him in an affectionate embrace. If they were just walking side by side, he could always play that one off and say Janessa was his cousin or some shit if questioned about it later on. He knew women were gullible, and he loved toying with their minds. He glanced over at Janessa, thinking she would do nicely as the freak of the week until she started expecting too much out of him.

Tempest almost tripped over a crack on the sidewalk when she spotted the Pleasure Palace on Wisconsin Avenue. "Wow, I've always wanted to go in there," she squealed with delight.

Janessa snickered. "Me, too. I know a lot of sistahs that spend mad dollars up in that store."

Geren and Dvontè exchanged glances, giving each other the expression meaning this-might-turn-out-to-be-a-freaky-night-after-all.

"Well, let's not stand out here peeking in the window. Let's go on in," Dvontè eagerly suggested, grabbing the door and holding it open for the rest of them.

Once inside, Tempest's eyes lit up like a Christmas tree. "Dang, look at all this wild stuff!" She giggled with delight. She picked up a satin case, opened it, and took out two silver balls. "Wow, Ben Wa balls!"

"What are those for?" Geren asked with piqued interest. Janessa and Dvontè had disappeared in the back of the store where all the S & M gadgets were located.

Tempest looked up at him innocently. "How the hell should I know?" She placed them back on the shelf and walked away, trying to hide the grin on her face. She knew exactly what they were for. In fact, she had a pair safely tucked away in her lingerie drawer. She wasn't ready to reveal her sexual prowess to Geren just yet. It was always good to keep a man guessing for as long as possible.

Tempest began to feel uncomfortable with Geren lurking over her shoulder. She was dying to buy some items that caught her eye; especially this book called *The Sex Chronicles* by some sistah named Zane. Several of the sexually active women at the gym where she worked out swore it should be required reading for any woman trying to get her freak on.

She almost creamed on herself when Geren picked up a pair of edible panties and inspected them. She could just envision him eating them off her and wondered if he was sharing the same thought. "What are you planning on doing with those?" she asked him seductively.

"Nothing you won't let me do with them," he replied, flashing his sexy grin. He held them up higher and pointed them toward the register. "Should I buy them?"

Tempest immediately got nervous. What if he was expecting some booty once he took her home? "Naw, that won't be necessary. Maybe some other time," she commented.

Geren chuckled and put them back on the shelf. "I was just joking. I told you I would never pressure you, and I meant it."

"I know," Tempest said, walking closer to him and looping her arm around his. "Let's go back here and see what Janessa and Dvontè are doing."

"Lawd only knows!" Geren laughed.

Before they could get to the back of the store, Janessa and Dvontè were already headed in their direction, loaded down with items to purchase, including a pair of handcuffs, a leather mask with zippers over the places for the eyes, nose, and mouth, and a leather whip.

"You are just so silly," Tempest giggled, smacking her lips at Janessa.

"No, I'm not," Janessa protested. "Dvontè and I just decided to put a little spark in our already sexsational love life."

Tempest looked at Geren, who was shaking his head at Dvontè. Dvontè just smirked at him, took the items from Janessa, and went to go pay for them. Geren wondered how Dvontè could swing for all of the sex toys but be reluctant to even buy the sistah a decent meal.

"Geren, can we head out now?" Tempest asked, pulling him even closer to her.

"Sure, sweetheart." He opened the door for her, and they said their quick good-byes to Janessa and Dvontè, who were so caught up in each other that they barely even noticed them leaving.

Tempest was a nervous wreck the entire drive back to her apartment. Since Janessa and Dvontè were so openly sexually active, she thought, Geren would expect the same thing from her. He had utilized a bunch of sweet talk about being willing to wait and all that, but her history with men warned her that he was not that damn patient.

He walked her upstairs to her door, took her by the hand, and swept his lips gently across her fingers before planting a kiss in her palm. "Thank you for the lovely evening, Tempest. I look forward to seeing you again."

With that said, Geren left Tempest standing there with a dumbfounded expression on her face. She masturbated herself to sleep that night, wondering what making love to him would feel like.

# 11

## one common goal

"Linda, we really need to get some more paper cups," Tempest complained, throwing away yet another one that had sprung a leak the moment she tried to pour some milk into it. "Half of these have holes in them."

"I'm trying, Temp," Linda replied, putting ginger snaps and apple slices on the small paper plates. "Mr. Saunders down at the corner store said he would donate some cups last week, and I haven't seen him since."

The two of them were in the kitchen of the center preparing for snack time. They always fed the young women a little something before each counseling session.

Tempest hated it when Linda called her Temp but never bothered to take issue with it. They had been working together at the teen pregnancy center for more than five years, and Tempest saw no reason to fall out over a nickname. Tempest knew Linda had grown up privileged in an all-white suburb of D.C. Linda wanted to save the world, but most of the young girls down at the center gave her a hard time. They couldn't fathom how a blond, blue-eyed Valley girl could relate to their problems in the hood. Yet and still, Linda hung in there through thick and thin. Tempest genuinely admired that.

"Mr. Saunders is always promising donations and backing down," Tempest said, adding her two cents. "It's such a shame that all of these merchants make a bunch of money off the community and refuse to give anything back."

"What can I say, Temp? Today's society is messed up like that."

"True!"

"By the way, how was the wedding you went to a couple of weeks ago?" Linda inquired.

"It was wild. I'll have to fill you in on the festivities after the session. Maybe we can go out and have a cup of coffee. It's been a long time since we actually sat down and had a one-on-one."

"Tell me about it." Linda chuckled, pushing her long blond hair behind her ear so it would stop falling in her face while she worked diligently on preparing the snacks. "There's never a dull moment around here. That's for sure."

As if to pay homage to that very statement, a loud scream sounded out down the corridor. Tempest and Linda practically bumped heads trying to get out of the kitchen at the same time. When they ran around the corner in the direction of the screams, a group of girls were gathered around the doorway of one of the center's rest rooms.

"What's going on here? What's wrong?" Tempest yelled out, pushing her way through the group of girls with Linda right on her tail.

"It's Brenda!" a young, curly-haired girl named Taneeka exclaimed. "I think she killed herself! She's not moving!"

As soon as Tempest got a good look in the rest room, she shouted out in panic. "Linda, call nine-one-one! Hurry!"

"Are you here with Brenda Watson?" an older female doctor with an Irish accent asked Tempest some three hours later in the waiting room of Children's Hospital.

"Yes, I am," Tempest replied, jumping up after being startled awake by the woman's voice. After the ambulance ride and filling out a bunch of forms, she must have dozed off on the couch. "Is Brenda going to be all right?"

"She lost a lot of blood when she slit her wrists, but she's going to be fine."

Tempest let out a loud sigh of relief. After walking into the bathroom and seeing what looked like a gallon of blood on the white linoleum floor, she'd thought Brenda might not make it. Her pulse had been extremely weak when Tempest felt for it while the ambulance was on the way to the center.

"We gave her a transfusion, and she's resting comfortably," the doctor continued. "You can see her in a little while."

"Thanks, doctor." Suddenly Tempest's heart started racing again when she remembered the reason behind the suicide attempt. Her mind had been drawing a blank up until that point. Probably from emotional burnout. "What about the baby? Is the baby okay?"

The doctor diverted her eyes to the floor. "I'm sorry. The fetus didn't survive."

Tempest collapsed back down on the waiting room couch, stunned beyond belief.

"We did everything we could," the doctor added. "Are you a relative?"

"No," Tempest quickly responded. "I am, at least I was, her counselor at a teenage pregnancy crisis center."

"What about the child's mother and father?"

"No father," Tempest replied, an edge of disdain in her voice. "Her mother leaves for weeks at a time to go stay with her boyfriend in New York City. I'll have to try to track her down."

"So when she's released, she'll be home by herself?" the doctor asked, obviously concerned about a repeat suicide attempt.

"She has a grandmother over in Northeast. I'll see if she can go stay with her for a while."

"Good idea. Meanwhile, she's going to need more intense counseling. Attempting to take one's own life is a very serious matter. We have a great support group here."

"I'll be sure to encourage her to attend the meetings," Tempest said, forcing the sides of her mouth into a weak smile. "Thanks so much for everything, Doctor—?"

"McTavish."

"Thanks, Dr. McTavish," Tempest said, shaking her hand.

The doctor turned to walk away. "I'll have the nurse come get you when Brenda is ready for visitors."

"Thanks."

Tempest was searching through her purse for thirty-five cents for the pay phone when Linda walked into the waiting room, looking just as exhausted as Tempest felt. Linda had volunteered to stay behind at the center and see that everyone got home okay. The session had obviously been canceled, but someone needed to shut the place down.

"How's Brenda? Is she okay? Is the baby okay?" Linda asked, rolling off three questions faster than Tempest could open her mouth to reply to the first one.

"Brenda will be fine," Tempest replied somberly. "At least physically. They're going to sign her up for suicide prevention counseling here at Children's. The baby didn't make it."

"Damn!" Linda exclaimed.

Tempest got up from the couch and put her arms around Linda. No matter what their racial difference, they were sistahs who shared the same goals and the same disappointments. Both of them had just lost the battle to save a young girl from the brink of disaster.

"This may not be the perfect place to share that cup of coffee, but how about we hit the hospital cafeteria?" Tempest suggested. "We could both use a pick-me-up."

"What about Brenda? Can't we go into her room?"

"Not yet," Tempest replied. "We'll stop by the nurses' station to tell them we'll be in the cafeteria so they can find us."

"Okay," Linda agreed as they walked out of the waiting room arm in arm.

"Temp, can I ask you something?"

"Sure," Tempest answered, taking a bite of the stale peanut butter cookie she'd purchased to nibble on with her cup of coffee.

"Why do you do this?" Linda asked.

"Do what?"

"Work with pregnant teenagers?"

Tempest shrugged her shoulders, not wanting to embark on a deep conversation about her past. "Let's just say I have my own personal reasons."

"So do I," Linda stated with an edge of nervousness in her voice. She took a sip of her own coffee before confessing, "I got pregnant when I was a teenager."

There was a brief silence while Tempest waited for her to expand on her statement. When she didn't, Tempest inquired, "What happened to the baby? Did you have an abortion?"

"Worse!" Linda lashed out at her. "My parents made me give my precious baby girl up for adoption. Just ripped her out of my arms and gave her away."

Tempest could see tears forming in Linda's eyes. She reached across the table and took her hand. "Look, we don't need to discuss this right now. We're both emotionally drained over the whole thing with Brenda. We can talk about this later."

"No, I want to talk about it!" Linda exclaimed. "I *need* to talk about it!"

"Okay, I'm listening," Tempest said, crossing her arms in front of her on the table and giving Linda her undivided attention.

"I was a junior in high school. A private school out in Potomac, Maryland. I first met Skip when we were in the eighth grade. By the ninth grade, I was totally infatuated by him." Linda took another sip of her coffee before continuing. "I made him pressure me for sex for a good two years before I finally gave in to him. I wasn't ready to have sex, but I knew if I didn't, he would just get it elsewhere.

"So we did it the first time in the backseat of my daddy's Rolls Royce. I snuck out to the garage late one night to meet him, and it was all over before I knew what hit me. In and out, you know?"

Tempest nodded her head. She figured two-minute brothas must come in all races. She could definitely relate.

"We went on like that for a few months until one day I realized my period was late. Real late!"

"How late?" Tempest inquired.

"Almost three months," Linda answered, lowering her eyes in shame. "I was just stupid back then. So caught up in the moments of passion that I didn't pay attention to much anything else."

"Were you using protection?"

"Yes, he was wearing condoms, but you know that story."

"Indeed, nothing is one-hundred-percent foolproof," Tempest commented, thinking about the dozens of young girls at the center who ended up pregnant in spite of birth control. "So then what happened?"

"I told Skip about the pregnancy, and he dumped me like I was the Bubonic Plague." A single tear finally escaped Linda's right eye and traced a trail down her pale cheek. "He stopped talking to me at school, he wouldn't accept any of my phone calls, nothing.

"I tried to have an abortion, but I couldn't for two reasons. First off, I couldn't do it without my parents signing a form, and secondly, it turned out I was too far along to have one anyway."

"What did your parents say when they found out?"

"I hid it for as long as I could. I wore baggy clothing and stayed in my bedroom most of the time when I was at home. Ironically, it was the headmistress at my school that called my parents and spilled the beans. She could tell I was pregnant despite the clothing. I was so scared when my mother came barging into my room. I thought she was going to strangle me with her bare hands. Instead, she just slapped me a couple of times across the face and told me, 'Just wait until your daddy gets home!' "

Tempest could pretty much guess the rest of the story, but she prodded Linda to finish it anyway. "So they insisted you give the baby up for adoption?"

"Absolutely!" Linda started wailing, and Tempest got up to walk around the table to sit directly beside her. The cafeteria was practically empty, since official visiting hours were over. "They wouldn't let me make my own decision. They made it for me. They told me I was going to college and making something out of myself, without a baby."

"Well, now I understand why you took on the task of working at the center. I admire your determination to get through to the girls, in spite of their disparaging comments toward you at times," Tempest said, rubbing the small of Linda's back. "You know what, Linda? You and I are not as different as you might think. We have an awful lot in common."

Linda dried her eyes with a napkin and darted them at Tempest. "Oh, yeah? Like what?"

Before Tempest could answer her question, which she planned to answer truthfully, a nurse came into the cafeteria and waved in their direction.

Linda jumped up from the table. "Brenda must be awake!"

Tempest got up to follow her out of the door. Linda suddenly swung around. "I'm sorry. Did you need to talk about your situation? If so, we can stay a few more minutes and see Brenda later."

"No, not at all!" Tempest replied quickly, glad to be saved by the bell. She had gotten caught up in the moment but really wasn't prepared to delve into her skeletal closet. "We'll talk about it some other time."

"You sure?"

"Positive!" Tempest grabbed Linda's elbow and led her out the door. "Let's go check on our girl!"

# 12

## makin' love

Geren knocked the charging base of the cordless phone off his nightstand when he reached for the handset in the darkness. His eyes slowly adjusted to the red light on his alarm clock. When he saw the time was 3:00 A.M., he wondered who in the world would be calling his house so late.

"Hello," he whispered groggily into the phone after pushing the talk button.

"Hey, Geren. I'm sorry to be calling so late. Did I wake you?"

"No, not at all," he lied, after realizing it was Tempest on the other end. "I was just watching some TV."

His television was on because he was used to sleeping with some sort of noise, but as usual, it was watching him instead of the other way around.

"That's cool," Tempest replied. She paused briefly before adding, "I just wanted to hear your voice."

"Is everything okay, Tempest?" Geren asked, propping himself up on one of his elbows and rubbing his eyes with his free hand. "It's not that I'm not glad to hear from you. You can call me any time of the day or night. I must admit this is a bit of a surprise, though."

He patiently awaited a reply but got no answer. After a phone sex commercial advertising a nine hundred number came on and went off, he said, "Tempest? Are you still there?"

"Yes, I am. Sorry," she anxiously replied. "I was just thinking about something."

"Is everything all right?"

"Yes and no," she responded, letting out a deep sigh afterward. "I'm fine physically, but I had an emotionally draining day."

"What happened?"

"One of the girls tried to kill herself," Tempest stated in dismay. "Right there in the center."

Geren sat straight up and threw his feet on the floor, flicking on a lamp in the process. He was wide awake now. "Sweetheart, I'm so sorry to hear that."

"Thanks."

"How is the girl?"

"Brenda's better, physically at least. I'm not sure about emotionally. She slit her wrists in the bathroom and lost a lot of blood."

"Oh, boy!" Geren exclaimed. "That's horrible!"

"I just left Children's Hospital," Tempest continued. "She's resting comfortably."

"That's good, and the baby?"

Geren could tell from the silence on the other end that the baby hadn't survived.

"She lost it," Tempest finally responded. "It was a little girl. Brenda was trying to kill herself and the baby, but now she's gonna have to live and face the guilt."

Geren rubbed his forehead, trying to prevent a sudden migraine from taking over. "Well, are they keeping a close eye on her? What if she tries it again?"

"They have her on a strenuous suicide watch. That's hospital policy."

"How are you holding up? That must have been such a traumatic experience for you."

"I'm all right. Just having trouble sleeping," Tempest said earnestly. "Just having a hell of a lot of trouble sleeping."

It suddenly dawned on Tempest that she was calling Geren at three in the morning. What if he wasn't alone? "I'm not interrupting anything, am I?"

"No, not at all," Geren quickly replied. "Tempest, I told you I'm not seeing anyone else."

Tempest blushed because he said anyone *else*. That implied he felt that he was seeing her. She was hoping he regarded her in such a fashion.

"In that case, I was lying here fantasizing about one of your awesome, spine-tingling massages."

"Oh, yeah!" Geren said excitedly.

"*Oh,* yeah!"

"If you're serious, that can most definitely be arranged. Just say the word."

"Word." Tempest giggled into the phone. She was ready for him. It was time. Life was too short. She needed someone. She needed Geren.

"Give me thirty minutes," Geren said before hanging up.

Geren headed to the bathroom to take a quick shower. Across town, Tempest did the same thing.

* * *

Geren's jaw almost hit his chest when Tempest greeted him at the door a little while later. He'd violated about a dozen traffic laws to get there. She was scantily clad in a black silk teddy and a short, sheer black robe.

"You're so damn beautiful," he finally managed to utter.

Tempest didn't respond. Instead, she grabbed Geren by the collar of his navy oxford shirt, pulling him inside into her arms before standing on her toes and gliding her tongue into his mouth. He eagerly accepted it.

She broke the kiss, took his hand, and led him to her bedroom. They collapsed onto Tempest's bed together, groping each other all over.

Geren palmed Tempest's breasts and drew her left nipple into his mouth through the silk fabric.

He was fidgeting with the straps of her teddy, trying to lower them when Tempest whispered, "You'll hurt me."

The statement took him completely off guard. He let go of her straps and propped himself up on his elbow so he would have an eagle's-eye view of her face. "What makes you say that?"

Tempest darted her eyes over to his and redirected them to the ceiling. "Just like the rest of them."

Geren let out a frustrated sigh. "Fuck all of those stupid ass-holes who tried to run a game on you!"

I did, Tempest thought to herself. I fucked every last one of them, and they dogged my ass out anyway.

"They didn't *try* to run a game on me, Geren," she replied, still gazing at the ceiling. "They *did* run a game on me. A very cruel game."

"Look at me Tempest," Geren pleaded. Tempest looked at him, though it was difficult. She was so confused, it was pathetic. She'd spent all that time in preparation to jump his bones, and now that he was here in the flesh, all the maggots from her past were invading her thoughts again.

"I'm not going to hurt you," Geren continued. "I'm not like the rest of them."

"That's what they all say," Tempest snidely remarked. How many times had she heard that one?

"Are you convinced we're going to fail? Are you?" Geren was just as confused as Tempest. Not about his feelings, but about her feelings toward him. "Because if you've already got it etched in your mind that our relationship is doomed, then it will be."

Tempest responded without hesitation, "I want this to work." She did want him. She just wasn't sure she was ready. "I want us to be together more than anything."

Geren let out a sigh of relief. He'd been on the verge of losing all hope. "So what's the problem, sweetheart?"

Tempest sat up and positioned her back against a pillow. Geren followed suit, taking hold of her right hand.

"I guess I've always had a problem separating the past from the present."

"You're going to have to learn to let go, or you'll never be happy with anyone." Geren prayed he was getting through to her. She was the one. There were no lingering doubts on his part. "Whether it's with me or somebody else."

"You're right," Tempest readily admitted. "I realize that."

"Do you want me to leave, Tempest?" Geren let go of her hand and got up off the bed. "I came over here to comfort you after a rough day. I honestly wasn't expecting anything else."

"No, I don't want you to leave!" Tempest exclaimed. She sat up on her knees. The last thing she wanted was to be left alone. "Please stay with me tonight."

Geren gathered Tempest's face into his hands and kissed her

gently on the forehead. "Not a problem. I'll stay as long as you like."

Tempest got up off the bed so she could turn down the covers. They both climbed in and cuddled. Tempest laid her head on Geren's chest. Ten minutes later, they were both sleeping soundly. It was 5:00 A.M.

At 8:00 A.M., Tempest's alarm clock blared out, interrupting the silence. She reached over Geren and slammed her palm down on the snooze button. Geren didn't budge. She cut the alarm completely off. She had no intention of going into the center that day—not after the incident the night before. There were no scheduled group sessions, and bottom line, people would just have to understand.

Geren looked so peaceful lying in her bed, like he belonged there. She ran the tip of her index finger over the well-defined features on his face. His eyebrows. The bridge of his nose. His thick, luscious lips. They looked so damn enticing.

Her lips on his stirred him from his slumber. Their kissing became more and more intense until they were both moaning loudly.

Tempest climbed on top of Geren and started unbuttoning his shirt and gyrating her hips on his dick.

Geren grabbed her by the wrists. "Are you sure?"

"Absolutely," Tempest replied, pulling her wrists free and getting the rest of the buttons unfastened.

"We don't have to do this," Geren whispered reluctantly, offering Tempest a way out but hoping she wouldn't take it. "I'll wait for you."

"I don't want to wait anymore." Tempest drove the point home by licking a trail across Geren's chest, nipple to nipple. She could feel him hardening underneath her and couldn't wait to take a ride. "I trust you completely."

"The feeling's mutual," Geren replied, deciding to make himself useful by palming an ass cheek in each hand.

"Good." Tempest sat up and lowered her teddy straps, exposing her firm breasts. Geren couldn't help but wonder how women always made it look so easy. "Now love me like I've never been hurt."

Tempest sucked gently on Geren's earlobe, something she'd been itching to do since she'd first laid eyes on him at the club. "Tell me your dreams," she whispered softly in his ear.

"My dreams?" Geren asked incredulously, finding it hard to believe Tempest wasn't totally spent after the hours of lovemaking they'd put in. They'd started at eight in the morning, and it was well after four in the afternoon before they finished. He was surprised to open his eyes and find her wearing a nightgown. He must have dozed off at some point.

"Yes, your dreams," Tempest replied, gazing into his eyes lovingly.

"You mean other than the one that just came true?" Geren flashed Tempest one of his perfect smiles, and Tempest blushed uncontrollably. "Hmm, let's see. My dreams. Well, I want to continue to climb up the corporate ladder in my career. That's a given."

"And other than your career?"

"Until recently, I was hoping to find the woman of my dreams."

"Until recently?" Tempest asked, practically grinning from ear to ear.

"Yeah." Geren took Tempest's hand and brushed his lips across her fingertips. "I'm pretty sure I have that one covered now."

Tempest started giggling like a teenager. "Stop making me blush."

"I love it when you blush." Geren leaned over and kissed her passionately. Once they came up for air, he added, "But seriously, let me make myself perfectly clear, so there won't be any doubts about what went down here today."

"You don't have to do this," Tempest said, not wanting him to think he had to declare his undying love for her after one roll in the hay. "You don't have to—"

Geren put his index finger over Tempest's mouth. "Shhh, you talk too much. Do you know that?"

"Only when I'm nervous."

"What are you nervous about?"

"This!" Tempest exclaimed, sitting all the way up and propping her back against a pillow. "You!"

"I want to be with you, Tempest. Not just today, not just tomorrow, but for the long haul." Tempest was taken aback by the conviction in his voice, and it showed all over her face. "What do you think about that?"

"I think we should take this slow," she replied, shrugging her shoulders. "I'm kind of rusty in the relationship department. At least, the *real* relationship department."

"We can take this as slow or as fast as you want to, as long as we take it somewhere." Geren sat up in the bed next to her, letting the covers fall away from his midsection so that he was fully exposed. Obviously, he wasn't as shy about his body as Tempest was. "Is that cool with you?"

"Yes, that's cool with me," Tempest replied in a near whisper, drinking him in with her eyes. "So tell me the rest of your dreams."

Geren let out a heavy sigh. "You just won't give up, will you?"

Tempest punched him lightly on the shoulder. "Nope."

"Eventually, I would like to get married and have a household full of kids. Maybe six or seven."

Tempest's eyes ballooned. "Excuse me, did you say six or seven?"

"Something like that," Geren replied without a second's hesitation. "I love kids."

"I see," was Tempest's only reply.

"What about you?" Geren asked, draping his arm around her waist.

"What about me?"

"Do you want kids, and if so, how many?"

"I guess I haven't really thought about it," Tempest replied, telling a complete lie. She thought about it more than she cared to let on. "Since I've never been in a truly committed relationship, I saw no reason to even ponder the situation."

"Well, maybe you should start pondering it."

"It just hit me," Tempest said, lying back down and turning her back to Geren.

"What did?"

"I'm exhausted. You wore my ass out."

Geren blushed and kissed Tempest on her shoulder blade. "I think it was more the trouble at the center and the hospital than me."

Tempest giggled. "Don't underestimate yourself."

"I guess I just feel like I haven't put in a full day's work." Geren actually felt like he had put in overtime, but he wanted to hear Tempest appraise his performance.

"Shoot, you must be kiddin' me." Tempest flipped over so that she could gaze up at him. "The way you just worked me over? Please! I almost needed to break out a hard hat to protect my head from the headboard!"

"You're wild." Geren guffawed. "Okay, it's your turn."

"My turn for what?"

"Tell me your dreams."

"Aww, do I have to?" Tempest asked, poking out her bottom lip.

Geren caressed her left breast through the nightgown, wishing she would take it back off so he could see all of her. "Turnabout is fair play."

"Other than the center, I really don't have any." Geren stared at her, prodding her to add more. She reluctantly continued, "I would like to make more progress with our teen pregnancy prevention program and maybe expand the center into an employment training facility for unwed mothers so they can find decent employment. Fast food places and things like that just aren't cutting it. How can someone survive on minimum wage when they have day-care bills and have to buy diapers and baby formula?"

"Good question," Geren agreed.

"The system really pisses me off," Tempest said angrily.

"You're amazing!"

"Why do you say that?"

"Because I asked you to tell me your dreams, what you want for yourself, and all you can talk about is helping others who are less fortunate. I really admire that."

Tempest stared at his dick and started rubbing it. "I'm thinking about myself right now."

"Is that right?" Geren asked, edging up the bottom of Tempest's nightgown to reveal her hips.

"Indeed." Tempest decided to help Geren out by sitting up and pulling her nightgown completely off. Geren's approval showed in his eyes.

"Should we break out the hard hat?" he inquired, licking his lips.

"Naw, that won't be necessary for this round." Tempest edged down farther on the bed. "You did a little favor for me earlier. I feel like I should return it." She took the shaft of his dick in her hand and started lowering her head down to it. "After all, like you said, turnabout is fair play."

"That it is!" Geren wholeheartedly agreed as she placed her warm mouth around him. "That it is!"

# 13

## sistahgurls

### three months later

"Dang, gurl!" Janessa exclaimed, returning to Tempest's living room from the kitchen with a can of Pepsi. "I guess it's true what they say. You can take the gurl out of the projects, but you can't take the projects out of the gurl."

Tempest glanced up from the television and stopped flipping through channels with the remote. "What the hell do you mean by that?"

"I'm talking about that big-ass can of used grease on your stove." Janessa chuckled. "All the money you have rolling in, and you're recycling grease? Shame on it all!"

"All what money? I know you didn't even go there," Tempest said, smacking her lips for emphasis. "You have a lot of nerve with your using-a-toothbrush-to-smooth-out-your-baby-hair-with-gel behind. If that's not ghetto, I don't know what is."

Janessa plopped down on the sofa next to her and slapped her on the knee. "Dang, that's cold! I thought social workers were supposed to go gentle on peeps."

They both had a good laugh.

"So what's on the tube?" Janessa asked. "Anything worth watching?"

"No," Tempest replied. "Just some Saturday-morning cartoons and kids' movies on all the premium channels."

"They need to show *Jerry Springer* on the weekends."

"I know that's right! I could sure go for watching some women call each other bitches and open up cans of whup-ass right about now," Tempest concurred, pushing the power button on the remote. "I'm about to cut this thing off so we can talk."

"That's cool." Janessa got up and headed toward the stereo. "You got any new CD's? I heard the Chaka Khan one is the bomb-diggity."

"Hmph, didn't I just say I was turning the television off so we can talk?"

"Yeah, and?"

"Well, isn't putting on music defeating the whole purpose?"

Janessa laughed and headed back to the sofa. "Good point." She plopped back down. "So what's new?"

"Not a damn thing," Tempest sighed, picking a piece of lint up off the sofa and plucking it on the carpet. "I'm thinking about checking out that play down at Crampton Auditorium tonight. Wanna come with me?"

"Gurl, I wish you had asked me before," Janessa replied, an edge of disgust in her voice. "I promised Shae I would go to the movies with her and her hardheaded-ass chaps tonight to see *Mighty Joe Young.*"

"I heard that was good. One of the teenagers down at the center was talking about it."

"Yeah, I heard it was good, too, but I'm still not even trying to go. Shae's kids get on my last nerve."

"How many kids does she have? I haven't laid eyes on Shae since high school. Since when have the two of you been hanging out, anyway?"

"Since you've been dissin' my ass on account of Geren," Janessa said sarcastically.

Tempest rolled her eyes. "You're seriously tripping. I haven't dissed you in any way, shape or form. Not because of Geren or anyone else."

"If you say so!" Janessa picked up the can of Pepsi, which was still unopened. "Shae has four kids. All girls."

"Get out of town!" Tempest exclaimed, drawn back in shock. "Gurlfriend has been spitting out about one a year, huh?"

"Yeah, and check this out." Janessa chuckled. "She named them all after luxury cars."

"You've got to be kidding! Is she married?"

"Nope! In fact, she's never even had a steady man. She just lets them hit it once or twice and never hears from them again. I always tease her and tell her she better not even look at a dick or she'll get pregnant. As a matter of fact, I have a theory. I think she names the kids after the type of car she gets knocked up in. She only dates drug dealers who drive fancy cars. Yet they're all still living at home with their mommas."

"Dang, momma's boys, that's bad!" Tempest watched Janessa struggle to get the Pepsi open. She wanted to laugh—her fake nails were too long to flip the top. "So what are the kids' names?"

"Oh, yeah, peep this! Their names are Lexus, Infiniti, Mercedes, and Jaguar, but they call her Jag for short."

"That's too funny." Tempest cackled, reaching for the soda. "Janessa, give me that so I can open it. You need to chill on the nail fetish. Those nails are longer than your fingers."

Janessa flipped Tempest the bird while she opened the can for her. "The better to say fuck you with, my dear."

"Aiight now, don't make me have to pull those extensions out of your damn head up in here," Tempest hissed, handing the soda back. "I guess I'll just go to the play by myself tonight, since you have plans."

Janessa eyed Tempest up and down suspiciously. "What about Mr. Super Lover? Why can't he go with you?"

"First of all, what makes you think I know anything about Geren being a super lover?"

"Gurl, I was born at night, but not last night. You and Geren are fucking, or my middle name's not Ethel. After all this time, I know you two are throwing down. Besides, I can see the difference in your eyes. Remember what I told you? The eyes are always a dead giveaway."

Tempest decided to let that one slide, since it was true. They were sexin' big time. "Geren has to work at the office all weekend to prepare for a big meeting on Monday."

"Uh-huh, sho' you right!"

"What do you mean by that snide remark?"

"Men always say they're at the office when they're really laid up in the bed with some other hoochie momma."

"Janessa, I'm not even going to go there with you," Tempest said indignantly. "Even if Geren *is* with someone else, he doesn't owe me an explanation—our relationship isn't that serious."

"Okay, gurlfriend." Janessa smirked. "If you say so."

Tempest flipped the coin on her. "Speaking of men, what's up with you and Dvontè?"

Janessa diverted her eyes to the black lacquer coffee table.

"Everything's straight. We see each other about once or twice a week."

"I see," Tempest said suspiciously.

"What does 'I see' mean?"

Tempest put her knee up on the leather sofa so she could look directly at her. "Janessa, I want to ask you something."

Janessa glared at her out the corner of her eye. "So ask!"

"First, you have to promise you won't get mad about it."

"Just ask the damn question already," Janessa said, sucking in her bottom lip.

"Okay, here goes." Tempest inhaled a deep breath and went for it. "Does Dvontè ever take you out on dates, or do you just go over to his place to have sex with him?"

Janessa jumped up off the sofa and headed down the hallway. "How dare you call me a hoe!" she blared. "That's what you're doing, right? Calling me a hoe?"

"Not at all." Tempest jumped up and followed her. "I was just wondering because Geren said whenever he calls Dvontè, you're always over there, but Dvontè never mentions you two going out anywhere. Except, of course, when the four of us hang out, but that's rare these days."

Janessa went in the bathroom and slammed the door. "So, because Geren put his two cents in, that makes me an automatic hoe?"

"See, I knew you were going to blow this shit all out of proportion. All I did was ask a simple question, and you're getting bent out of shape." Tempest hesitated, then added through the door. "It *must* be true. Otherwise, you wouldn't be offended."

"Dang, can a sistah take a leak in peace around here?" Tempest heard Janessa pull her jeans down and plop down on the toilet seat. "Why is Geren all up in my beeswax anyway? Tell him to get a life! For that matter, you need to get one, too, heifer!"

Tempest laughed off the heifer comment. "Whatever, tramp!" She could hear Janessa let out a slight giggle from the other side of the door. "Just know that I love your crazy ass and don't want to see you get hurt. If Dvontè is trying to run a game on you, his ass will have to deal with my wrath before it's all over and said and done. They don't call me Tempest for nothing!"

The toilet flushed and the faucet started running. A moment later, Janessa came out of the bathroom. "For your information, nosy ass, Dvontè and I *do* go out places. However, Dvontè doesn't make a grip like Geren, so we have to stay within a budget."

"That's bullshit," Tempest said, leaning against the hallway wall. "Even a dog deserves a walk. This is Washington, D.C. The nation's mofo capitol. There are tons of free things to do around here. Especially on the weekends. You need to set him straight from jump, or he'll let his current behavior dictate the rest of your relationship."

Janessa pouted. "I will agree with you to a certain extent, but I still can't believe the nerve of Geren. Who does he think he is, telling you all my business? If he tells it all, what the hell am I going to have left to tell you? That's what being best friends is all about. Spilling the beans."

"I agree," Tempest said, throwing her arms around Janessa and kissing her on the cheek. "Now, let's kiss and make up."

Janessa laughed, glancing down at her watch. "Dang, we still have the whole day left before I have to meet Shae. What are we going to do?"

"I have a great idea." Tempest headed toward the kitchen. "Why don't we make some Rice Krispies treats and cherry Kool-Aid? We can spend the rest of the afternoon doing each other's hair in some fucked-da-hell-up hairstyles."

Janessa nodded in excitement. "Sounds good, but you have to

promise to put at least two cups of sugar in the pitcher of Kool-Aid," she said jokingly. "I bet you have some Mason jars we can drink it out of, too. If you have that grease can on the stove, I know your ghetto ass has some Mason jars hiding around here some-place."

Tempest fell out laughing. "I damn sure do. My mother gave them to me when I moved in."

Janessa smirked. "I tell you what. You make the Rice Krispies treats while I make the Kool-Aid. I don't trust your ass. You might try to skimp on the sugar."

"You're a trip." Tempest slapped her gently on the arm. "I don't know about you doing my hair with those long-ass nails. You might draw blood on a sistah."

"No, I won't," Janessa said, obviously offended. She reached for the glass pitcher on top of the refrigerator and started search-ing for the packets of Kool-Aid. "You remember that time, when we were about ten, when I put your hair into that waterfall hairdo?"

"Yeah, that style was fucked-da-hell-up and then some." Tempest chuckled, remembering the way it looked like it was yes-terday. "My poor mother came home from work and thought some crackhead had broken into the house. She didn't even recog-nize me. I had to show her the birthmark on my right shoulder so she wouldn't call 5-0 on a sistah."

They both fell out laughing. "Those were the good old days," Janessa added. "Why can't things be as much fun now?"

"They can be," Tempest interjected. "We just have to live our lives to the fullest while we still have lives to live."

"Amen to that, gurl. Let's start by throwing down on some of these goodies. Make sure you don't put the mixture on the wax paper while it's still hot. Last time, we had to pull the Rice Krispies treats off the wax paper with forks."

"Yeah, but those bad boys were good," Tempest objected. "You just make sure one of those witch fingernails doesn't fall off in the Kool-Aid while you're stirring. I don't want to choke up in here."

Janessa held up her middle finger. "The better to say fuck you with, my dear."

# 14

## reciprocity

"Hang on for a second, Trisha." Dvontè tossed the phone on his love seat and went to look out the peephole, wondering who would be bold enough to knock on his door unannounced. He knew it wasn't Geren. Geren had phoned earlier to say he was taking Tempest out of town for the weekend.

Dvontè cursed under his breath when he realized it was Janessa. She was really becoming a nuisance.

He went back to his living room and picked up the phone. "Umm, Trisha, let me call you back in a few."

"I thought you were coming through tonight?" Trisha asked seductively. Dvontè got an automatic hard-on, thinking about drowning his face in her 42DDD tits. "I bought a new bra and a thong today from Body and Soul over in Prince George's Plaza. I want to get your opinion."

"Oh, I will be there with bells on, beautiful," he replied excitedly. "You can bank on that. Just make sure you have the handcuffs and whipped cream ready. We have some unfinished business from last week."

Janessa started banging on the door again and calling out his name. He was hoping like all hell Trisha wouldn't hear her and start asking a bunch of questions. He wasn't even trying to get cold busted before he could crawl up between Trisha's creamy thighs again.

"Okay, baby, I'll have everything waiting for you," she cooed. "Just hurry up. My pussy is throbbing, and I want to give you a tongue bath."

That did it! "Never mind me calling you back," he whispered into the phone, licking his lips in anticipation and scoping his watch. "I'll be there in exactly one hour. Later!"

He hung the phone up just as Janessa started abusing his door for the third time. "Dvontè, I know you're in there!" she yelled. "I can hear you moving around."

"I'm coming!" he snapped back, headed toward the door. It became painfully clear it was time for his ten-minute overstepping-the-homie-lover-friend-boundary chat.

Dvontè yanked the door open, not even trying to fake the funk. He was highly upset and wanted her to know it.

"Janessa, what are you doing here? Did we have plans for tonight? If so, I completely forgot."

"No, we didn't have plans, Dvontè," she replied in a mousy voice. Damn right, we didn't have plans, he thought to himself. *I have a set of 42DDD breastesses, a can of whipped cream, and a pair of handcuffs waiting on my ass across town.* "I decided to surprise you." She flung her arms open, flashing him her radiant smile. "So surprise!"

He tried to force a grin but only managed to conjure up a

smirk. She bent down and picked up a few plastic grocery bags from the carpeted corridor, practically knocking him down to get inside his crib.

"Can you grab my overnight bag for me, baby?" Janessa was headed toward the kitchen with the groceries, making herself at home like Florida Evans from *Good Times*. Dvontè couldn't help but notice she looked damn sexy. She was wearing a skintight black hoochie dress that didn't leave an inch of thought to the imagination.

Overnight bag! What da hell? He looked out in the hall, and Janessa wasn't fronting on the overnight bag. It was more like an overmonth bag. He picked up the black duffel and calculated that it weighed every bit of fifty pounds.

"Damn, what do you have in here?" Dvontè asked sarcastically. "You planning on moving in or something?"

Janessa pulled the bag away from him, walked into the living room, and set it on the sofa. She grabbed the collar of his white Armani dress shirt, a definite no-no in his book, and kissed him on the lips. "Only if you want me to."

Dvontè was speechless. Things were getting way out of hand. "Janessa, we need to talk," he declared, sitting down on the love seat and positioning her on his lap. He didn't want to be too cold about it. After all, she was fine as all hell. "I think you got the wrong impression about things somewhere along the way."

"I was kidding about moving in, dufus." She giggled, rubbing her long fingernails through his curly brown hair. "The reason the bag is so heavy is because I have several surprises in there for you."

"Aren't you just full of surprises tonight." Dvontè glanced at his watch and felt a panic attack coming on. He had a booty call to make, and things weren't looking too good. "What type of surprises?"

"You'll just have to wait and see, but I will tell you this. You're going to enjoy every single one of them." Janessa started gyrating her ass on his lap, reaching her hand between her own legs to caress his dick. "I see your dick is already hard. That's a good thing."

Damn, what was a brotha to do! Even though Dvontè wanted to bone Trisha in the worst way, Janessa had this habit of turning him on like no other. He decided that his ten-minute overstepping-the-homie-lover-friend-boundary chat could wait one more day. As for Trisha, he knew she would be mad if he didn't show, but that was guaranteed pussy. Bottom line: she wasn't going to refuse him whenever he did go over there for some ass.

"So, what's in the grocery bags?" Dvontè asked her. "Can you at least tell me that, or is that top-secret info too?"

"Well—" she chuckled. "You're always talking about how you miss your grandmother's pepper steak."

"Yeah, I can't wait to go to Mississippi for Thanksgiving so I can throw down."

She teased him with her bedroom eyes. "Thanksgiving is more than a month away, so I decided to make some for you tonight. I looked up the recipe in a cookbook and got all the ingredients."

"How did you get over here anyway?"

"I caught a cab." She slipped him the tongue and then yanked it away just as he was about to slobber her ass down. She was such a tease, but he loved to be teased on occasion. "I hope you're not upset with me for coming by without calling."

"No, not at all." Dvontè lied. He was waiting for the lightning to strike. Instead, the phone rang. He knew it was Trisha. No way was he picking up.

Janessa looked at Dvontè strangely when he ignored the phone. He opted to let the answering machine pick up in the bedroom. She knew what was up. "Aren't you going to get that?"

"Nope, not at all. Who needs distractions?" Dvontè pulled Janessa's head down to his and drew her succulent bottom lip into his mouth. "Before you start cooking, how about we go into my bedroom?"

"Umm, sounds yummy, but let me get something out of my bag first." She jumped up from his lap and unzipped the bag, standing with her back to him so he couldn't see what she was getting out. "Ta-dah!" she exclaimed, revealing an 8mm camcorder. "Still have that fantasy about making a movie?"

Dvontè's dick expanded three more inches in his pants. "Damn right I do!" He stood up and put his arms around her waist. "You would do that for me?"

She looked him dead in the eyes and replied, "I would do anything for you."

Something ran through Dvontè right at that moment. He wasn't sure what the hell it was, but it scared the living daylights out of him. No woman had ever said that to him before. They had said a lot of things, ranging from "Cum all over my tits" to "Make it bounce, daddy," but never that. For a brief moment, Dvontè thought Geren might have been right about him settling down. It was a fleeting moment. Once it was over, he just wanted to fuck as usual.

Dvontè picked Janessa up and carried her into the bedroom, camcorder and all. "Where should I put it?"

"The camcorder or your dick?" They both laughed. "Put the camera over on your dresser and make sure it is on. I wouldn't want to miss getting anything on tape."

While Dvontè was setting the camera up, he noticed Janessa messing through the drawer of his nightstand, another definite no-no. A pair of lace panties was shoved in the back of it that some piece of ass he met at a club left over his place. He'd been meaning to throw them away and prayed Janessa didn't find them. He'd waited damn near thirty years to make a porno tape and didn't want a jealous rampage to ruin it.

The phone started ringing again. Dvontè rushed over to the nightstand and turned the volume completely down on his answering machine before Trisha could leave a message.

"Must be your woman calling," Janessa stated sarcastically. "If you need to answer it, go ahead."

"Naw, I'm cool." Dvontè reached for the wall plate to unplug it altogether. "I just want to eat you like a piece of black licorice."

"Speaking of eating—" Janessa pulled a black fountain pen out of his drawer, obviously what she had been looking for. "You're always saying you have nothing good to eat between Thanksgiving and Christmas when you go visit your grandma."

She took the pen and drew the word *Thanksgiving* on her right inner thigh and *Christmas* on the left one. She sat up on her elbows and gave him that damn sexy smile again. "Now, how about ripping off my panties and joining me between the holidays?"

Dvontè almost came in his pants. Janessa was about to turn him out for real. She was saying and doing all the right things. That "join me between the holidays" line was probably as old as he was, but he appreciated her freakiness anyway. He stood there for a brief moment, letting his eyes linger over her body, and then did what came naturally.

Janessa lay there in a daze, not really enjoying what Dvontè was doing between her legs. She was more worried about where things were going in their relationship.

Some of the things Tempest said to her had really hit home, and it bothered her to no end. When she showed up at Dvontè's apartment without calling, she was a nervous freakin' wreck. She just knew one of three things would happen. Either he would be pissed off and kick her to the curb, he would have another woman up in there, or he would pull a booty bandit switcharoo on her and be up in there banging another man like Tempest's ex, Trent.

Much to her delight, none of that happened, although it did take him almost five minutes to answer the door. Janessa figured he was probably taking a nap when she showed up, so she'd banged on his door louder and louder until she heard him stirring around in there. He was fully dressed when he answered and looked downright fuckable as usual. She began to worry that he was on his way out to be with some other hoochie.

Lucky for her he didn't have any other plans for the evening, because she'd spent over fifty bucks on groceries to make him this pepper steak recipe. She'd brought some red potatoes and fresh asparagus to go with it and a bottle of red wine to wash it down. Ironically, she didn't get to even turn the stove on until the next morning. They ended up having it for breakfast.

By the time the sun came up, Janessa had convinced herself that Tempest was wrong. Tempest was her gurl, but she'd let Geren put all those silly ideas in her head about Dvontè using her for sex. Granted, they didn't hang out all the time, but they went to movies on occasion and ate out once or twice.

She'd done something completely outrageous with him during the night by borrowing Shae's camcorder and making a porno tape. That had always been a fantasy of Dvontè's, and she wanted to make it come true for him. She would be lying if she said it didn't turn her ass on too.

Janessa was past turned on. Just the mere thought of the camera running made her want to impress somebody. The way she deep-throated his dick would have made Vanessa Del Rio bow down to her in envy. She'd posed for the camera, she'd vogued for the camera, and she made sure her valiant ride on his gratifying dick made it onto film. Yes, the dick was gratifying. Over the past few months, Dvontè's up time had seriously improved. They watched the tape about four in the morning and were so pleased, they decided to do the sequel.

Tempest was straight-up tripping, Janessa concluded. For once, Janessa just knew Tempest's ass was reading a man wrong. After all, Tempest didn't exactly have a spotless track record with men herself.

# 15

## mirror images

Tempest pretended to be completely preoccupied with the manila folder placed in front of her, a folder she'd read cover to cover an hour earlier. She was actually racking her brain, trying to think of something to say to the young girl sitting across the desk from her.

The girl was fourteen but looked old enough to walk into a club without being asked for identification. She had smooth, ebony skin and long, wavy black hair down to her bra strap. Tempest couldn't help but notice that the girl's breasts were larger than hers. She was also taller than Tempest, at least five-foot-nine, and had legs for days.

Most of the young girls who came into the center seeking help were talkative, outspoken even, but not this one. She'd barely uttered a word. Tempest knew she would have to tread carefully.

"Are you comfortable?" Tempest eyed the gray metal folding chair the girl was seated on. "We really need to get some better chairs, but we just don't have the funding right now."

The girl made eye contact with Tempest for the first time. She had dark brown cat's eyes. "I'm fine," she whispered.

Tempest exhaled. A small response was a far cry better than none at all. "So your name is Kensington?"

"Yes, ma'am."

"And you're fourteen?"

"Yes, ma'am."

She's polite, Tempest noted. "How many months pregnant are you, Kensington?"

The girl winced, sending a shudder up Tempest's spine.

"I don't know, ma'am," Kensington answered reluctantly. "Five or six, I guess. Something like that."

"I see. Any prenatal care?"

"No, ma'am. All I know is I'm too far along to have an abortion."

Finally, we're getting somewhere. "How do you know that? You tried to have an abortion?"

Kensington nodded. "My momma took me to that clinic over on Georgia Avenue."

Tempest glanced back down at the folder. Kensington Sparks. Age fourteen. Raised by a single mother on welfare. Paternity unknown. Straight-A student.

"Well, Kensington, there are other options we can explore. You don't have to raise this baby."

Kensington bit her bottom lip. "I know, ma'am."

"But you want to raise the child? Is that it?"

"I don't know!" Kensington burst out, showing symptoms of the frustration Tempest was all too familiar with, which immediately put Tempest more at ease. She was used to the outbursts; it was the quiet ones that made her nervous. "I'm confused! I didn't mean for this to happen!"

No one ever does, Tempest said silently to herself. "Everyone makes mistakes, Kensington. Don't beat yourself up because of it."

Kensington started crying. Tempest got up and walked around the desk, grabbing three tissues out of the dispenser on her way. She handed them to Kensington and then rubbed the girl's shoulders.

"What about the baby's father? Is he still in the picture?"

Kensington shook her head in disgust. "Jeremy's with Chantel now. I hate her. I hate both of them."

"It says you're a straight-A student in your folder."

That perked Kensington up. She blew her nose, sat up straighter, and even cracked a slight smile. "Yes, ma'am."

Tempest grinned. "Any plans for college?"

"Mr. Casey, my counselor, said I have a good chance of getting a full scholarship if I keep my grades up. I'd be the first one in my family to get a college degree."

"That's wonderful!" Tempest exclaimed, glad to see that Kensington was goal-oriented. That was a good sign.

The mood changed quickly when Kensington looked down and rubbed her belly. She was showing big-time. "But that was before—"

Tempest let go of Kensington's shoulders and sat on the corner of the desk so she could face her. "What about your mother? How does she feel about this?"

Kensington started crying again. Tempest handed her some more tissue. "She says I'm no good. That I should've kept my legs closed. That I'm nothing but a tramp." Kensington gazed at Tempest helplessly. "Jeremy's the first boy I slept with. I swear it."

"Would you like for me to call your mother? Maybe I can reason with her."

"Please don't do that, ma'am," Kensington pleaded. Tempest saw fear written all over her face. Damn, when would parents learn to comfort their kids when they make mistakes, not crucify them? "I just needed somebody to talk to. My mother doesn't understand me."

"Well, I'm your woman," Tempest proclaimed, forcing a smile. "You can talk to me about anything."

Kensington fell silent for a few moments, and Tempest pretended to busy herself with odds and ends around her desk. She'd extended the invitation to Kensington to discuss any matter, and she hoped she would take her up on the offer; there was more than just the pregnancy bothering her, she was sure.

Kensington finally spoke. "There is one thing I'd like to know, ma'am."

"What's that?"

"Can I ask you a question?"

"Like I said before, you can ask me anything," Tempest replied eagerly. Helping young girls was what made her life so fulfilling. "What would you like to know?"

"Ma'am, if my mother hits me, and I call the police, what will happen to her?"

Tempest crumbled up the piece of paper she was holding in her left hand, her way of venting her anger without showing it on her facial expression. When a child brought up abuse, any form of abuse, Tempest immediately wanted to hunt the culprit down and open a can of whup-ass.

Kensington stared at Tempest, awaiting a reply. Tempest exhaled and answered, "Has your mother ever hit you, Kensington?"

"Maybe," Kensington whispered, lowering her eyes to the floor. "Maybe not."

"I see." Tempest knew the child was scared to death.

"I'm just saying, what would happen to her if she did and I told someone?"

Tempest decided to come clean, even though she knew it would bring about a less-than-desirable reaction. "The Department of Social Services would investigate, and depending on the results of the investigation, they might press charges or place you in a foster home or both."

"A foster home!" Kensington exclaimed, jumping up out of the chair, startling Tempest. "That means I would have to live with strangers?"

"Temporarily. At least until the matter could be resolved by a court."

Kensington slowly sat back down in the chair, trying to regain some composure. "Thanks for answering the question."

"You're very welcome." Tempest got up from her desk to open a window. The office was getting stuffy. When she sat back down on the edge of the desk, she asked, "Kensington, are you sure there's not something you'd like to tell me?"

"I'm positive," Kensington responded, flashing a phony smile. "I'm just scared about this pregnancy and all."

"Don't be afraid, Kensington." Tempest held out her hand, and Kensington took it. Tempest rubbed Kensington's knuckles with her free hand. "You'll find nothing but friends here at the center."

Kensington gazed into Tempest's eyes. "I feel like I have a new friend already."

"You do." Tempest grinned. "You do."

Tempest spent another thirty minutes alone in her office with Kensington until the girl felt comfortable enough to tour the center and meet the others. There was a group session going on, and surprisingly, Kensington jumped right into the conversation with the rest of the expectant mothers. While Tempest had nothing but compassion for all the girls at the center, Kensington claimed a special place in her heart immediately—probably because she reminded Tempest so much of herself.

Over the next several weeks, Tempest and Kensington became very close. Tempest took Kensington shopping for maternity clothes but told her to keep it a secret from the other girls down at the center. She'd never taken such an interest in a pregnant teen before, and she didn't want the other girls to be envious.

Tempest also helped Kensington with her schoolwork and discussed possible college scholarships with her, even though college was still years down the road. Janessa and Geren both took a liking to Kensington right off the bat as well. Dvontè was missing in action except for during booty-call hours as usual. Geren even offered to teach Kensington how to Rollerblade once she had the baby. Tempest said she would watch from the sidelines; one busted ass bone in a year was enough for her.

After much prodding, Kensington finally broke down and admitted to Tempest that her mother had been beating her on and off, even during the pregnancy. Tempest immediately handled the situation, deciding to pay Kensington's mother, Pauline Sparks, a home visit the sistah would never forget.

"Ms. Sparks?" Tempest asked, rapping lightly on the open door of the small apartment. There were two women in the kitchen area, one propped up on a stool while the other one stood behind her, braiding her hair. Tempest instantly knew the one standing was Pauline Sparks; Kensington was her spitting image. "Ms. Sparks, my name's Tempest Vaughn. I'm a friend of your daughter's. I'm the director of the—"

"I know who the fuck you are! I'm surprised I didn't smell your prissy ass coming a mile away!" Pauline Sparks hissed at her. Her friend started laughing. Pauline snatched her head back, causing her to shriek out in pain. "Kensington's not here. She's in school."

"Actually, I came to see you," Tempest said, entering the apartment uninvited. She walked over to the kitchenette and reached out her hand. Pauline refused to shake it, rolling her eyes and continuing to work on a thick braid instead. "I was hoping we could discuss Kensington's pregnancy. Among other things."

"What the fuck is there to discuss?" Pauline asked with an edge of sarcasm in her voice. Tempest picked up a whiff of beer on her breath. "The little hoe got knocked up. End of story."

The woman on the stool started cackling again. Tempest wanted to go upside both of their heads but willed herself not to. She headed over to a sofa in the middle of the living room and pointed to it. "Do you mind if I sit down?"

"Help yourself." Pauline flung her head in Tempest's direction, looking her over from head to toe. "Excuse me if our furniture isn't as fancy as that to which you are accustomed."

Tempest sat down on the tattered sofa with weak springs and immediately grew concerned. It was the same sofa Kensington had to sleep on every night, and it definitely didn't have enough support for her back, especially in her condition. She noticed *Divorce Court* was on TV and then looked back over at Pauline, trying to establish eye contact. "Can we talk?"

Pauline rolled her eyes at Tempest again. "We are talking."

"I mean alone." Tempest diverted her eyes to the sistah on the stool, who was so large that she almost needed two of them. "Can I speak with you in private?"

Pauline seemed to ponder the request for a few seconds. "Dawna, let me see what Miss Thang wants right quick." She hit the sistah on the stool lightly on the back, pushing her up off the stool. "Why don't you go down to the corner store and get us another pack of beer?"

"With my hair lookin' like this?" Dawna asked, staring at Pauline like she'd lost her mind. Only half of her hair was finished. The other half looked like she'd just lost a wrestling match. "No fuckin' way!"

"Aw, come on, it's my treat." Pauline reached into the pocket of her jeans and pulled out a ten-dollar bill.

"What? Your treat?" Dawna asked, smacking her lips and putting her hands on her rotund hips. "Must be snowing in hell today."

Pauline plucked Dawna on her chunky arm. "Bite me, bitch!"

Dawna smacked her lips once more time for effect, rolled her eyes at Tempest, and headed for the door. "I'll be right back, heifer!"

"So what's so damn important that I had to kick my homegurl out the crib and spring for a pack of beer?" Pauline asked, once Dawna was out of their line of vision. "It's not like Dawna doesn't know Kensington spread her legs one time too often. She's showing big-time. Her ass better not be having twins either. I can tell you that much right now."

"You know what, Ms. Sparks?" Tempest asked from the sofa, feeling herself getting even more hot under the collar than she was before she came over there. "Pauline, rather. Can I call you Pauline?" Pauline shrugged her shoulders, giving Tempest a look of disdain. "I came over here with the intention of having a nice, warm, civilized chat with you, but—"

Pauline plopped down on the stool, taking Dawna's place. "But what, Miss Thang?"

"I can see that's not going to happen, so let's just throw tact and everything else that comes with it out the damn window."

*"Damn,* Miss Thang said 'damn'!" Pauline exclaimed.

Tempest jumped up off the couch and walked over to the stool. She'd had enough of the Miss Thang comment. "Oh, I got your Miss Thang, aiight!" Tempest shouted, poking Pauline in the shoulder blade with her index finger.

Pauline appeared stunned that Tempest would step to her in such a fashion. "I know you're not even trying to break bad with me. You better take your fancy ass up out of here before things get ugly. This is the hood, and we don't play that shit."

Tempest threw her head back and chuckled. She wasn't hardly impressed. "First of all, this situation has already turned ugly. Second of all, I'm not going any damn place until I speak my mind, and thirdly, I grew up in the hood, and I don't play that shit either. You can't intimidate me, bitch."

Pauline leaped up off the stool and tried to increase the distance between them by grabbing Tempest's arm and pushing her backward. "Bitch? Who the hell do you—"

"Shut the fuck up!" Tempest yelled, standing her ground. Pauline was taller than her, just like Kensington, but she didn't care. She would kick off her shoes and take off her earrings if need be. "Look, I'm just gonna throw the shit right on out there. Enough bullshittin'."

"Well, throw the shit on out there then," Pauline spewed back at her, saliva flying out of her mouth as she spoke.

Tempest stared at her dead in the eyes. "I know you've been beating Kensington."

"I haven't touched that child!" Pauline exclaimed, giving Tempest that no-you-didn't-even-go-there expression. "She's my baby girl! How dare you accuse me of—"

Tempest circled around Pauline and sat down on the stool. She refused to engage in some silly Mexican standoff. She noticed a roach crawling out of a dirty cereal bowl that looked as if it had been sitting in the same spot for more than a week. "Save your pathetic lies. I know you've been hittin' her, and the only reason I came knocking on your door instead of Social Services and the police is because Kensington begged me not to call them. She's afraid they'll make her a ward of the state and place her in foster care."

Pauline leaned against the counter and crossed her arms across her chest. "So why the hell did she tell you, then?"

"Oh, so you're admitting it?" Tempest asked with contempt.

"Let's get something straight right now." Tempest perceived something in Pauline's eyes right at that moment, something resembling love and compassion. Pauline must have sensed Tempest reading her mind; she lowered her eyes to the floor. "I've never beaten Kensington, as you put it. I may have slapped her around a time or two when she wasn't listening, but that's my damn business. I gave birth to her, gave up my own childhood for her, and I can do whatever the hell I want."

It was then that Tempest noticed how young Pauline Sparks really was. While she had signs of age, probably due to acute alcoholism, it was still obvious the woman wasn't a day over thirty. Tempest did a quick calculation in her brain and gauged that Pauline must have had Kensington when she was about fourteen or fifteen, the same age range as Kensington. She was about to try to reason with her but decided she needed to continue to take the hard approach, whether the woman was young or not. Abuse was abuse and inexcusable. "No, you can't do whatever the hell you want."

Pauline looked like she was about to spit fire, she was so angry. She stomped over to the door and swung it open wider. "Get out of my house!"

"Fine, I'm leaving, but let me make myself perfectly clear before I do." Tempest adjusted her purse strap on her shoulder, stood and walked over to her, getting as far up in Pauline's grill as she could stand without being nauseated by her breath. "If you ever lay another hand on Kensington, pregnant or not pregnant, I *will* call the police."

"No, you won't." Pauline giggled. "You already said Kensington's afraid they'll take her away. The last thing she wants is to leave up from around here."

"Oh, I will call. You can bank on that." Tempest hadn't even thought that far ahead, so she was improvising. She had hoped to reason with Kensington's mother, but things weren't going too well. "Not only that, but I'll also file for temporary custody of Kensington myself."

"Bullshit!" Pauline hissed at her, rubbing one of her bloodshot eyes.

"I'm not a foster parent, but I'm sure if I file expedited papers, they'll go through, and I'll take her from you," Tempest stated with conviction. "Raise her myself if I have to."

"Kensington's overreacting." Pauline, realizing the sistah just might be serious about taking her daughter away, was going on the defensive. "So I slapped her for being lazy or not doing the dishes. Big fuckin' deal. My mother used to beat my ass all the time."

"Well, that's probably part of the problem. Are you proud of what you're doing to her?" Tempest spotted a tear in the corner of Pauline's right eye, but Pauline wiped away the evidence quickly. Deducing that Pauline wasn't as hard as she pretended to be, Tempest reached over and gently caressed her cheek, pleading to Pauline with her eyes. "Kensington has a real shot at making something of herself. She has a bright future ahead of her. Don't make this a vicious cycle."

"Everything okay in here?" Dawna asked.

"Everything's fine," Tempest replied. Neither she nor Pauline had noticed Dawna standing in the doorway, holding a paper bag full of their afternoon sustenance. Tempest spotted some pork rinds sticking out of the top of the bag and figured it must be their lunch. "I was just leaving."

Dawna put the bag down on the kitchen counter, eyed the same roach Tempest had seen earlier, picked up a copy of *Jet* magazine, and slammed the hell out of it until nothing was left but a carcass.

Pauline walked back over to the kitchen makeshift beauty parlor and busied herself by cleaning out a brush with a comb.

Tempest glared at her from across the room. Pauline glared back. "Remember what I said. Don't ever let it happen again, or I'll take Kensington, and then you better pray you never run up on me in a dark alley."

Dawna ripped open the bag of pork rinds and started shoveling them into her mouth, enthralled by the conversation like she was watching her favorite soap. She was hoping Pauline wouldn't be in too fucked-up a mood to finish her hair; she was planning to go to the male strip show at the Black Screw that night.

Pauline laughed, trying to save some face even though she was beginning to get scared. The sistah, fancy clothes and all, really was from the hood, and definitely didn't play that shit. She could tell that much. "Are you threatening me?"

"Don't let it happen again, or you'll feel my wrath." Tempest stormed out of the apartment and slammed the door behind her.

"Damn, do you do this shit with the parents of all the girls down at the center?" Pauline yelled out through the door.

Tempest started crying before she hit the parking lot, and she cried all the way home.

# 16

## a lovers' christmas

"Wow, sweetheart!" Geren exclaimed, checking out the number of hat-and-glove sets Tempest was tossing into their shopping cart at Kmart. "How many of those are you planning on getting?"

"About fifty, if they have them," Tempest replied. "I'm trying to get all the girls at the center the same thing. You know how females can get. If I get even three or four of them a different Christmas present, the others will swear I'm playing favoritism."

"True!" Geren grabbed Tempest by the waist and kissed her gently on the forehead. "You know what I adore about you most?"

"What?" Tempest asked, blushing.

"Your compassion." He let go of her and started picking out sets to add to the pile. "That very first night at your apartment, when you described what you do for a living, I could see the excitement and dedication in your eyes. Not many people would commit themselves to doing what you do. It takes a special kind of person."

"Well, I have my reasons, Geren," Tempest said somberly. "Don't make me out to be some sort of saint, because I'm not. I just don't want to see teenage girls sink into depression and assume their lives are over simply because of an unplanned pregnancy. This isn't a new problem in society. Did you see that HBO movie, *If These Walls Could Talk?* It spoke volumes."

"No, I missed it. What was it about?"

Tempest gazed up at him, and he got an uneasy feeling. It was almost as if there was pure hatred in her eyes. "It was about three women who resided in the same house during different decades who all had to deal with an unplanned pregnancy. One was a nurse who had an illegal abortion right on her kitchen table, one was a married woman with one too many kids already, and the third was a college student who had an affair with a professor. When she went to an abortion clinic to have the procedure done, an antiabortionist shot and killed the female doctor right in front of her."

"Damn, that sounds real deep!"

Tempest looked away and threw a few more glove sets in the cart. "It was not only deep but extremely realistic. The crazy part is these men—the ones who say anything to get into a woman's pants and then run for the hills when she ends up pregnant. The ones who think birth control is solely the woman's responsibility. I hate men like that!"

"So I gather," Geren said cautiously, hoping she wasn't implying he was in the same category. He couldn't wait to have kids. With the right woman, of course. He went to the opposite side of the display stand and picked up a pair of navy insulated gloves. "How do you like these?" he asked, trying his best to change the subject. "Do you think they match the jacket I have on?"

Tempest took a good look at the jacket he had on, which was ablaze with a kaleidoscope of colors. She wanted to tell him that jacket was not half as fly as he thought it was. It was downright unattractive, which surprised Tempest, since Geren usually dressed very stylishly. Instead, she just said, "Naw, I think black will look better if they have them. Black matches everything. By the way, that jacket is the bomb-diggity."

"You really like it?"

"Hell, yeah!" Tempest exclaimed, lying her ass off but wanting to make him feel good about himself.

Geren's face lit up as he put the navy pair back and rummaged through the pile until he found a black pair. "Here we go." He held them up to his jacket and did a quick inspection. "You're right. These do look better."

Tempest grinned at him and started pushing the cart, satisfied she finally had enough hat-and-glove sets to cover everybody at the center. "Before we check out, I want to look down the Christmas decorations aisle."

"I thought you already had a bunch of them." Geren recalled how Tempest had asked him to pull several boxes filled with ornaments down from the hidden storage area at the top of her hallway closet.

"I do. I just want to see what they have. I collect African-American ornaments and Santa Clauses," Tempest boasted. "Just wait until you see my collection. It's taken me years to accumulate them all."

Geren blushed. "Does that mean you're going to let me help trim the tree?"

Tempest looped her arm around his and rubbed her cheek against the shoulder of his ugly-ass coat. "Among other things."

"Umm, sounds promising!"

"Oh, it is. Wait until you see what I plan to do with the leftover frosting from the cookies I'm decorating for the center." Tempest continued to hold on to his arm while they strolled down the aisle of Christmas decorations. She didn't see any African-American items. "I have big plans for that frosting."

"Big ones, huh?"

"Huge ones!"

"By the way, you're going to attend the Christmas party at the center, aren't you?" Tempest poked her bottom lip out, letting Geren know there was a temper tantrum lurking around the corner if he said no. "All the women and girls there are dying to meet my man."

"I'll be there with bells on my toes," Geren replied.

"Bells on your toes? That sounds sexy."

Tempest let go of his arm and picked up a box of greeting cards with African-American carolers on the front. She immediately found another package with African-American elves. "These are great! I'm going to send these out this year. I'm glad I didn't already put stamps on the other ones I have at home."

Geren felt compelled to confess, "I'd do anything for you."

"Really?" Tempest asked suspiciously, trying to conceal a grin.

"Yes, really," Geren replied in a mocking voice. "Just try me."

"Okay, I will." Tempest giggled. "The other day when I was in Landover Mall, I had this lightbulb go off in my head."

"I hope it didn't short-circuit anything."

Tempest punched him gently on the chest and laughed. "Silly ass! Anyway, they have an African-American Santa Claus there, and I was wondering if you would dress up as Santa for the party."

Geren frowned slightly, uncomfortable with the idea of putting on a red velvet suit and beard. Before he could say no, Tempest added, "I'll be your wife."

Geren bent over and gently swept his lips across hers. "I never thought I'd hear you say that."

"Umm, I did-did-didn't mean it like that," Tempest stuttered. "I meant I would dress up like Mrs. Santa Claus."

"Oh, I thought you meant something else," Geren said, disappointed.

Tempest took off for the checkout counter like she was a contestant on *Supermarket Sweep*. She wasn't prepared for a conversation about marriage, even if it was in a joking manner. The problem was, she wasn't sure whether Geren was joking or not.

Geren yanked gently on the back of her sweater. "Slow down, Tempest. I didn't mean to make you nervous."

"I'm not nervous," Tempest said, flashing a strained smile. "I just remembered that I promised Kensington I would stop by and check on her today. Her mother's still giving her a hard time about the pregnancy."

Geren chuckled, knowing that wasn't the real reason she took off like a bat out of hell. "What was that you said about not showing favoritism to any of the girls at the center?"

Tempest shrugged her shoulders in embarrassment. "Well, I have to admit that Kensington's very special to me. I'm not sure why. Maybe it's her innocence, but they're all innocent. None of them ask to end up in this predicament. Yet there's something about her that reminds me a lot of myself."

"So does this mean she won't get the hat-and-glove set?" Geren asked with an edge of sarcasm.

"She'll get one of those, but I would be lying if I said I didn't plan to give her something else on the sly. In fact, I already bought it."

"Oh, yeah? Do tell!"

"Uh-uh, you'll just have to wait and see," Tempest said, getting in one of the long checkout lines. "Dang, we're going to be here all day!"

Geren grabbed a *National Inquisiter* off the rack at the end of the counter.

"You read that trash?" Tempest asked in shock.

"Heck, yeah!" Geren exclaimed, flipping the pages. "They have some good stuff in here."

"Yeah, right."

"Really, they do. Here's an article about a famous movie star who had a baby by her cousin."

Tempest yanked it out of his hand. "Let me see that!"

By the time they checked out, Tempest was hooked. She purchased a copy of every tabloid she could find.

"Boy, that was so much fun!" Geren admitted, plopping down on Tempest's sofa in his Santa costume. "I never thought I'd like dressing up like this. In fact, I just knew I would hate it, but I was wrong. I loved it!"

"That's great!" Tempest unbuckled her black granny shoes and kicked them off in the middle of the floor. Her dogs were barking. "You were wonderful with all of the kids. The real shocker was the batch of cookies you baked. Are you sure you didn't buy them?" Tempest asked suspiciously.

"Hey, hey now, I told you I baked those cookies from scratch. I worked my kitchen over all afternoon."

"Maybe now you can work me over," Tempest said seductively.

"Did Janessa tear into my cookies or what?"

Tempest laughed. "She ate at least ten of those bad boys. I thought she was going to have to waddle out of there."

"I wonder what happened to Dvontè. He said he was coming through."

"He's your boy," Tempest replied snidely. "Probably out hoeing."

Geren didn't know what to make of that comment, so he changed the subject. "Where did all of those people come from? I thought it was just going to be the girls who get counseling at the center."

Tempest wrinkled her nose, trying to restrain a laugh. "I kind of, sort of, omitted the fact that we have a big community party every year. I thought you might back out if you knew half the neighborhood was coming."

"You would have been right, too." Geren pulled Tempest down on top of him on the sofa. "You look mighty sexy in that outfit," he said, pulling the gray wig off her head so her silky brown hair could outline her face.

"That outfit you have on is kind of turning me on, too," Tempest replied jokingly. "Especially the pillow stuffed in your shirt. There's nothing like having something soft and cuddly to snuggle up with."

"Is that right?" Geren pulled her face closer to his so he could kiss her, but she pulled back from him. "What's wrong?"

"Nothing." Tempest anxiously removed his hat, wig and beard. "I just don't want a mouth full of synthetic hair."

"Don't stop there!" Geren protested. "Take everything off me, and then I'll take everything off you."

"And then?"

"And then we'll make love until the sun comes up."

"Hmm, are you sure you're not taking Niagra on the sly?" Tempest teased. "All these nights of endless lovemaking are beginning to arouse my suspicions."

"Naw, I don't need any Niagra," Geren replied. "Just looking at you makes my dick hard."

Tempest blushed. "In that case, take me to bed."

* * *

Tempest was aroused the next morning by the mouthwatering aroma of freshly baked apple-cinnamon muffins. She threw the covers off, climbed out of bed and reached for her white cotton bathrobe, which was hanging from a dowel on her bedroom door. She slid her feet into a pair of fluffy slippers and headed to the kitchen to investigate the scent.

"What smells so scrumptious?" she asked, rubbing remnants of sleep out of her eyes while they adjusted to the bright fluorescent lighting of the kitchen.

"You mean other than you?" Geren responded, taking a fresh batch of muffins out of the lower oven.

"Very funny." Tempest giggled.

"It wasn't meant as a joke." Geren threw the oven mitts on the counter, grabbed Tempest by the waist and slipped her the tongue. After a deep, passionate kiss, he added, "You do smell sweet. Sweet enough to eat."

Tempest pulled away from him, playing hard to get, if only for a few seconds. She tried to take a muffin out of the pan, but it was too hot. "Hmm, if I'm not mistaken, you already did that last night," she whispered, licking the stickiness off her slightly seared fingertips.

Geren cracked an evil grin, undressing her with his eyeballs. "What? Are you imposing limitations or something like that?"

Tempest couldn't help but be amused. She looked at him, standing there in a pair of form-fitting white silk boxers and nothing else. "Not at all," she stated, realizing she still craved more sex, even after the hellified dick action he threw on her the night before. "Chez Tempest is open twenty-four/seven."

"Oh yeah, what's on the menu at Chez Tempest?" Geren got an instant erection from the possibilities alone.

"Well," Tempest drawled, surveying her kitchen counters, "for starters, we have honey-dipped breasts sprinkled with powdered sugar."

"Sounds yummy."

"Would you like to try some?"

"Hell, yeah!" Geren exclaimed.

Tempest picked up a jar of honey with one hand and untied her robe with the other one. She let it fall open, exposing her bare breasts, and then spread honey on her nipples with her fingers. She followed that up by sprinkling some powdered sugar on them.

Geren bent down and hungrily licked the sweet confection off her nipples, first one at a time and then simultaneously, pushing her breasts together and moving his tongue back and forth between them.

Once done, he stood up and asked, "Can I have some more, please?"

"Nope!" Tempest replied. Geren pouted, and she burst out laughing. "Now it's time for the main course."

Geren's eyes lit up like firecrackers. "Which is?"

Tempest thought for a second, trying to conjure up some creativity, picked up a jar of orange marmalade, and then answered, "Pussy à la orange."

"Ew, damn, hold up!" Geren exclaimed. He opened up one of Tempest's lower kitchen cabinets, the one where she kept serving dishes. "Let me get my plate."

Tempest giggled when Geren retrieved a large silver platter out of the cabinet. "That's not a plate. That's a platter."

Geren caressed the nape of her neck and stared lovingly in her eyes. "Let me eat you off a silver platter. You deserve to be treated like royalty. Today, tomorrow, and always."

Tempest was overwhelmed with excitement. Geren was

always full of surprises when it came to lovemaking. "In that case, let me get you a bib," she said jokingly.

Geren pulled the rest of Tempest's robe off with his free hand and then lifted her up by placing his arm under her buttocks. He suckled on her sticky nipples while he carried both her and the platter to the dining room table so he could eat his breakfast.

"I think now is a good time to give you my present." Geren had a satisfied look on his face as he climbed up off the sofa. He had made love to Tempest for the better part of Christmas Day, and dinnertime was about to roll around. They had a turkey breast, along with some sweet potatoes and corn-bread stuffing baking in the oven.

"Present?" Tempest said, faking astonishment. She knew her boo would buy her the bomb-ass present, and she'd been waiting anxiously to find out what it was. She didn't want Geren to know that she'd been on pins and needles, though.

"Yes." She is not even fooling me, Geren thought to himself. He knew Tempest was the typical woman and loved presents just as much as the next one. "Of course I bought you something."

"Where is it?" Tempest demanded to know. She jumped from the sofa butt-naked, having long gotten over any inhibitions she had around him.

Geren laughed and waved his index finger back and forth in front of her face. "Uh-uh-uh, you have to find it."

"Aw, come on. No fair!" Tempest protested, pushing her bottom lip out as far as it could possibly go.

"I'll give you a clue."

"A clue?" Tempest rolled her eyes. "Why a clue? Just tell me where it is, you silly goose."

"If you take fifteen steps forward from the front door, take forty steps to your left, and then twelve steps backward, where would you be?"

Tempest gawked at him in disbelief. His clue was downright ridiculous. "Hmm, how about another clue?"

Geren sat on the arm of the sofa and crossed his arms. "Okay, but just one more. If you don't get it this time, too bad."

"Okay!" Tempest reluctantly agreed.

Geren decided to go easy on her and let her off the hook. "It's under your bed."

Tempest took off speed-walking down the hall, tits swinging and all, to her bedroom. She got down on her knees and started looking under her bed. Geren, who had followed her, was enthralled by her bare ass bouncing up in the air. It made him horny all over again.

Tempest came back up with a box wrapped in African-American Santa Claus paper. "I see you pulled one of my numbers with the African-American Christmas stuff, huh?"

"Sure did," Geren admitted. "Maybe your habits are rubbing off on me."

Tempest smiled lovingly at him while she ripped the paper off the box and tore the lid off.

"Oh, my goodness!" Tempest exclaimed, pulling out an ugly-ass kaleidoscope jacket identical to the one Geren owned.

"You threw such a fit over my jacket the other night at Kmart that I decided to get you one just like it," Geren stated with pride. He felt it was the perfect gift for her.

"Thanks, baby," Tempest said, still in shock. She had no intention of wearing that jacket out in public, but that was the least of her problems at the moment. "I don't know what to say."

"Try it on," Geren insisted. "I want to make sure it fits."

"Okay."

Tempest let Geren hold the jacket open for her while she slipped her arms in. While comfortable, it was still ugly as all hell.

"I love it!" Tempest lied. "Thank you, baby!"

"I knew you would, and you're welcome."

"Umm, listen," Tempest whispered, a nervous wreck in the making. "I haven't gotten your present yet. I had to special-order it, and it won't be ready until Monday. I'll pick it up then."

"That's strange." Geren stared at her suspiciously. *"Real* strange."

"What is?"

"I could've sworn I saw a big present with my name on it in the bottom of your closet."

Tempest clamped her eyes shut. Damn, damn, damn, he saw it, she thought to herself. "Is that so?"

"Yes. Gold wrapping with African-American angels. Red bow. Sound familiar?"

"Uh—uh—uh—" Tempest stuttered, struggling for a response that wouldn't come.

"You're up to something," Geren proclaimed, wondering why Tempest would go through the trouble of buying him a present and then deny she even had one.

"Who, me?" Tempest asked, still holding out hope that the nightmare would go away.

"Yes, you." Geren snickered at her. "I can always tell."

He walked over to Tempest's walk-in closet, swung the door open, and moved her clothes hamper in the rear of her closet to the side, exposing the gift-wrapped box they both knew was there.

"See, here it is," he said, carrying it back out of the closet and setting it on the bed.

"So it seems." Tempest started biting her nails profusely.

Geren waited for Tempest to tell him to open it, but she never did, so he asked, "Mind if I open it? It does say 'For Geren' on it, after all."

"What if I say, Hell no, you can't open it?" Tempest blurted out.

Geren ignored her, ripped the paper off and opened the box. It was an expensive black leather jacket.

"Aw, thank you, baby!" he said with glee, pulling it out of the box and trying it on. "I guess we'll both be warm this winter. I still want us to wear our twin jackets out somewhere though."

Tempest's eyes fell on the card in the box. She debated about trying to snatch it out and hide it before Geren could see it but knew it was useless. He would see her.

"Geren, there's something I have to tell you."

"What's that, sweetheart?" Before she could answer, Geren spotted the card and picked it up. "Let me read your card. How sweet of you. I must admit I forgot your card, but I'll get you a special one tomorrow."

"Geren, please don't read that!" Tempest pleaded to no avail.

Geren opened the card and read the handwritten inscription out loud. "Baby, here's a REAL JACKET to replace that ugly-ass, 'flicted-looking one you had on when we were shopping. Please burn that damn thing. Love, Your Boo."

At first Geren had an expression of hurt on his face. Less than three seconds later, he fell out laughing. Tempest was relieved. In fact, she was so relieved that she laughed, too.

"Come here, you fool!" Geren shouted, pulling her to him and taking off the jacket he'd given to her so she was naked again. "Take off that ugly-ass, 'flicted jacket, as you put it."

"You're not mad?"

"A little, but you can make it up to me," he replied.

"Name it and I'll do it." Tempest pushed the leather jacket off him and noticed his dick was hard. She rubbed her belly button up against it and licked a trail from his chest up to his chin. "So how can I make it up to you?"

Geren moaned with delight. He pushed her backward on the bed, tossing the boxes and wrapping paper on the bedroom floor. "I'm sure I'll think of something."

"Where were you last night?" Janessa screamed into the receiver.

"Excuse me?" Dvontè screamed back at her from the other end of the phone line.

"You heard me, Dvontè!" Janessa put down the bottle of nail polish she was using to do her toes and put her feet on the floor, taking them off her bed. "Where were you last night?"

Dvontè blew hard into the phone, trying to keep his cool in front of his guest, who was lying on the bed beside him. "Look, Janessa, don't even start this shit with me!"

"What shit?"

"Callin' my place, trying to interrogate me!"

"You were supposed to come to the center last night for the Christmas party. What happened?"

"I never promised you I was coming!"

"Geren was there," Janessa stated with disdain, trying to make Dvontè feel bad. "He even played Santa Claus and baked home-made cookies!"

"Well, whoop-de-do! Good for him!" Dvontè said sarcastically. "When I'm ready to be domesticated, I will let you know, but don't hold your breath."

Janessa decided the bitch-mode attitude wasn't working well, so she lowered her voice. "There's no need to be nasty."

"Then don't come at me like that, dammit!"

Janessa just wanted some sort of explanation, even though she figured it would more than likely be a straight-up lie. She needed to believe in him. "Just please tell me why you didn't come."

"I had something come up," Dvontè glanced over at the nude figure on the bed. "It's as simple as that."

Janessa didn't respond. She wanted to drill him with twenty questions but figured all she would get was a bang in her ear when he slammed the phone down. It wouldn't be the first time he'd hung up on her. It was becoming a common occurrence, one she hoped Tempest didn't find out about. Sometimes Dvontè's behavior was downright confusing.

Dvontè quickly grew tired of listening to Janessa breathe over the phone. "Look, I have to go, Janessa. I'll call you later."

"Can I see you today?" Janessa blurted out.

"I don't think so. I have other plans."

"I'm sorry I snapped at you."

The woman beside him started tugging on his arm, making no bones about the fact that she didn't appreciate him talking to another woman while she was there. "No problem, but let me holla at you later."

"Okay," Janessa reluctantly agreed. "Dvontè?"

"Yes?"

"What about New Year's? We're going to spend it together, right?"

Dvontè's first thought was to say, Hell no. He never wanted to be put on a leash, but he felt one tightening around his neck just the same. He cared for Janessa, and it was scaring the shit out of him. "Yeah, we'll spend New Year's together, aiight?"

"Great!" Janessa exclaimed. "Tempest said Geren was taking her to a club down on the waterfront for New Year's Eve. Can we hang out with them?"

"Whatever you like, okay?" he said in a monotone. "Just set it up with them, and I'm down."

"Okay, call me later."

"Okay, later."

Janessa hung up the phone and lay back on her bed, kicking and giggling; Dvontè had said he would spend New Year's with her. She convinced herself that Dvontè must've really had something important to do the night before. She had wanted to spend Christmas with him, but she would settle for New Year's.

"Who in the hell was that?" Melinda or whatever the hell her name was yelled at Dvontè.

"Don't you start with me!" Dvontè couldn't believe the nerve of the heifer. She was nothing but a piece of ass, and they both knew it. "I told you last night when I met you that I just wanted to fuck. Don't trip, or you can get the fuck out!"

She got up off the bed and stomped into the bathroom naked, leaving the door open while she peed. Dvontè thought that was so disgusting. Looking at her now, with the mismatched fake braids and cellulite-infested thighs, he wondered why the hell he'd even brought her home.

"You men are nothing but dogs," she said, continuing her rampage as she came back out.

"Then what does that make you?" Dvontè asked nastily. "You're the one who came on to me at the club. You wanted some dick just like I wanted some pussy."

"Yeah, and it was good dick, too," she professed.

Dvontè grinned at the comment. She may have been a hoochie, but she knew good dick when she got some. "Glad you liked it."

Melinda or whatever the hell her name was sat back down on the bed and started rubbing the shaft of Dvontè's dick. It easily hardened, but not because he thought she was special. It was just habit. "I want some more," she said, lowering her mouth to the head of his dick.

"Just get dressed, please. I'll drop you off wherever you want to go," Dvontè said, pushing her head away. "I'm done with your ass."

Janessa was looking better and better to him every day. Maybe it was time for him to make a commitment to one woman, although he dreaded the mere thought. Yet and still, after he got rid of the tramp in his bedroom, he planned to call Janessa up and ask if he could go over to her folk's crib for Christmas dinner.

# 17

## new year's eve

"This party is the bomb!" Janessa squealed, shaking her ass to the music at the Zanzibar on the southwest waterfront.

"Damn sure is!" Tempest agreed, admiring the decor. The place was jam-packed for the New Year's Eve party. "I'm glad Geren and I came. We were about to back out."

Janessa gave Tempest a love slap on the arm. "Gurl, if you'd pulled a no-show, I would've given you a serious beatdown."

"What's the big deal?" Tempest asked snidely. "Dvontè's here with you."

Janessa smacked her lips. "Yeah, but only because he knew you two were coming."

"It's New Year's Eve. Where else would Dvontè be, if not with you?"

Tempest started running possible realistic answers through her mind, all of them unpleasant. Since the day she'd confronted Janessa in her apartment about Dvontè, she'd refrained from asking anything else, but things obviously weren't all peaches and cream.

"Oh, he would've still been with me," Janessa stated, trying to save face even though doubts lingered heavily in her mind. "He probably would be at his place getting his eat on instead of hanging at this party." Tempest didn't seem impressed, so Janessa added, "I plan to ration his ass a pint of punanny juice later tonight, though."

"Dang!" Tempest shook her head and rolled her eyes. "You make it sound like homie hangs downtown twenty-five/eight."

"Sumptin' like that," Janessa boasted with pride. "Eating my pussy is definitely Dvontè's favorite extracurricular activity."

Tempest tried to visualize Janessa sitting somewhere with her legs spread eagle and Dvontè's head buried between them for hours on end. The mere thought of it made her stomach turn. "Shame on it all!" she hissed. "That shit can't be healthy." She searched the club for Geren, spotting him standing beside Dvontè at the bar. After waiting in line for more than ten minutes, they'd finally gotten around to ordering drinks.

"Shame on you if you're not sitting on Geren's face every chance you get!" Janessa snapped back at her.

Tempest was about to take the topic on full force when a sistah with bleached blond hair brushed past her, hit her in the shoulder blade, and almost knocked her down.

Before Tempest could ram a foot up her rude ass in return, she was halfway across the room with two other bleached blond, weave-wearing, fake-contact-sporting hoochies trailing behind her. Only one word came to mind when she looked at them in clothes that were too damn tight: *Skank!*

Janessa was eyeing them, too. Both Tempest and Janessa's mouths gaped open when the head hoochie walked up to Dvontè, grabbed him around the neck, and tried to tongue the shit out of him. He quickly pushed her away, but not before he saw the expression on Janessa's face and realized he was busted.

"What the fuck is up with that?" Janessa screamed at Tempest.

"Don't look at me," Tempest replied, shrugging her shoulders and holding her palms face up. "I don't know the Lil' Kim triplets."

Janessa stormed off. "I'll be right back!"

Tempest debated about going after Janessa, but noticed Geren was already making his way over to her. Apparently, he didn't want any part of the scene that was inevitably about to go down. He was empty-handed, having left their drinks on the bar beside Dvontè. He slipped his arms around Tempest's waist and whispered in her ear, "May I have this dance?"

Tempest loved the slow jam pumping from the speakers but didn't feel like dancing. "Who are those women?" she demanded to know.

Geren tried to play dumb. "What women?"

Tempest pointed over to the bar. "The ones crowded around Dvontè."

"I don't know, and I don't care," Geren replied sarcastically. "I'm here with you tonight, not with Dvontè."

"He's cheating on her, isn't he?"

Geren kneaded Tempest's neck with his fingertips. He didn't want their first New Year's together to be ruined. "Sweetheart, let Janessa handle her own business." He pulled Tempest toward the dance floor, and she followed with great reluctance.

Back over at the bar, the head hoochie was busy trying to get into Dvontè's pants.

"You still coming over tomorrow?" she asked, seductively rubbing her fake nails up and down his biceps. "I want to show you my new bedroom set."

"Let me holla at you tomorrow, aiight?" Dvontè never took his eyes off Janessa, who was pushing through the crowd twenty feet away and closing in hard.

"Why you tryin' to diss me, baby?"

"I'm not dissin' you," Dvonte stated, lying his ass off.

"Good, because after that bomb-ass blow job I gave you last night, I deserve a fucking medal," head hoochie boasted.

Her two friends cackled while some other more conservative sistahs standing nearby rolled their eyes in his direction.

He pulled a twenty out of his pocket to pay the bartender waiting patiently on the opposite side of the bar. When he turned back around, Janessa was within striking distance, her arms folded across her chest.

Janessa looked the head hoochie up and down, giving her the once-over. Head hoochie returned the favor. "Dvontè, who is this skeezer?"

"Who the fuck are you?" the head hoochie yelled back, getting all up in Janessa's grill.

"Dvontè's woman!" Janessa stated proudly.

"Woman?" head hoochie chuckled. "Well, if he's your man, he wasn't last night."

Janessa unfolded her arms and pushed Dvontè on the chest, ramming his back into the bar. "What the hell does that mean?"

"Yeah, Dvontè." Head hoochie sucked on her teeth. "What *am* I talking about?"

Dvontè wanted to smack the shit out of the tramp, but hitting women wasn't in his nature. He grabbed Janessa's wrist. "Janessa, let's go someplace where we can talk."

"I think I've heard quite enough," Janessa whispered, fighting back tears. "I trusted you. I thought you were different."

All the hoochies started laughing, while everyone else just gawked and stared. One of the other two, the one with purple contacts, yelled after Janessa as she pushed her way through the crowd to the exit, "Chile, he's a male hoe just like the rest of them! Cash that reality check, gurlfriend!"

Dvontè told the hoochie, "You need to shut your *unbeweavable* ass up!" He started after Janessa. "Come here, Janessa! Janessa!"

Tempest and Geren had been watching from the dance floor. They couldn't hear the argument over the loud music, but the basics were obvious.

"I'm going after her," Tempest announced, heading for the door.

"Shit," Geren huffed under his breath. He left the dance floor and caught up to Dvontè, swinging him around by the arm. "You're fuckin' up big-time, *and* messing with my relationship in the process."

"It's just a misunderstanding, Geren!" Dvontè proclaimed, trying to look innocent. "I swear!"

"You're not even fooling me! Tell that bullshit to someone who can't read you like a book!"

Dvontè waved Geren off. "I need to find Janessa."

"Let Tempest deal with Janessa." Geren glanced over at the bar. "You deal with that trash over there *permanently*."

Dvontè looked at the head hoochie standing over by the bar, profiling and basking in her glory while her trifling-ass friends gulped down the drinks he'd paid for. Damn shame—she'd sucked his dick the night before, and he couldn't even recall her name.

Geren asked, "We understand each other?"

Dvontè made a fist and pounded it over his own heart. "As always, we're right here."

Not lately, Geren thought to himself. "I'll make sure Janessa gets home safely."

Dvontè gave Geren a man-to-man hug. "Thanks, man. I appreciate it."

Geren headed for the exit. He turned around, throwing one last look of disdain in Dvontè's direction. "Don't call Janessa anymore. Not until you get your shit together."

# 18

## just two black chicks shootin' the breeze

"I can't believe they made you pay a quarter for a shopping cart," Janessa said, shaking her head in dismay. "That woman had the nerve to get nasty with us, at that."

"Isn't that ridiculous? As if losing a measly twenty-five cents would deter someone from stealing a cart," Tempest replied, equally disgusted.

She and Janessa had decided to stop by the Value-Added Supermarket on the way back from the gym because it was less crowded than Giant and Safeway on Saturdays. Janessa had reluctantly agreed to submit herself to another session of cardio-karate, and every muscle in her body was sore. They were both surprised when one of the employees told them they had to deposit a quarter in a slot to get a cart to slide out.

Janessa clucked her tongue and rolled her eyes in the direction of the frog-faced woman who followed them inside. She purposely raised her voice so the woman would hear her. "If peeps want to walk off with a cart, they're going to do it regardless. I know. I did it once my damn self."

"Really?" Tempest followed the direction of Janessa's eyes and glared at the woman. "Is there a problem?"

The woman stopped dead in her tracks, sneered at them, and walked away.

"Yeah, Momma gave me this long-ass grocery list. I wasn't about to lug all that stuff home on the bus, so I took a cart, strolled home, and got some exercise in, all in one shot."

"Why didn't you just call a cab?"

"A cab? The cabdrivers around here try to rip a sistah off. The last time I took a cab, bro man almost hit a truck, ran three lights, and then had the nerve to demand a tip on top of the eight-dollar fare."

"Dang! You're lucky you got home," Tempest giggled. "Did you give him a tip?"

"Hell, yeah! I told him he needed to learn how to freakin' drive. That was his mofo tip."

Tempest and Janessa both snickered while Tempest picked up a box of instant oatmeal off the shelf and read the label. They only had one brand, a generic one, and Tempest decided against it, since Quaker Oats were her favorite.

"Besides," Janessa continued, "Momma only gave me about twenty bucks for ninety dollars worth of groceries, so I had to come up with the rest."

"That's messed up."

They went down the frozen food aisle, and Tempest was disappointed again to find out they didn't sell the low-fat frozen dinners she liked.

"I wouldn't mind if the food was for my parents, but Fred and his crew of fart-infested friends eat up the majority of the food at the crib."

"Damn, not fart-infested?" Tempest chuckled.

"Mega-fart-infested!" They both fell out laughing. "I don't see how in the world the sistahs they date deal with their funky asses. If they were smart, they wouldn't let them mofos eat anything gaseous within two hours of bedtime."

"What about Fred?" Tempest asked, already assuming the answer. "Does he have a woman?"

"Hellz naw! What kind of woman would date a skank, crater-skinned, elephantine, stinking troll like him?"

"Damn, sis!" Tempest shook her head, wondering how Janessa and Fred managed to reside in the same house without killing each other. "You sure are hard on your brother!"

"He did have a woman once, but that was way back in the day."

"Word?" Tempest tossed a loaf of wheat bread in the cart. She'd never heard of the brand, but bread was bread, and she was down to the ends of the loaf at home. "I've never seen Fred with a woman, or maybe I just don't remember her."

"Well, I'll never forget the desperate hoochie." Janessa picked up a package of pecan twirls and threw them in the cart. Tempest wanted to tell her that eating sweets after a workout was defeating the purpose but decided to let it slide. She was just glad Janessa had been going to class and keeping her company. "She was about four-foot-nine, 360 pounds, high yella like me but she had freckles, an orange hair weave and more teef than a set of quintuplets."

Tempest slapped Janessa lightly on the arm. "You're so stupid!"

Tempest headed to the checkout line and got behind a woman in the express lane who was well over the limit of ten items.

"Is that all you're getting?" Janessa inquired. "Why the hell did we come in here? We could have gotten a loaf of bread at 7-Eleven."

Tempest put the two items on the belt and threw a copy of the *National Inquisiter* in for good measure. She was surprised they even carried tabloids. "Yep, this is it. I'm scared to eat half of the generic stuff they have up in here. Plus, I don't like the way that woman was eyeing us. I'm not about to give this place a bunch of my money."

"I heard that!" They waited patiently for the cashier to ring up the customer in front of them. "Tempest, by the way, I want to run something by you."

"What's up?"

"I've made a decision."

"What type of decision?"

"After what happened on New Year's Eve with Dvontè, I realize I'm concentrating on the wrong things in life."

Tempest put her arm around Janessa's shoulder and gave her a loving hug. "That's a good thing. What do you plan to concentrate on?"

"School," Janessa blurted out. "I've decided to apply for the fall semester."

Tempest squealed, and suddenly all eyes were on them. "That's spantacular! What school?"

"I'm thinking about Howard, if I can afford it."

"I have some information about scholarships at my office. We can stop there on the way home and get them." Tempest was so excited, she wanted to jump up and down and do cartwheels. Janessa going back to school had always been a dream of hers, but it had never been Janessa's dream. Not until now. "This is so cool!"

"Thanks, sis!"

The cashier started ringing up their three items. "What are you going to major in? Have you decided?"

"Pharmacy," Janessa replied. "I've always wanted to be a pharmacist, ever since we were little."

"I never knew that."

"That's because I never told you, dufus!" They both giggled and chided each other until they got outside.

Tempest started pushing the cart back to the lock-up. "Whatever happened to the cart you took home?"

"Fred gave it to one of his homies, Benito. He uses it to collect soda cans."

Tempest wondered why a man Fred's age would be collecting soda cans. "Dang, is he homeless?"

"Naw, he's shacking with his girl, but he doesn't work. Trifling ass!"

"So he uses the money from the cans for food?"

"Naw."

"Drugs?"

"Naw."

"Then what?"

"Niagra." They both cackled. "He must have that limpdicki-tus," Janessa added.

Before Tempest could push the cart back on the rack, they heard someone shout, "Hey, gurls!"

Both of their eyes almost popped out of their sockets when they spotted Janessa's grandmother, Mrs. Porter, approaching them, all hugged up with a man.

"Hey, Grandma!" Janessa exclaimed, immediately giving the man in the burgundy polyester slacks and black leisure jacket the once-over.

"Hello, Mrs. Porter," Tempest said once they got within a few feet of them. She also looked the man over and decided he was attractive for his age. He looked to be considerably younger than Mrs. Porter. She had at least twenty years on him. "Fancy seeing you here."

"Why's that?" Mrs. Porter asked. "Senior citizens have to eat, too." Everyone laughed except the man on her arm. She realized she was being rude and started the introductions. "This is Mr. Roscoe Munroe," she said, caressing his forearm seductively. "Roscoe is one of my neighbors."

Tempest and Janessa both gazed at him with pasted-on smiles.

Mrs. Porter pointed at Janessa. "Roscoe, this here is one of my grandbabies, Janessa, and her best friend, Tempest."

Roscoe flashed his dentures. "Nice to make the acquaintance of you lovely young ladies."

There was a bunch of nervous energy while everyone just stared at each other and the customers walking in and out of the store.

Janessa broke the silence. "Grandma, I was just telling Tempest I plan to go back to school in the fall."

Mrs. Porter let go of Roscoe's arm and flung her own arms around Janessa. "You're going to college?" she asked proudly. "That's wonderful, baby!"

Tempest noticed Mr. Munroe continuously glancing down at his watch. "Claudine, we better get on in here and get the whipped cream," he insisted, giving Janessa and Tempest a little more information than they cared to know. They both almost freaked when he added, "We can still make it to the video store before all the *special* movies get checked out." Mrs. Porter blushed and giggled, and Janessa had to fight the urge to go upside the man's head. "You know most of the good ones go fast on the weekends."

Mrs. Porter noticed the killer look on Janessa's face and Tempest's agape mouth and decided it was time to part ways. She held her hand out. "Roscoe, give me a quarter for a buggy."

Tempest pushed her cart toward them. "Mrs. Porter, you can have this one. Save your quarter."

"Thanks, baby," Mrs. Porter said, still blushing as she took ahold of the cart.

"Nice meeting you," Mr. Munroe proclaimed, walking off through the automatic doors of the store.

"Same here," Tempest uttered, her mouth immediately falling back open the second the words left her lips.

As soon as he was out of earshot, Janessa lit into her grandmother. "Grandma, is that your boyfriend?"

Mrs. Porter threw her humongous purse in the upper part of the basket and snickered. "Let's just say that dildo you gave me awakened feelings in me I thought were long dead."

"Oh, my!" Tempest whispered, trying not to let images of Mrs. Porter fucking herself with a dildo flash through her head.

Mrs. Porter laughed. Janessa leaned up against one of the columns and took in air like she was sucking it through a straw. "Like I said before, it's just like riding a bike." She winked at them and reiterated. "Just like riding a bike."

They watched her saunter off, switching with a pep in her step they didn't recognize.

"Damn, your grandmother's been getting her freak on!" Tempest exclaimed.

"Big-time," Janessa agreed, walking off to Tempest's car.

Tempest squinted into the store and spotted the two of them walking down one of the aisles. She shook her head when she saw Mr. Munroe slap Mrs. Porter on the ass. "That's too deep for me!"

# 19

## the baby's here

Tempest slammed on her brakes, barely missing the trash truck in front of them. She adjusted her rearview mirror so she could peek into the backseat.

"You okay back there, Kensington?"

Kensington reached over the seat and yanked on Tempest's hair. "No, I'm not okay!" she screamed out, another contraction kicking in.

"Damn," Tempest stated to no one in particular. She made a quick assessment of their situation. Traffic was at a complete standstill. There was road construction about a mile ahead, and two lanes were closed, forcing everyone to merge into one.

Kensington yelled out again. "Please hurry, Tempest! I'm not sure how much longer I can keep it in!"

Tempest giggled slightly. Didn't Kensington realize she couldn't keep a baby inside when it was ready to come out?

"Just hang in there with me, Kensington. We're almost there," Tempest fibbed. They were still more than four miles from the hospital. "Just take deep breaths."

Tempest grabbed her cell phone off the passenger seat again. Just like before, it gave two short beeps when she hit the power button, letting her know the battery was low.

"Shit!" Tempest was bordering on a panic attack.

"Why are you cursing? I'm the one in labor," Kensington managed to utter between breaths.

"Why didn't you call me sooner?" Tempest demanded to know. "Why'd you wait until you were so far along?"

"I wasn't sure it was labor!" Kensington snapped back at her. "My water never broke!"

Tempest rolled her eyes in disgust and clamped her hand over her mouth. She felt like screaming, but realized it wouldn't resolve anything. She was just glad Kensington had phoned her at all. It showed a degree of trust, and it meant Kensington had grown to depend on her. She wouldn't let her down. She couldn't.

"Kensington, lay your head back against the door and elevate your feet on the seat," Tempest instructed. She pulled the car over into the closed-off lane nearest to the curb, put it in park, and opened the driver's-side door. "I'll be right back."

"Where are you going?" Kensington yelled out after her, all the while obeying the instructions she was given. Another contraction kicked in, this one stronger than the last. She yelped out in pain.

Tempest ran up to a group of men standing on the sidewalk. It didn't take a genius to deduce they were slanging dope.

"Listen, I need your help," she blurted out.

"With what?" one gold-toothed nucca in a three-hundred-dollar jacket and a two-hundred-dollar pair of basketball shoes asked out of curiosity. He looked her up and down, sizing her up. "You're not 5-0, are you?"

"No, I'm not 5-0," Tempest hissed at him.

"Don't get bitchy with me," was his only reply. He reached up and scraped something off his gold tooth with the nail of his pinky finger—the nail bamas always keep long so they can pick their noses.

Tempest wanted to curse him out but opted for the polite approach. She scanned the other faces in the group. All babies, she concluded. None of them looked a day over twenty-one. Two of them were twins.

"Look, guys," Tempest began, trying to sound as pleasant as possible. "I have a young sistah in the back of my car about to have a baby."

"Oh, shit!" one of them exclaimed.

"Word? Fa real?" another one shouted.

"So what you want us to do?" Gold Tooth asked, making his way over to Tempest's car to take a look-see. He glanced back at his friends. "Damn, she's not lyin' homies."

"I know one of you has got to have a phone," Tempest pleaded. She knew good and damn well drug dealers didn't bother with pay phones anymore.

Miraculously, every last one of them pulled out a wireless phone. Tempest clasped her hands together and looked up at the sky. "Thank you, Lord!" She looked at Gold Tooth, since he seemed to be the leader. "Can you call 911, please? We need an ambulance."

"Sure," he quickly agreed. "But if you think they're going to send an ambulance out here anytime soon, you can forget it."

They all chuckled.

The statement confused Tempest. "What do you mean?"

"Take a look around you, sistah," one of the other ones stated. "This is Dodge City, not Georgetown."

Tempest did take a quick look around. They were standing in

one of the roughest parts of D.C. If rumors were true, the response time on 911 calls was pathetic.

"Well, call anyway," she insisted.

Gold Tooth sucked his teeth and started dialing. "Okay, as you wish."

The other one continued his soliloquy on emergency services while Kensington let out another scream from the car. "If this were Georgetown, you could open your front door and find the police and fire department standing there," he stated avidly, following Tempest back to her car. "Around here, you have to wait damn near an hour for them to show."

Tempest swung the back door open and almost lost her stomach contents. Blood was everywhere, mixed with a clear liquid. "Shit, her water broke!"

"Tempest, please help me," Kensington begged.

"They're on their way," Gold Tooth announced. "For what it's worth." He cut the phone off and glanced at his watch. "I'm timing these mofos, too."

Tempest couldn't believe that none of them seemed the least bit frazzled about the blood. Then again, they were probably used to the sight of blood.

"Looka here, I have an idea." Gold Tooth pointed to the twins. "Ronnie and Ray-Ray both got bikes."

"Bikes?" Tempest asked incredulously.

"Yeah, motorcycles. They can cruise right through all this traffic shit."

Tempest spotted two Harley Davidsons leaning up against the side of the building. "You've got to be kiddin'?"

"Hey, I'm just making a sug-ges-ten. It's up to ya'll. Wait around here for another two hours. Up to you."

Tempest had to make a split-second decision. She surveyed the traffic. It hadn't budged. The trash truck had moved maybe fifty feet.

"Kensington, listen to me," she said, trying to remain calm while she pulled Kensington out of the backseat, legs first. "Everything's going to be okay."

"Tempest, I can't ride on the back of a motorcycle," Kensington blurted out in agony.

"You don't have a choice," Tempest proclaimed. "I'll be right behind you. I promise."

Gold Tooth gave swift instructions to the twins. "Yo, go get the bikes, man!"

By the time Tempest got Kensington out of the car with the help of Gold Tooth and one of the others, the twins were waiting right beside the car, mounted on their bikes.

"Be careful," Tempest pleaded while they lifted Kensington onto the back of one of them. Ray-Ray was spray-painted on the side of the engine casing. "You be careful with her, Ray-Ray."

"I will," he replied, taking off with a jolt in the direction of the hospital. Kensington was holding on to his waist for dear life.

"Not too damn fast, man!" Gold Tooth yelled out.

Tempest hopped on the back of Ronnie's bike. "Hurry! Please hurry!"

Tempest's legs felt like they were about to fall off as she wobbled out of the recovery room. They'd delivered the baby girl by cesarean section less than ten minutes after they'd arrived. They were just in the nick of time, too; the cord had been lodged around the baby's neck.

Tempest waited in recovery with Kensington until she woke up. Kensington was in great spirits. She was just glad it was all over. So was Tempest.

She asked a passing lab technician for directions to the nursery and wobbled down there to see the baby. Much to her astonishment, Gold Tooth, the twins, and the rest of the crew were all gathered around the window, tapping on the glass and cooing at the babies.

"I don't know how to thank you guys." Tempest hugged them all one at a time like they were long-lost relatives. "We wouldn't have made it in time without your help."

"Don't mention it, sistah," Gold Tooth said, cracking a smile. He pointed to the tiny baby wrapped in a pink blanket, lying in a bassinet marked Baby Sparks. "That little honie in there was well worth it."

Tempest pressed her face up to the glass. Kensington's baby had smooth, caramel skin and a head full of black, curly hair. "She's beautiful!"

Ray-Ray agreed. "Yeah, her daddy's gonna have to beat the lil' knuckleheads off with a stick when she gets older."

Tempest grimaced. What damn daddy?

"We're about to roll out," Gold Tooth announced, looking a bit teary-eyed.

Suddenly, it hit Tempest. "Oh, no! My car! My purse! They're still out on the street!"

"Naw, it's all good." Gold Tooth dangled Tempest's keys in front of her face. "I drove your ride over here. I figured you wouldn't mind."

Tempest couldn't believe it. They were so thoughtful. One of the others came forward and handed Tempest her purse.

"Your car is in the visitors' lot, row B," Gold Tooth added. "I gotta tell you, though. You're gonna need one hell of a cleanup job on your backseat. It's mad nasty."

Tempest opened her purse to get her wallet. Everything was still intact.

"Let me give you fellas something for your trouble. I don't have much cash on me, but if you give me your addresses—"

"Naw, sistah." Gold Tooth shook his head dramatically. "We like to do a little community service e-ve-ry now and then."

They all shared a good laugh, even Tempest.

"Besides, that girl Kensington—she could've been one of our baby sisters or sumptin'," Ronnie said.

They began to walk off down the hall to the elevator. No sooner had they turned the corner than Geren appeared. Tempest was overjoyed to see him. She'd asked one of the nurses to contact him but didn't think she'd succeeded.

Tempest ran into the safety of his arms. "I'm so glad you're here."

"Kensington?" Geren asked, holding Tempest snugly.

"She's fine."

"The baby?"

"She's fine, too."

"A girl, huh?" Geren let out a sigh of relief. "So what happened, sweetheart?"

"Baby, do I have one hell of a story to tell you." Tempest pulled him toward the nursery. "First, I want to introduce you to the newest Nubian queen."

# 20

## memories

Geren reached over and pushed the handle on the passenger door until it was slightly ajar.

"Hop in!" he shouted out to Tempest. The heavy rainfall had already begun to invade the car in the span of a few seconds. "You're getting soaked!"

Tempest swung the door open wider, hopped in, and slammed it quickly. She was indeed soaked, and she could have kicked herself for not tossing a compact umbrella in her briefcase that morning. It must have been all the butterflies fluttering around in her stomach. The day had started out stressful and gone downhill from there.

The mere sight of Geren immediately lifted her spirits. He always had that effect on her.

"Thanks for picking me up. I really appreciate it."

"Don't mention it." Geren took Tempest's briefcase out of her arms and tossed it in the backseat. "I'll use any excuse I can find to see you."

Damn, great minds really do think alike, Tempest thought to herself. She could have just as easily taken a cab home, but she chose to call Geren instead. She wanted to see him. No, scratch that. She *needed* to see him.

Tempest eyed Geren seductively, wishing he were inside her that very second. "The Toyota dealer said my car, rather my birth mobile on wheels, should be ready by seven."

Geren chuckled. "Birth mobile on wheels. That's funny."

Tempest found nothing amusing. The incident with Kensington had been nothing short of traumatic for everyone involved. Fortunately, both Kensington and baby Sydney were healthy and unharmed.

She opted to change the subject. "Maybe we can kill a little time, and you can drop me by there before they close."

"Sure," Geren eagerly agreed. "What do you have in mind? An early dinner?"

Tempest shook her head. "I'm not really hungry. Are you?"

"Naw, I'm still full from lunch."

An aggressive driver behind them started pressing heavy on his horn. Geren had on his hazards in a lane restricted to no parking from four to six.

He merged into the rush-hour traffic. It had been a quick shower; the rain was already tapering off a bit.

Tempest looked out the window at all of the people rushing to their cars, the bus stop, or wherever, trying their best not to get wet. One expensively dressed sistah was on the corner doing battle with an umbrella turned inside out by the strong wind gusts. She was glad that wasn't her.

She diverted her eyes to Geren, who was concentrating on the traffic. "I have an idea."

"What's that, baby?"

"Let's go antique shopping or some other bourgeois thing like that."

"Sounds good, but—"

"But what?"

"Does the evening have to end there?" Geren asked hesitantly. "When you pick up your car? I was hoping we could be together tonight."

Tempest blushed uncontrollably. "I thought you'd never ask."

Geren lifted her hand to his mouth and kissed her gently on her palm, taking a long whiff of the pear-scented lotion he'd grown so accustomed to. It smelled like heaven to him.

"So what brings you down to Georgetown anyway?"

Tempest sighed heavily. She really didn't want to discuss her stressful day. "I had a meeting with the board of directors of the Shearer Foundation."

Geren turned the busy corner at Wisconsin Avenue and M Street. "I've never heard of them," he stated, keeping an eye out for an antique store.

"That's not too surprising. They prefer to keep their affairs on the down-low."

"Kind of like the Mafia, huh?" They both cackled. "What does the foundation do exactly?"

"Several things. Among them, handing out fat grants to non-profit organizations."

"Ahhh, like the teen pregnancy center?"

"Uh-huh. They're one of our largest benefactors. The city gives us some money, but not nearly enough to get by on."

"I see."

"Today was our annual review." Tempest took another deep breath and exhaled. "I had to get up in front of a dozen filthy rich people and account for every penny of the money they so generously forked over to us."

"Sounds thrilling," Geren said, an edge of sarcasm in his voice. Tempest looked at Geren like he'd lost his mind.

"Ha, are you kiddin'? I have a migraine that won't quit."

Geren started rubbing her knee. She was as stiff as an ironing board. "Don't worry. I'll hook my baby boo up with one of my award-winning massages and fix you right up. Make you feel like new."

"Ummmmmmm," Tempest moaned, relaxing her head against the headrest of the car, relishing the thought of Geren's hands all over her. "As long as it's a full-body massage."

Tempest opened her eyes just in time to see Geren winking at her. "That can definitely be arranged."

Tempest couldn't stand it one more second. She reached over the gearshift and caressed Geren's dick through his pants. "Why don't we just head to your place?"

"What about your car, sweetheart?" Geren asked, even though he couldn't have cared less about the car. His dick was already rock-hard. He'd been fantasizing about being with her all day.

Tempest brushed her lips across his right cheek, slid her tongue in and out of his ear, and whispered, "I'll get it in the morning."

Geren got frustrated with the traffic on M Street and decided to cut over to P Street. It was an entirely different story now; he was trying to get some sex. He wanted to get Tempest back to his place, but quick.

The situation on P Street was a little better. Tempest was still rubbing Geren's dick and undressing him with her eyes. He inched up her skirt and had the elastic of her panties halfway pushed over so he could finger her when Tempest almost made him wreck the car.

"Wait! Stop the car!" Tempest exclaimed.

"What's wrong?" Geren asked after losing control of the steering wheel for a second and regaining control.

the heat seekers 207

Tempest let go of Geren's dick and started beating on his arm. "Stop! Stop right here!" she squealed. "It's for sale! I don't freakin' believe it!"

Geren put on his right ticker and began parallel parking. Tempest jumped out of the car while his front end was still out in the street.

Geren finished parking and joined Tempest on the curb. It was barely drizzling by that time, but Geren winced when a messenger on a mountain bike swished past them, almost splashing a puddle of water on them in the process.

The near miss didn't seem to bother Tempest. She was too busy staring at a huge brownstone with a For Sale sign attached to a stake on the front lawn, along with a Lucite box containing pamphlets of information.

"You know the people who live here?"

"No, not really," Tempest replied solemnly. "Not the ones who live here now, but my grandparents used to own this house."

"Really?" Geren took a longer, more detailed look at the house. All of the windows had antique beveled glass, and there was a huge front porch. He also noticed a second entrance on the side and assumed it was a basement apartment—most of the older houses in the district had them. Geren had always admired their architecture.

"They passed away about twelve years ago," Tempest responded without turning around to look at him. She didn't want him to bear witness to the tears she was attempting to fight back. "My grandfather died of lung cancer. He was a heavy smoker." Geren walked up close behind her on the sidewalk and rubbed her shoulders. "My grandma passed less than six months after he did."

"Cancer, too?" Geren asked.

"No. For all intents and purposes, she was in perfect health. I've always believed she died of a broken heart." Tempest wiped her nose with the sleeve of her gray blazer. "Loving someone for more than half a century and having him suddenly ripped from her arms must've been devastating for her."

"I'm sorry for your loss," Geren whispered, kissing Tempest on the top of her head.

"Thanks, but death is a part of life." Tempest turned so she could gaze into Geren's eyes, wondering if he would be willing to love her for half a century. "My mother wanted to keep the house in the family, but my two uncles wouldn't hear of it. All they saw were dollar signs. Property in Georgetown is extremely valuable these days. My grandparents bought the house when it was still fairly reasonable."

Geren ran his fingers through Tempest's hair and kissed her on the forehead.

"Anyway, they insisted on selling it to a young corporate lawyer and his family. My mother literally begged them not to. I've never forgiven my uncles for that. They're so damn selfish."

Geren's curiosity about the house grew stronger by the second. "I wonder why they're selling it?"

"I haven't a clue." Tempest turned her attention back to the house. So many wonderful memories—her grandma baking homemade brownies in the kitchen, her grandfather reading the Old Testament to her by the fireplace in the den. "Maybe they're leaving the D.C. area."

Geren desperately wanted to see the inside of the house. Something about it just drew him to it. Maybe it was the love for it he heard in Tempest's voice.

He pointed at the house. "There's a light on in the rear of the house. Want to go knock?"

"That's pointless!" Tempest seemed agitated at the mere suggestion. "I could never afford a house like this. Not on my salary. Not in my wildest dreams."

Geren knew Tempest was right on point with her assessment. Several of his clients lived in Georgetown, and being their investment broker, he was well aware of the market value of their homes.

A lightbulb went off in his head. "Would you buy it if you could?"

"Without question. Some of the fondest memories of my childhood involve this house."

"Tell me about them," Geren prodded, just as a clap of thunder exploded over their heads.

Tempest glanced up at the sky. It was dark gray. An electrical storm was impending.

"Maybe later. Let's go," she insisted, heading back to Geren's car. "This is only depressing me."

Once she got in, she noticed Geren was all the way up on the lawn by the realty sign. "Geren, you coming?" she shouted.

"Here I come," Geren replied, shoving one of the pamphlets into his left pants pocket.

# 21

## when the other shoe falls

It was pouring down rain when Tempest pulled into the gravel parking lot of the playground. She glanced at the digital clock on her dashboard: 2:35. Janessa had left a message with Linda, asking Tempest to meet her there at two-thirty.

Figuring there was absolutely no way Janessa would be out in that weather, Tempest reached into the glove compartment to get her cell phone. She had the first four digits of Janessa's home number punched in when she noticed someone sitting on a swing on the far side of the picnic shelter.

"Janessa!" she said to herself, pushing the car door open and unbuckling her seat belt simultaneously. She looked on the back floor of her car to see if she had an umbrella but remembered she hadn't replaced it after the last shower. It was in her office. The continuous rainfall in D.C. was becoming frustrating.

Tempest sloshed through the mud, unconcerned about damage to the heels of her navy pumps. She had to get to Janessa. She'd had this terrible feeling in her gut the second she got the message, and now, seeing Janessa drooped on the seat of a swing in the middle of a shower made her heart speed up.

"Janessa, what are you doing out here?" Tempest shouted, while there was still about ten yards between them. "Linda gave me your message!"

Tempest stood in front of Janessa, but Janessa didn't even acknowledge her presence. She kept her eyes glued to the ground. She had on her postal uniform, so Tempest asked her, "Why'd you ask me to meet you here, and why aren't you at work?"

Still nothing! Tempest kneeled down in the mud, letting the left leg of her taupe pantsuit absorb the dirt. She grabbed both of Janessa's shoulders and shook her. "Janessa, look at me, dammit!"

Janessa finally raised her eyes, and Tempest was startled by their blank, lifeless expression. She stood up, forcing Janessa to get up off the swing, and guided her toward the covered picnic shelter. "Come on, let's go over here under the shelter. We're both going to get pneumonia if we stay out here."

As soon as Tempest forced Janessa down on a bench at a picnic table, an earsplitting clap of thunder came out of nowhere. Tempest had always been afraid of storms. She remembered when the lightning used to dance through the house when she was a child. She would always bury herself under the covers and pray she wouldn't get struck.

But now, the pitiful look on Janessa's face made Tempest reconsider her priorities. Her first duty was to help her friend get through whatever was bothering her. She had to get Janessa to open up to her.

"Please talk to me," Tempest pleaded. "You're frightening me, sis!"

Janessa looked out toward the jungle gym and finally uttered some words. "Remember when we used to play here?"

"Yes, of course I remember," Tempest replied. The playground was located within a ten-block radius of the homes where they both grew up. "We used to spend every Saturday afternoon having a ball on the play equipment."

Janessa grinned slightly. "Hmph, that's not how I recall it. You were too much of a punktress to go down the giant slide at first. We all used to tease you something terrible."

"Yes, and your skank ass pushed me down it one day while I was sitting at the top trying to get the nerve to come down it by myself."

They shared a laugh. Tempest was glad Janessa wasn't totally withdrawn. She still had her sense of humor.

"Janessa, it's not that I mind reminiscing about the good times, but it's the middle of a workday, and we're sitting out here in the middle of a thunderstorm. What's up with that?"

Janessa took Tempest's hand. Tempest noticed that Janessa was trembling, and her hands were practically icicles. "You're freezing, Janessa!" she said, releasing her hand and removing the jacket of her suit, leaving herself exposed to the elements with nothing but a thin, silk blouse on. She placed it around Janessa's shoulders and rubbed her arms, trying to generate some body heat.

"You know what's ironic about life?" Janessa asked.

"What's ironic?"

Janessa leaned against Tempest, placing her cheek on Tempest's breastbone. "Whenever things start to look up for me, something horrible happens to ruin it all."

Tempest wanted to babble off fifty-eleven questions but refrained and limited herself to one. "I'm lost, sis. What's going on with you?"

"This should be the happiest day of my life, other than the day

I first met you." Tempest smiled. Meeting Janessa was also the best thing that had ever happened to her. "Instead, my life has turned into a complete nightmare."

"Janessa, I'm not sure what this is all about, but you're a wonderful woman and a great friend. Whatever this is, we'll work through it together. First, you've got to tell me what's going on. What nightmare are you talking about?"

Janessa sat up, looking at Tempest through tear-drenched eyes, leaving a trail of them on Tempest's blouse. "Do you want the good or the bad first?"

"Good," Tempest replied without hesitation.

"I got accepted into Howard for the fall semester," Janessa blurted out.

"That's fantastic news!" Tempest exclaimed, suddenly feeling better.

"I even got a full scholarship," Janessa added. "The one you suggested I apply for."

"Gurl, that's wonderful! I'm so proud of you!" Tempest gave her a huge bear hug. "Why do you consider that a nightmare? Are you worried about making good grades? If so, you can cut that out right now, because you've always been smarter than I have. You just never applied yourself."

Janessa was flattered by the compliment, but it didn't help the situation any. "School's not a problem, Tempest, because I won't be attending. Not in the fall. Not ever."

Tempest was confused. She thought getting a college education was what Janessa wanted. "Why not?"

"Because I can't deal with going to school, going to work, studying, and—"

"Janessa, I told you I'd help you out financially if need be. We agreed you would go to school during the day and work part-time in the evening."

"Let me finish!" Janessa snapped.

Tempest went quiet and waited to hear the bad news that was apparently still lurking around the corner. Janessa had mentioned good *and* bad.

Janessa stood up and leaned up against one of the wood beams supporting the roof of the shelter. She didn't want to look Tempest in the face. She was so ashamed. "I can't go to college because I'm pregnant!"

Janessa clamped her eyes shut, expecting Tempest to start yelling all sorts of disparaging comments at her, but none ever came. Finally she turned around and saw that Tempest had laid her head down on the table, engulfing it with her arms. Probably trying to hide her anger, Janessa figured.

The thunder was getting closer, and Janessa saw a flash of lightning in the near distance. "Hmph, now you're the one that has nothing to say, huh, Tempest?"

"It's not that," Tempest whispered, her voice barely audible. "I'm just thinking."

Janessa went over and sat on the top of the picnic table with her feet on the bench beside Tempest and her knee touching Tempest's shoulder. "What's there to think about? My life's finished, over, kaput."

Tempest looked up at her, and Janessa could tell she was fighting back tears. "On the contrary, your life is just beginning."

Janessa smirked. "How do you figure that? The last thing I need right now is a baby. I was just beginning to get my shit together so I could become independent enough to get my own place and a car, and most importantly, so I could get a college degree. At first I didn't give two shakes of a rat's tail about going to college. You know that! But finally I got excited about the whole thing and was ready to go for it." Janessa fingered her well-toned stomach. "Now this."

"Did you tell Dvontè already?" Tempest saw the eye-roll, lip-smack combination Janessa threw at her and guessed she had. "Well, what did he say?"

"What *didn't* he say is more the question! First, he started cussin' like all hell. Not necessarily at me, but at life in general. Then he said he would call an abortion clinic the next day and set up an appointment, like it was a given I would get rid of it."

"Is that what you want to do? Have an abortion?"

"I don't know what the hell I want! I'm so confused, but I know you can relate to what I'm feeling. We've been here before, you and me."

Tempest didn't even want to go there, but it was inevitable. "Yeah, but this time the shoe is on the other foot." She reached out and rubbed Janessa's knee. "If you're not ready to handle this, then we'll deal with it together. You were there for me, and I'll be there for you. Just say the word, and I'll go to the clinic with you. I'll even pay for it if you need me to."

"That's the one thing Dvontè has no problem with. Giving me money to have an abortion." Janessa wiped the tears off her left cheek with the sleeve of Tempest's jacket. "I told him we needed to think this through. He became belligerent and threw me out of his car on the Fourteenth Street Bridge."

"I sincerely hope you're kiddin', Janessa." Tempest was appalled at the thought of him tossing her out like a piece of trash. "He put you out on the street?"

"Yes, he treated me like a tramp, a nobody. Dvontè and I have been seeing each other just as long as you and Geren. I knew he didn't love me. I'm not even sure I love him. But I never thought he would diss me like that."

"I'm going to kill him!" Tempest barked. "Nobody treats you like that! Wait till I get my hands on him!"

"Forget about it," Janessa insisted. "It's over. Whatever I do about this baby, I can't and don't expect Dvontè to have anything to do with it. He made himself perfectly clear, and I hope I never have to lay eyes on him again."

Tempest decided becoming violent wasn't a viable solution. Geren was in NYC on business, but as soon as he got back, she would fill him in and let him deal with Dvontè. If nothing else, Tempest knew how Geren felt about kids. The mere thought of him expressing how much he wanted children to her the first night they made love proved that.

"You know what's really ironic, Janessa?"

"What's that?"

"You becoming pregnant when Dvontè doesn't want a baby, and me knowing that I'll never be able to give Geren the ones he craves so badly."

Janessa ran her fingers through Tempest's damp hair. "You haven't told Geren about what happened that summer, have you?"

"No, I don't know how to." Tempest broke out in tears, and Janessa slid down on the bench beside her, taking Tempest into her arms to comfort her. "How can I tell him something like that?"

"Things are getting serious between you two. Eventually he's going to pop the question, and you're going to have to fess up."

"I know," Tempest admitted. "I love Geren, but I can't marry him. Maybe the best thing to do is just break it off before I allow him to buy into an impossible dream."

Janessa started laughing. Tempest looked at her like she had gone mental. "What's so funny?"

"Us! If we're not the queens of drama, then I don't know who is!"

Tempest giggled, wiping away her tears. "Well, I guess drama *is* what makes life interesting."

Janessa got up and headed to the car. The rain was finally letting up. "Come on, we'll deal with our issues later. Right now, let's go to Baskin-Robbins and get some triple-scoop ice cream cones."

Tempest got up and followed her out into the mud. "I'm with that! You know *stressed* is *desserts* spelled backward!"

# 22

## *reactions*

The first thing Geren noticed when Tempest answered her door was the strained expression on her face. She favored a deer caught in a pair of headlights.

"Tempest, what's wrong?" he asked in growing concern, having never seen her look so desolate before.

"Shhhhhh!" Tempest placed her forefinger to her mouth and made no effort to open the door wider so he could come in. "Janessa's sleeping."

"Janessa? What's she doing here?"

Tempest rolled her eyes. "She's sleeping, like I just said."

Geren sighed heavily, a symbol of his growing irritation. "Tempest, aren't you forgetting something?"

Tempest was clucless. "Not that I know of."

"You were so adamant about me taking you to the charity

benefit tonight that I cut my business trip short so I could be here."

Tempest clamped her eyes shut. Damn, how could she have fucked up so royally?

"Geren, I'm so sorry, baby! It completely slipped my mind. This whole thing with Janessa has me trippin' hard."

It took Geren all of three seconds to put two and two together, but he decided not to jump the gun. He'd warned Dvontè on numerous occasions to always wear a raincoat with the ladies he dealt with, but to no avail. "What whole thing with Janessa? What's going on, Tempest?"

Tempest glanced behind her to make sure Janessa was still asleep on the couch. She could hear light snoring, and Janessa's legs were sprawled out like scissors as usual, so she came out into the hall, leaving her door slightly ajar. "Let's talk out here."

Geren followed her down the hallway to the landing and sat down on the stairs beside her. He waited patiently for her to break the silence.

"Janessa's pregnant," she finally blurted out.

"How many months?" Geren asked, a little too casually for Tempest's liking.

"How many months? Is that all you have to say?"

Geren shrugged. "It seemed like a logical question. What else am I supposed to say?"

Tempest stood up and took off like a bat out of hell down the stairs. Geren caught up to her at the bottom.

"Tempest, come on, baby. Don't be like this."

"Like what? Concerned?"

"I know you're concerned. So am I, but what's done is done. The only thing left to do now is live with the consequences."

"That's easy for you to say. Janessa's been so excited lately, making plans for her future. She was all set to enroll in college in the fall, and now this."

"Well, there's no reason why she still can't go."

"Is that right?"

"Yes, and you should know that better than anybody. You see this every day."

"You're right, I do, and as much as I hate to admit my failure rate, a lot of the women who come to me for help have to let go of their dreams when a baby enters the picture."

Geren chuckled. Tempest didn't see a damn thing funny.

"Tempest, those are young girls. Some sorry-ass boys that are still sucking on their mommas' tits knock them up. They don't know anything about responsibility. At least Janessa got pregnant by someone like Dvontè. He might be a playa at times—well, most of the time—but this will settle him down. He'll do the right thing by her."

Tempest smirked. "Well, obviously you don't know your boy half as much as you think you do."

"What the hell is that supposed to mean?"

Tempest started pacing around Geren on the sidewalk. "It means Dvontè told Janessa to basically fuck off and die."

Geren was speechless.

"He told her that he never wanted to hear from her again unless it was to accept the abortion money he offered her," Tempest added snidely. "He even put her ass out of his car on the Fourteenth Street Bridge."

Geren grabbed Tempest by the wrists to hold her in place. "That must've just been his initial reaction. Dvontè's never been through this before."

"Neither has Janessa!" Tempest snapped back at him. "I should've known."

"What?"

Tempest tried to free her wrists, but Geren tightened his grasp.

"I should've expected this. You're making excuses for him."

"No, I'm not!" Geren let go of her wrists and hugged her around the waist. "Look at me, baby!"

She did. "How can you stand here and defend him? You know what I think about shitty-ass men like him. Men who abandon their children."

It hit Geren like a ton of bricks. The problems between Janessa and Dvontè might possibly cost him the one woman he'd ever truly loved.

"Listen to me." He placed his forehead on top of hers. "Promise me that no matter what happens, this won't affect our relationship."

"I love you, Geren. I do, but—"

"I love you, too, and I won't lose you over this."

Geren closed his eyes, trying to fight back tears. Tempest kissed him gently on each eyelid and then on the mouth. Their lips parted, and a passionate kiss ensued.

Geren ended the kiss suddenly and started for his car, parked a few spaces down from the building entrance. "Go back inside. I'll be back in a little while."

"Where are you going?"

"To take care of something," was his only reply.

Tempest watched him pull off, knowing exactly where he was going and hoping his mission turned out a success.

# 23

## them there are fightin' words

        Dvontè knew it had to be Geren the second he heard the banging on his door. He came out of the bedroom and took a deep breath before unlatching the dead bolt, hoping they wouldn't end up having a full-blown altercation.

"Geren, what's up, man?" Dvontè asked cautiously, as if he didn't already know.

Geren stormed into his apartment. "Don't even pretend you don't know why I'm here! I just left Tempest's, and Janessa's an emotional wreck!"

They stood in the foyer for a few seconds, shooting daggers at each other with their eyes.

Dvontè kicked the door shut with his left foot and headed into the living room. "Janessa knew what this shit was about from jump! I never promised to love or respect any damn body! She just needs to forget about me and move on!"

"Forget about you?" Geren barked, walking right on his tail. "How in the world can she forget about you when she's carrying your child inside of her?"

"Not for long," Dvontè stated confidently. "I'm hoping she takes my suggestion and gets rid of it. I made myself perfectly clear. I have no intention of becoming a daddy." He sat on the couch and picked up the opened beer off his coffee table. He'd been drinking heavily for the last couple of days, trying to make the whole nightmare go away. "Not now, anyway," he added. "Maybe further on down the road, when I find the right woman."

Geren sat on the coffee table, facing him. "Do you even hear yourself? First of all, we're not discussing an *it*. We're talking about a human being. Secondly, you should've never made love to her if she wasn't right for you."

"Made love?" Dvontè smirked, raising an eyebrow in disgust. "Hmph, we never 'made love.' We fucked. Pure and simple."

"I can't believe you," Geren said, equally disgusted. "I knew you were a serious poon hound, but I never thought you'd turn your back on a baby."

"Well, I guess you don't know me half as much as you think you do."

Geren folded his arms across his chest, trying to hide the fists his hands had involuntarily become. "I guess not," he agreed. "All of this time, you sure had me fooled."

Dvontè didn't want to lose their lifelong friendship over what he felt amounted to a bunch of bullshit and drama. He took another swig of the beer, trying to calm his own flared temper. "Look, Geren, it's not that big of a deal. I've been through this drama before. I'm more than willing to shell out the cash to get this over and done with."

The word *before* hit Geren like a ton of bricks. "What do you mean, you've been through this before?"

Dvontè sighed, realizing his slip. He mistakenly dug up a past he intended to leave buried. "You remember that fine girl Yvonnè from high school?"

"Yeah, I remember her. What about Yvonnè?"

"She and I used to kick it every now and then."

"I never knew that," Geren said, recalling Yvonnè Lewis, a timid bookworm who seemed scared of her own shadow most of the time. He couldn't imagine her hooking up with Dvontè. He was nothing but a pussy bandit, even back then. "You never mentioned it. How come?"

"There was nothing *to* mention. It was strictly a sex thing. That's when I first figured out that most of the shy-acting sistahs are really kinky in the bedroom." Geren rolled his eyes and sighed. Dvontè could tell he didn't want the long, drawn-out version, so he got to the point. "Anyway, she lied about being on the pill and got knocked up. I pawned a couple pieces of my stereo equipment and took care of *my* business."

Geren thought back to the day Dvontè went into hysterics after they went into his garage after school and some of the equipment he used for mixing rap albums had disappeared. "You said your stuff was stolen. You called the police, filled out a report, and everything."

Dvontè threw his hands up in the air, spilling a little of the beer on his red Fubu tee. "I had to make up *something* to tell my moms. She would've strung my ass up if she knew the real deal. She always told me to keep my dick in my pants before I got someone pregnant. You remember all those lectures she used to give both of us around the kitchen table?" he asked rhetorically, knowing there was no way either he or Geren could ever forget them. She used to practically go ballistic on them.

"I can understand about your mother, but why'd you lie to me?"

"I felt it was a need-to-know thing, and you didn't need to know. Shit, I just wanted to get rid of the nightmare and go on with my life." He paused and then added, "Which I did. Yvonnè and I both did. All of that studying paid off for her. I hear she's some big-time journalist in L.A. now."

Geren was stunned, but he figured Dvontè and Yvonnè had a mutual agreement about terminating her pregnancy. Yvonnè didn't strike him as the type that would be willing to admit an unplanned teenage pregnancy to her parents. "So you think that since things went your way the first time, they will again? Janessa's not a teenager. She's a grown woman, and you're a grown man. This isn't hardly the same situation."

"I don't know what'll happen, but I do know this. If Janessa insists on having that baby, she's raising it by her damn self, because I have better things to do."

Geren's fists tightened even more. "You bastard!"

"Whatever, man!" Dvontè said indignantly, picking up the remote and flicking through the channels until he got to ESPN. "I do like the honie, but not enough to play house with her. She should've protected herself, and this shit would've never happened."

"You sound like one of those ignorant brothas on talk shows. She didn't get pregnant all by herself. Where the hell was your protection? You can buy condoms just as easily as she can."

Dvontè leered at Geren out the corner of his eye and slightly chuckled. "Look, if I've told you once, I've told you a thousand times. I don't do rubbers! I'm sick of your judgmental ass getting in my business. If you got a woman knocked up you didn't want to be bothered with, you'd drive her ass straight to the abortion clinic. Don't even front! You've just lucked out all of these years."

Geren had to admit to himself that he had been lucky. There had been rare occasions when he'd bedded down women he wasn't romantically interested in. "That's where you're wrong. If I did accidentally get a sistah pregnant, I would see it for the blessing that it is and cherish my son or daughter."

"Yeah, right! Maybe if it was Tempest. It's obvious your ass is pussy-whipped, but if it was one of the sistahs you used to have casual sex with, things would be different."

"Not really!" Geren insisted. "Even if I wasn't in love with the person, I would still love and take care of my child. You don't have to marry Janessa or shack up with her, but you damn sure better be there for the baby if she has one."

"Damn, did I stu-stu-stu-stutter the first time? I'm not taking care of *jack!* My daddy never did shit for me, and as far as I'm concerned, turnabout is fair play."

Geren lowered his eyes to the carpet. He couldn't even stand the sight of Dvontè right at that moment. "Your mother would turn over in her grave if she heard you say that."

"My mother was a damn fool for having me!" Dvontè yelled, getting up off the couch and going out on his third-floor balcony. "She had to give up everything to raise me! She could've been a famous singer, but she went to the grave a nobody instead! You heard her sing, man! She could blow!"

Geren joined him on the balcony, watching the kids swimming in the apartment complex outdoor pool. "Yes, she did have a beautiful voice. No argument here about that."

They shared a moment of silence while both of them ran favorite memories of her through their minds.

"I'm not making the same mistake, Geren. Things are going well for me at work. I'm hoping to make systems analyst in a few more months."

"That's wonderful news, man!" Geren slapped him lightly on the back. "That means you'll get a raise and can help Janessa out with the baby."

Dvontè shook his head. "I'm going to live out all of my dreams, and none of them include changing dirty diapers."

"It's not like you have any options about the money. If she has the baby, the courts will make you pay child support. Your best bet is to arrange it between the two of you and keep the legal system out of it."

"Her ass better not try to haul my ass into court," Dvontè said angrily. "I'll just tell everyone what a big hoe she is and deny the child is mine. For all I know, it might not even be my baby in the first damn place. After all, she did fuck me after the first date."

Geren had heard enough. Men who spoke such ignorance enraged him. He never thought Dvontè would stoop so low. His mother had raised him alone, and Dvontè should've been chomping at the bit to make sure his child didn't have to live through the same pain. "In all the time I've known you, I've never once felt the urge to hit you, but right now I want to beat the living daylights out of your pathetic ass."

Dvontè bent over the railing in laughter. "You aren't man enough to hit me. Besides, if you're willing to let some pussy come between us, then we're better off going our separate ways." He dreaded losing the only real brother he'd ever had, but claiming a child just wasn't in the cards. "Maybe you should just leave, Geren. I'm sure Miss High and Mighty is waiting for your return."

"You're right! I should leave, but I fully intend to pick this up later. Neither of us is in the right frame of mind for this discussion." Geren headed back into the living room to get his keys off the coffee table. "Now you've resorted to talking about Tempest, and only bad things can come from continuing this."

"Damn right, I'm talking about Tempest. I know she sent your ass over here. I must say, you're obeying her like a good little puppy." Dvontè plopped back down on the couch. "Hell, you have the imprints of her ass cheeks blistered on your lips!"

That did it! Geren punched Dvontè in the nose, sending him hurling over the back side of the couch.

It took a second for it all to register with Dvontè. Once it did,

Geren was halfway to the door. Dvontè jumped up off the floor and rammed into Geren's back, causing him to slam headfirst into the door frame.

"I can't believe you hit me, man!" Dvontè exclaimed, still in shock. "Over a bitch?"

"I've got your bitch!" Geren swung around and landed a fist on Dvontè's rib cage, knocking the air out of him.

They went at it for a full five minutes, scrambling around on the floor like a couple of WWF wrestlers and practically destroying the apartment.

Geren was straddled over Dvontè, who was beaten to a bloody pulp, getting ready to land a punch that would inevitably shatter his jaw to bits. Geren took a good look at him and his two swollen eyes and said, "Fuck it, man! You're not even worth it!"

He got up and barreled out of the apartment, wanting to get as far away from there as possible.

He was getting into his car when Dvontè appeared on the balcony, screaming at him. "Get the fuck out of my life! Tell Janessa to call me if and only if she wants some money to get rid of it. Otherwise, tell that skank bitch to kiss my black ass!" Geren glared up at him and rolled his eyes. "Besides, who are you to judge me, man? You haven't even told Tempest the truth about you, have you? How dare you judge me if you haven't walked in my shoes?"

Geren couldn't help but notice all the kids staring from the pool and their mothers shaking their heads in disgust. He could only hope the next generation of brothas would know how to be real men. He started his car up and left.

# 24

## facing demons

"Janessa, you really don't have to do this," Tempest said, turning around to stare at Janessa, in the backseat of Geren's car. "Let's just go back to my place, and you can stay there for a few days."

Geren had agreed to drive Janessa home despite Tempest's objections. He was sitting in the driver's seat, trying to keep his mouth shut. He was still severely upset about his fight with Dvontè.

"Tempest, stop treating me like a child." Janessa stared out of the window, elated there wasn't a bunch of riffraff hanging out in front of the crack house across the street. A pleasant change. "I'm not one of those teenagers from down at the center. I'm a grown woman."

"I understand that, Janessa. Of course you're grown. I'm not trying to sound condescending, but you and I both know how your parents are going to react to your pregnancy. Especially your mother."

"Oh, well, such is life." Janessa sighed. "I'm just gonna have to deal with the drama."

"I have a suggestion," Geren said, interrupting their conversation against his better judgment. "Why don't you just hold off on telling your parents until you can clear your head and make some final decisions?"

Janessa had to fight the urge to slap Geren on the back of his head. Instead she unlocked and opened the rear door and got out. She leaned down so she could glare at him.

"Are you implying I should kill my baby?" she shouted. "That is what you're saying, right?"

Tempest flung off her seat belt and jumped out of the car just as Janessa slammed the back door as hard as she could. The entire car shook.

"Janessa, calm down." Tempest grabbed Janessa by the elbow so she couldn't walk away. "Geren didn't get you pregnant. Dvontè did. The two of you created this predicament, not us."

Janessa yanked her arm away from Tempest. "Hmph, I see. I forgot you were Miss Perfect."

"Janessa, I'm not per—"

"Then again, you don't have jack shit to worry about anyway. After all, there isn't a chance in hell of anything like this happening to you."

Janessa's expression turned cynical as Tempest met her gaze. Tempest felt like her heart had just been ripped out. They both fell silent.

Geren yelled at them through the ajar passenger door. "You ladies please stop fighting! This isn't going to solve anything!" He got out on the driver's side and joined them on the curb, touching Janessa lightly on the shoulder. She flinched. "Janessa, I wasn't implying you should have an abortion. On the contrary, I think a child is the greatest gift a woman could ever give to a man."

Neither Janessa nor Tempest would even look in his direction. They just stared each other down, but Geren continued anyway. "I'm just saying that all of this is new. Everyone's emotions are still riled up. If your parents are likely to make things worse, which is the impression I'm getting, then you might need to wait a few days before you compound the issue."

Geren waved his arm up and down in between Tempest and Janessa. Still no visible reaction. They didn't even blink.

"I'm in shock myself, and I really don't have shit to do with it," Geren added, taking a few steps away from them and sitting down on the hood of his car. "I'm not so shocked that you're pregnant. You and Dvontè have been going at it pretty hard, and these things happen. What I can't get over is Dvontè's lackadaisical attitude." He crossed his arms and cupped his elbows. "My best friend and I got into a fight today," he said, shaking his head in disgust. "A fistfight, at that."

"Dvontè is a piece of shit," Tempest hissed, finally breaking away from Janessa's stare to look into Geren's eyes. "Don't even start blaming yourself for what happened today. I'm glad you gave him an ass-whupping. He deserved everything you laid on him and then some."

"Right now, I can't dispute that. Hopefully he'll come to his senses. I think Dvontè is more scared than anything."

Tempest threw her hands up in the air and then slapped them loudly on her hips. "And Janessa's not scared?"

Before Geren could respond, Janessa said, "Look, I'm about to get this over with. Tempest, I'll holla at you tomorrow."

"You sure?" Tempest asked, raising her right eyebrow. "You

don't have to do this. You can just go in there and pretend like nothing's happened until we can talk about it some more."

"I'm sure. There's no sense in running from it. They might as well know about it tonight." Janessa put her arms around Tempest and embraced her. "I'm sorry I snapped at you. I'm stressed the hell out, but I love you the same as ever."

"I love you too, sis."

Janessa forced a smile as she walked backward up the front walk. "You know you're my shero."

Tempest managed to giggle, even though she didn't feel like much of a superhero that night.

"Take it easy, Janessa," Geren said. "If you need anything, you know where to find me."

Janessa winked at him and shook her finger. "Yeah, I know where to find you, aiight! Up in Tempest's bed!" Geren blushed, and then she added, "On the real, though, thanks for the ride home."

"Not a problem. Anytime."

"More importantly, thanks for trying to talk to Dvontè on my behalf."

Geren diverted his eyes to the ground briefly, ashamed that he had failed at his task. "I just wish things had gone better."

"Janessa unlocked the front door and waved. "Good night."

"Good night," Tempest called, repressing the urge to run after her and make her come back.

Geren said, "Peace," as Janessa disappeared inside and closed the door.

Geren waited patiently for Tempest to get back in his car so he could close her door but she didn't budge.

"You're really worried about her, huh?"

"That's an understatement. Don't be surprised when I have black bags underneath my eyes from lack of sleep and patches of my hair start falling out."

Geren wrapped his arms tightly around Tempest from behind. He kissed her on her left earlobe. "Oh, baby, everything's going to be okay."

No sooner had the words left his lips when the shouting started. They could hear the words *heathen, whore,* and *slut* being thrown around interchangeably by Janessa's parents.

"I'm going in there!" Tempest yelled out, breaking away from Geren and speed-walking to the door.

Geren caught up to her midway and pulled her back toward the car. "No, Tempest. Janessa said she wanted to talk to them alone."

"That's her prerogative, but they better not lay a finger on her. I respect Janessa's parents, but I will get in their asses if need be."

Geren tried to prod Tempest to get in the car. "Let's just go. This is only upsetting you."

"Can we just stay for a few more minutes?"

Geren was about to say no when he spotted a tear in the corner of her eye. He put his arm around her and pulled her close. "If it'll make you feel better."

Tempest buried her head in Geren's chest, listening to the ruckus coming from within and trying to hold back the rest of her tears.

# 25

## the confession

Tempest stared out of the beveled window of their suite at the Pines Bed and Breakfast Inn in Portland, Maine. The view was magnificent, but Tempest was lost in thought, dreading the moments to come.

Geren had insisted on the weekend getaway, making plane reservations before she could blink twice. He told her that he had something important to ask her. They both knew the deal. The only thing left was a formality.

Geren couldn't have chosen a more romantic place to pop the question. Their suite was adorned with antique furniture well over a hundred years old. A wooden sleigh bed on a three-step riser was the main attraction of the suite.

Geren came into the bedroom, smelling fresh from the shower and clad only in a towel around his waist. "Shall we have dinner in the room tonight, or would you like to go out? I heard there's a great seafood restaurant a few blocks away with a deck overlooking the ocean." He got no response. "Tempest?"

"Sorry. What did you say?" Tempest turned from the window to face him. "I was distracted by the beautiful view," she added, lying.

"I asked if you wanted to dine in or out."

"Actually, I'm not hungry."

"You should be starving. I am. We haven't eaten a thing since breakfast."

"Geren."

"Yes?"

"We need to talk." Tempest walked over and sat on the edge of the bed. "Before you ask me whatever it is you want to ask, there's something I really need to tell you."

Geren splashed on some aftershave and then searched through his toiletry kit for his deodorant. A twinge of nervousness shot up his spine, but he tried to act nonchalant.

"Go ahead, sweetheart. I'm listening."

"This is so difficult. I don't want to lose you, but I'll understand if I do."

Geren chuckled. He found her statement ludicrous; he had no intention of ever breaking up with her. "You're not going to lose me, Tempest. I promise you that."

"Please don't make me promises you can't keep."

"Oh, but I can keep that one. I adore you." Geren flashed his cinematic smile at Tempest, but he could feel the tension rising in the room. "You know that, don't you? That I adore you. In fact, that's what I wanted to—"

"Please, Geren!" Tempest shouted at him. "Just let me get this out before I lose my nerve. I should've told you everything a long time ago." Tempest sighed heavily. "Before we ever became intimately involved."

Geren was putting his deodorant back in his bag on the dresser when the last comment froze him in place. He looked at Tempest's reflection in the mirror. "You don't have a disease, do you?"

Tempest sucked in her bottom lip and glared at him. "No, no diseases. We discussed that already. I'd never put your health in jeopardy, Geren. You should know that. Maybe you don't really know me at all."

Geren came and sat down beside her on the bed. "Not only do I know you, I love you." Tempest didn't respond. She edged farther away from him on the bed. He didn't know what to make of it. He had planned out the weekend perfectly in his mind, but as usual, things were never the way he dreamed them up. He felt like their relationship was all of a sudden bordering on disaster. "Okay, so what is it? Are you seeing someone else? Did one of your ex-boyfriends come back into your life?"

Tempest couldn't hold it in a second longer. "I'm sterile, Geren," she whispered in a barely audible tone. Geren's eyes widened in stunned disbelief. "I can't give you the household full of children you're always talking about. I would sell my soul if I could, but I can't. I can't."

Geren's throat was extremely dry. He reached over on the nightstand to get a bottle of springwater. Tempest moved back farther on the bed when his fingertip accidentally brushed against her thigh. She made him feel like he'd done something wrong.

"I don't know how to respond, sweetheart. I'm stunned. Are you sure about this, baby?"

Tempest pulled a pillow up in front of her chest and crossed her legs Indian-style on the bed. "Unfortunately, I'm positive."

"It's okay," Geren said without hesitation. "I still love you, and I want to be with you always."

"That's very admirable, and I guess I shouldn't have expected anything less from you, but I need to tell you everything. Once I'm done, you'll probably think I'm the stupidest sistah in America and kick me to the curb."

"Why do you keep saying that?" Geren asked, getting irritated by Tempest's assumptions. "I'm not dumping you. It sounds like you almost want me to."

"Part of me feels like I deserve it," Tempest said, the first tear finally escaping and making a caravan down her right cheek. "Losing the one man I've ever truly loved seems like just punishment for what I did."

"What did you do?"

Tempest fell silent for a few moments, searching for the right words—words she should've spoken months earlier. "Geren, the reason I went so ballistic when Dvontè abandoned Janessa and the reason I'm so determined to help Kensington is because I know how they both feel. I know how it feels not to have anyone to talk to, anyone to help you."

The truth hit Geren like a Mack truck. "You were pregnant before?" he asked rhetorically, already knowing the answer.

Tempest took the pillow she was holding, placed it on the bed, and lay down, facing away from Geren. She felt so ashamed she couldn't even bear to look at him.

"I was seventeen. Kenny was the father. You know, my ex who's shacking up with my aunt now? I told you about him. You remember?"

"Yes," Geren responded, reaching over to rub her back. He was elated that she didn't flinch. "I remember you telling me about the dumb bastard."

Tempest giggled slightly. Kenny was a dumb bastard. "I found out I was pregnant less than two weeks after I found out they were sleeping with each other. I was devastated."

Geren began to cry silent tears. He didn't want Tempest to know he was weeping. "You've been through too much, baby. Too damn much!"

"Not only had I lost the only person I'd ever cared about and the only lover I ever had, but I lost him to my own flesh and blood. I never thought she would ever hurt me like that. When I was little, Aunt Geraldine would spoil me and take me places my parents refused to go. Then she turned around and stabbed me in my back."

"I'm so sorry, baby." Geren lay down on the bed beside Tempest, draping his left arm over her waist and burying his nose in her hair. It smelled sweet, as usual. "What happened once you found out? Did you tell him?"

"Hell, no. I panicked. The only person who knew was Janessa, but she couldn't help me. It was like the blind leading the blind. I was too embarrassed and ashamed to even tell my parents about it."

Geren brushed her hair with the fingertips of his other hand. "So what happened to the baby you were carrying?"

Tempest sucked in a deep breath. Geren could feel her heart racing through her back, which was pressed against his chest.

"Geren, looking back on it now, I realize I made so many crucial mistakes, but I was just a child myself. I've been dealing with the emotional and sometimes physical scars ever since."

"Take your time, sweetheart."

"I didn't have enough money for an abortion clinic, and having the baby was out of the question. I would've died from shame if everyone found out, especially since the whole world, at least my whole world, knew about Kenny and Aunt Geraldine. Kenny made me feel like the dirt on the bottom of his shoes, and so—"

"So?" Geren didn't want to press Tempest, but he knew from experience that getting things out in the open always helped to alleviate stress.

"Janessa found out about this place in Southeast where they did abortions dirt-cheap: just fifty dollars. I knew it sounded shady from the start, but that's about all I had to my name after scraping together loose change from my mother's dresser drawers and the little bit I had in mine."

"So you had an illegal abortion?"

Tempest startled Geren when she flipped over suddenly. She was equally as startled to discover his face was just as tear-drenched as hers.

"Geren, you should've seen the place. It was absolutely horrid. We got to the building, and it looked like it should have been condemned. There were these huge rats everywhere, and the carpet smelled like urine. People were shooting up in the hallways, and girls, babies really, were sucking men's dicks on the stairs for drug money."

Tempest started trembling in fear. "You don't have to finish," Geren said, rubbing his hand up and down her arm and kissing her on the bridge of her nose. "This is making you too uncomfortable. I understand where this is going."

"No, I need to tell you," Tempest pleaded.

Geren sighed. "Okay, if you must."

"We got into this apartment on the third floor, and it was the filthiest, most disgusting place I'd ever seen. This older, nasty-looking man with a mouthful of rotten teeth demanded the fifty dollars and then told me to lie on this table in the middle of the living room floor. The table was already covered with bloodstains." Tempest wiped her face on the edge of the pillowcase before continuing. "I did it, and the entire time he was torturing me, Janessa held my hands. I kept my eyes shut. I didn't want to see. It hurt like hell. Later, Janessa told me he used this rusty coat hanger and a pair of pliers."

Tempest started weeping loudly, and Geren drew her tightly to him, kissing her lightly all over her face.

"I could barely walk straight when we left there. He didn't

even let me rest five minutes before he kicked Janessa and me out. I saw another girl coming up the stairs who looked even younger and more frightened than me. She was all alone. I wanted to tell her not to do it because I knew something was terribly wrong the second I got up off the table. My insides felt like they were about to fall out, and there was blood trickling down both of my legs."

"Oh, baby!" Geren exclaimed, unable to keep his emotions under control. "If I ever find that butcher, I'll kill him!"

"Somehow, Janessa managed to get me home. My parents were still at work. I passed out in pain. Janessa stayed with me and tried to keep my mother from coming into my room that evening, but she demanded to be let in. I guess it was her sixth sense or something. My mother's screams woke me up. My entire mattress was soaked in blood. I remember my father barreling into the room and bursting out in tears. That was the first and only time I ever saw him cry. They called 911, and an ambulance took me to the hospital.

"They stitched me up and gave me all types of painkillers. The entire time, all I could worry about was the shame I felt. Now everyone knew, or they would know, and I just wanted to shrivel up and die."

"I wish I could have been there for you, sweetheart. That must've been so devastating."

"It was, but not half as devastating as when the doctor told me that my reproductive organs were damaged beyond repair, and that I would never be able to conceive another child." Tempest reached down and rubbed her flat stomach. "I killed my baby that day and all the babies I might have had, all in the space of one afternoon." Tempest gazed at Geren and felt like only half of a woman. How could he possibly still want to be with her? "So there you have it. That's why I flinch in pain sometimes while we're making love, and that's why I'm so adamant about taking care of Janessa and Kensington and the rest of them."

"And that's why you work at the center?"

"Yes, I never want another young woman to feel like she has no one to talk to. I never want to see someone else go through what I did. But they do. Tens of thousands of them every year. I can't stop it, but I can try."

Geren kissed Tempest passionately on the lips. She hesitantly reciprocated.

"It's okay, baby. You have me now. Everything's going to be okay from now on. I promise you that!"

They lay together in silence for about thirty minutes. Geren was taken aback when Tempest straddled him and started kissing him hungrily. That was all the motivation he needed. They made love for the remainder of the evening, and in the morning, they went down to the Portland waterfront to catch the ferry to Nova Scotia.

Once they were on board and standing at the helm, overlooking the ocean, Geren decided to go for it. "Can I ask my question now?" he inquired, reaching into the right pocket of his denim carpenter pants.

"Please, Geren. Not right now," Tempest replied adamantly, holding a finger up to his lips. "If you ask me now, I'll feel like you're only doing it because you pity me. Because you think I'm pathetic."

"How can you say that, baby? After the way we made love last night?"

"I just want you to take some time to think about this."

"I don't need to think about anything."

"I want you to think about the things I told you yesterday, because they will influence the rest of your life. I know you want kids, Geren. Don't even try to pretend otherwise."

Geren removed his hand from his pocket and ran his fingertips over Tempest's cheek. "I do want kids, and just because you're physically incapable of having them doesn't mean we can't adopt."

"I realize that, but it wouldn't be the same. I can't give you a child with your own flesh and blood."

"Listen to me very carefully, Tempest. I can live without having a child, but I can't live without you. I have no intention of living without you."

"Please, just think about it," Tempest pleaded.

Geren reluctantly postponed asking her the question, even though he didn't want to wait one more second. He didn't want her to have any doubts about his intentions, so he decided to wait. They went back to watching the ocean.

# 26

## the proposal

"You know, these quarter-ouncer burgers from Raoul's place aren't half bad," Geren commented, plopping another miniature burger into his mouth.

"For real!" Tempest agreed. She washed down the remains of one, taking a long sip of cherry cola through a straw. "If you can get past the way they look, it's all good!"

Geren chuckled. "Well, they have to make them small. Most of the clientele are midgets."

Tempest slapped him gently on the arm and giggled at his remark. "You're so silly!"

"I'm serious. The place is so far out of the way." Geren picked up his own soda out of one of the built-in cup holders in his car and drank some. "How many people do you honestly think pass up Burger King, McDonald's, and Checkers to get food at Raoul's?"

"I don't know," Tempest answered, pondering the question. "Maybe a bunch of horny women hunting for midgets with huge dicks."

Geren looked at her suspiciously out the corner of his eye. "You sure you don't want a big-dicked midget?"

"All I want is you," Tempest replied without hesitation.

"That's my sweetheart."

"Why are we out here in the boondocks?" Tempest asked, surveying the dirt road where they were parked and the surrounding area. "We're not trespassing on personal property, are we?"

"No, not really," Geren responded, growing more nervous about coming clean than he had been when he suggested they drive out there. Dvontè was right about one thing. He hadn't been totally honest with Tempest, and it was time to fess up.

"Okay, if you say so. As long as we don't get locked up in the county jail," Tempest joked.

Geren pointed to the north. "You see that building over there on the hill?"

Tempest's eyes followed the direction of his finger. There was a big black glass building with a high security fence all around it. Being the weekend, only a few cars were scattered around in the parking lot. "The Phoenix Corporation building? What about it?"

"You know how you're always commenting on all the Phoenix electronic equipment I have?"

"Yeah." Tempest giggled. "Sometimes I think you single-handedly keep them in business."

"There's something I need to tell you, Tempest." Geren took a deep breath. "Before I ask you my question, and I fully intend to ask it today—no matter what."

"What do you need to tell me, Geren?" Tempest asked, taking another sip of her soda.

"Well, for starters, most of the Phoenix equipment in my home and office, even this stereo in my car, is not available on the open market yet."

"But how can that be?" Tempest inquired, totally confused. "Are you part of a beta testing program or something?"

"Beta testing!" Geren said with a hint of sarcasm. "I guess you could call it that."

Tempest didn't like the way the conversation was heading. She hoped he wasn't about to confess to being an electronics dealer—"hot" electronics, that is. Even with all the money he was making at the investment firm, some things still didn't quite add up to her, and it had been bothering her for some time.

"The fact of the matter is that I've been less than truthful with you, sweetheart."

Oh, shit, Tempest thought to herself. He's a damn criminal. I might see his ass on *America's Most Wanted* or some shit. "About?" she asked calmly, trying not to show her true attitude.

"My past. My future. Our future. Everything."

She liked the way he said "our future." "Geren, I'm not quite following you. You've got me confused like a whore in church."

"These business trips I keep taking to New York are not all related to the brokerage firm. I am a broker. That's strictly legit but—"

"But?" Oh, God, I hope he's not about to tell me he's a drug dealer or something, Tempest thought, working herself up into a panic. "Please tell me you don't have a woman in New York."

"Oh, baby, it's nothing like that." Geren reached over for her hand and gripped it tightly. "You're the only one for me."

Tempest didn't respond. She just stared at him with a clueless expression on her face.

"This is very difficult for me," Geren whispered. "Let me start from the beginning."

Tempest lifted his hand to her mouth and kissed it gently. "Take your time."

"My mother died of leukemia when I was in elementary school. I told you that before."

"Yes, you did."

"But my father——"

"Your father lives in Seattle, right?"

"No, he has a home in Seattle, among many other places, but his main residence is in New York."

"New York?" Tempest asked, taken completely by surprise. In all the time they'd been dating, Geren had never mentioned his father having a place in New York, rather less a main residence, as he put it.

"Yes."

"So why did you lie to me?"

"I didn't lie," Geren stated avidly. "Not exactly."

Tempest wondered what a not exactly lie was.

"My father's name is Phoenix Kincaid."

"I thought you said his name was Ralph?"

"Technically, it is. Ralph was his given name, but he legally changed it when he was in college."

"Why did he change it to Phoenix?" Tempest asked. Things were getting more complicated by the second. "Granted, Ralph is not the most exciting name in the world, but Phoenix?"

"My mother grew up in Phoenix, Arizona. He fell in love with her the second he laid eyes on her. Kind of the same way I fell in love with you."

He kissed Tempest's hand, but the expression on her face said it all. She was pissed and not even trying to hide it.

"Anyway," Geren continued, "Momma wouldn't have a thing to

do with him. She thought he was the most arrogant man that ever walked the earth. At least, that's how the story goes."

"You take after him," Tempest snidely remarked. She had thought Geren was arrogant when she first met him, too.

Geren sucked his teeth. "Very funny."

"Finish telling me the story," Tempest prodded.

"He tried everything to get her, from tattooing her name on his chest to serenading her in the college cafeteria. Nothing worked, so finally he changed his name."

"To Phoenix?"

"Yeah, well, he couldn't change it to Angelica like hers, so he did the next best thing. He changed his name to symbolize the place she was born."

"That's deep!"

"Want to hear something even deeper?"

"Sure!"

Geren braced himself and then blurted it out before he lost his nerve. "My father owns Phoenix Corporation."

Tempest gawked at him. "You're kidding, right?"

"No, not at all," Geren said hesitantly. "All of my business trips to New York were really board meetings. My father makes me come because he believes I need to keep abreast of everything so that once he retires, I can step right into his shoes."

Tempest didn't say a word. She just pulled her hand away and moved as far over on the seat as possible.

"Does this change things between us?"

"Should it?" Tempest asked with a raised brow.

"I don't know," Geren replied. "Look at your body language, though. Obviously, it does."

"Why didn't you just tell me?"

Tempest waited patiently while Geren tried to concoct a viable answer, one that wouldn't make her cuss him out.

"Because all of my life, once a woman found out about my father, she would become obsessed with getting me down the aisle so she could get my money. *His* money."

"Is that what you thought of me?" Tempest rolled her eyes and looked down at her lap. "Never mind, don't answer that."

"Tempest—"

"No, this explains a hell of a lot. Like the conversation we had in your office about gold diggers."

"Can I please make a comment?"

"No, but what you can do is take me home."

"Absolutely not! Not until I do what I came here to do!" Geren reached for her, but she knocked his hand away. "I just wanted to tell you everything about me first, so you would know what you're getting into."

"I'm not getting into anything. I just want you to take my gold-digging ass home."

"After the weekend in Maine and everything we've been to each other, you still think this comes down to money?"

"Like you said before, obviously it does. If it didn't, you would've told me this months ago."

"My opinion of you has never faltered. I knew you were strong-willed and independent from the day we met. And you're right. I should've said something months ago, but I just didn't know how to."

"It's simple. Just open your mouth and speak."

"Tempest, if I can forgive you for not telling me about your inability to have children before we got involved, can't you forgive me for this?"

Tempest frowned, and Geren could tell she was fighting back tears. That was a low blow, and he immediately regretted it.

"I'm sorry. That came out wrong."

Tempest wiped her eyes with a napkin and shoved all the

hamburger trash into a bag. "Can you just take me home, please?"

"You are so damn stubborn!" Geren blared out in frustration.

Tempest sighed and rolled her eyes in disdain. "Today!"

"Not until you answer a question for me."

"What question?" Tempest replied, not particularly interested in anything he had to say at the moment.

"Will you marry me?" Geren whispered, saying a silent prayer. The moment wasn't perfect, but he'd held off on proposing long enough. "Will you marry me, Tempest?" Geren reached for her hand again. This time she let him take it. She was in shock. "I love you. I adore everything about you, and I could search the earth for a million years and never find another woman like you."

"Geren, I—"

"If it's about the kid situation, like I said before, we can adopt." He could tell from the expression on her face that he'd hit the nail on the head. "There are tons of children out there who need loving parents. You know that from working at the center."

No response. Tempest's hand started trembling something fierce, and he held it tighter.

"We could wait a couple of years after the wedding to adopt, if you want. Whatever you want. I just want you."

Still no response.

"Look at me." Geren lifted Tempest's chin so she had to and gazed into her eyes. "I love the way you laugh. I love the way you cry. I love the way you walk. The way you talk. I love the way you poke your bottom lip out when you're trying to get your way. I love that little birthmark on your ass. I love the way you moan, the way you cum, the way you hold me when I need to be held."

Tempest blushed but still refused to respond. She was too busy deciding if she was experiencing a dream or a nightmare. How could she expect him to give up his dream of having a house full of kids?

"I couldn't get used to the idea of changing my name to Washington, D.C. Why couldn't you have been born in Chicago? Naw, that sounds like a pimp's name. Or Tempe, Arizona? Then we could have been Tempe and Tempest Kincaid."

Tempest chuckled and pulled away from him. "You're so crazy!"

"Crazy over you!"

Tempest got out of the car and sat down on the hood. All sorts of things were running through her mind at the speed of light.

Geren got out and came around to join her. He pulled off his shirt, exposing a tattoo of a heart on his chest. The name *Tempest* was placed in the middle, directly over his heart.

Tempest reached out nervously to finger it. "Is it real?"

"It's real, and it's permanent—just like my love for you." Geren reached into his left pants pocket and pulled out a velvet box. He snapped it open. "And so is this!"

Tempest almost choked on her own saliva when she saw the ring. The diamond had to be at least six carats. She finally managed to utter, "It's gorgeous."

"Give me your hand." Geren took it before she could offer it, pulled the ring from the box, and placed it on her finger. "Say yes."

"Geren—"

"Say yes, or my life is over." He kissed each one of her fingertips, kissed her gently on the forehead, and whispered in her ear, "Save my life, Tempest. Don't force me to live in a world without you. I could never do that."

She was still trembling, so Geren gathered her up into his arms. "You're sure you don't mind adopting, Geren?"

He brushed her hair back out of her face and gazed at her lovingly. "Say yes!"

"Yes!" Tempest finally yelled out, grinning from ear-to-ear.

Geren kissed her on the lips. "Thank you!"

"For what?" Tempest asked.

"For saving my life."

They made love for the remainder of the afternoon on the hood of his car and then went home to start making calls, informing their friends and family of the good news.

# 27

## you've got a friend in me

Tempest glanced across the table at the Florida Avenue Grill and noticed Janessa had barely touched her fried chicken wings and fries. "Janessa, you've go to eat *something*," she implored.

"I'm not very hungry." Janessa put her elbows on the table and held her head. She was battling a serious migraine. The stress from the unwanted pregnancy had really gotten to her.

"But you need to maintain your health, Janessa. Especially during your pregnancy."

Janessa sucked her tongue and snapped at Tempest, "Sis, I don't need you to remind me that I'm pregnant. It's all I ever think about."

Tempest slammed her glass of iced tea down on the table. "Well, shoot me for being concerned."

Janessa looked at Tempest, who was sitting across from her, pouting, and realized she was taking her frustration out on the wrong person. When Tempest had showed up at the Brentwood Post Office to take her out to lunch, Janessa was very rude to her and almost refused to go.

"I'm sorry, Tempest. I didn't mean to cop a 'tude with you." Janessa reached over and patted Tempest lightly on the hand. "You know I love you."

"I love you, too," Tempest responded, intertwining their fingers. She noticed that the older, gray-haired sistah behind the counter was staring at them as if they were dykes and pulled her hand away. "Have you at least been keeping up with your ob/gyn appointments?"

"Yes, like clockwork." Janessa picked at a chicken wing and put a morsel into her mouth in an attempt to make Tempest happy. "I've got a great doctor at the Columbia Hospital for Women."

"Oh, yeah?" Tempest was glad to know Janessa was at least seeing a doctor. From her experience at the center, she was all too aware that a lot of young women neglect to go to an ob/gyn in hopes that the pregnancy will just miraculously go away. "What's his name?"

"*Her* name is Tamika Brown. I made it a point to request a female doctor because the last thing I want is another man, any man, looking in the direction of my coochie."

"Tamika Brown?" Tempest chuckled. "Now she's got to be a sistah!"

"Yes, she is," Janessa confirmed. "She's one of those African-American women who got through the hard times, went for the golden ring, and made it." Janessa stared at Tempest with envy. "Just like you."

Tempest took a bite of her cheeseburger and looked out the window. There was a young girl, probably no older than fifteen, struggling to get up the steps of a Metrobus with a baby in her arms and a toddler holding on to her pants leg.

"Too bad I won't be able to do the same," Janessa continued. "I really wanted to become a pharmacist. Instead, I'll be stuck in the postal system until I'm old and gray."

Tempest took a deep breath and decided it was time to reveal her plans. "Not necessarily, sis. In fact, that's the main reason I invited you to lunch."

Janessa raised a curious eyebrow. "Oh, yeah?"

"I think I've worked out a feasible solution to all of your problems. Maybe not all of them, but a couple of the major ones."

"What are you talking about, Tempest?"

"Good afternoon, ladies!" Tempest and Janessa looked up to see who had spoken to them. A tall, handsome, dark-skinned brotha was walking past their table.

"Good afternoon," they both replied in unison.

He sat down on a stool at the counter and got a menu out of the metal holder in the center. He kept darting his eyes at Janessa, and she couldn't help but blush from the attention. Maybe she did still have it after all!

"That guy's checking you out big-time," Tempest observed. "He's a cutie-pie too."

Janessa smirked and went back to her chicken wing. "Yeah, but he's probably married or bisexual or just a plain ole dog like the rest of them."

"Janessa, I hope you won't let what happened with Dvontè turn you against all men. I mean, look at me and all the crap men put my ass through before Geren."

"You're right, gurl," Janessa said, even though she felt Tempest was wrong. She doubted she would ever trust a man enough again to date him. "But still, you must admit there are a lot of pit bulls running around D.C."

"True," Tempest wholeheartedly agreed. "Maybe they should just install metal detectors at the entrance of all the hangouts in D.C. to detect the thousands of wedding rings stuffed in men's pockets."

"Naw, too many gold teeth would set those bad boys off." Janessa and Tempest both snickered.

Once the laughter wore off, Tempest decided to get back to the matter at hand. "As I was saying, I think I may have it all figured out. You can still go to school and work, even with the baby coming."

"How do you figure that?" Janessa inquired, thinking Tempest must have forgotten to cash her reality check that week.

"Well, you have a scholarship, so you don't have to worry about tuition."

"But what about the big-ass baby-sitting bill I'm going to have?"

"I'm glad you asked," Tempest said with a sanguine smile. "Check this out. When you're in school during the day, I can arrange for your baby to go to the day care next door to the center. I've already talked to Sharrice Johnson, who runs the place. She has a long waiting list, but she's agreed to take your baby in as a favor to me."

"But how much is it?" Janessa asked sullenly, still wondering how this solved anything.

"Absolutely nothing!" Tempest exclaimed. "The day care center is fully funded, so your child could go for free."

"Really?"

"Yes, that's why the waiting list is so long. As far as you working in the evening, I have that figured out also."

"How?"

"I'll watch the baby at night!"

Janessa's mouth flew open. "I can't ask you to do that, Tempest. You're about to get married."

"Come on, Janessa. It will only be for what, four or five hours an evening? I can handle it," Tempest insisted. "If it gets to be too much, then I'll hire a sitter to come in and watch the baby at my place."

Janessa couldn't find the right words to express her gratitude.

"Bottom line is this," Tempest added. "I haven't seen you this excited about anything for a long time, and I am hell bent on making sure your dreams come true. So is Geren. He is behind this one hundred percent."

"I can't believe this," Janessa said with a flustered glance. "You mean I can really go to college?"

"You can go. You *are* going, or I'm going to kick your ass. After you deliver the baby, of course."

Janessa and Tempest jumped up, squealing and hugging each other over the table. The older woman behind the counter gave them the evil eye and cleared her throat. She kept her hands on her hips until they sat back down.

"I don't know how I could ever thank you or Geren."

"You can thank us by making good grades and becoming the best pharmacist this city has ever seen." Tempest was happy when Janessa finally started digging into her food. "See, I knew your behind was hungry."

They both giggled.

"I'm starving," Janessa confessed, picking up the drumstick part of the wing and sucking all the meat off it.

"You're not lifting anything heavy down at the post office, are you?" The thought suddenly hit Tempest that Janessa's job might put too much physical strain on the fetus.

"Naw, they have me on light duty until I go on maternity leave. I only sort envelopes."

"Good!" Tempest exclaimed with a sigh of relief. "When are you planning to go on leave?"

"My due date is February 15, so probably sometime in mid-January."

"Oooooooh, you might mess around and have a Valentine's baby. That would be so romantic."

Janessa grimaced. "Romance. What a crock of bullshit. Love is nothing but a delusion." Janessa saw the disappointment on Tempest's face and added, "Except in your case, of course."

Tempest smiled at her and finished off her glass of tea.

"How are the wedding plans coming along?" Janessa asked. "I've been so caught up in myself lately, I haven't even asked. When's the date?"

Tempest almost choked on the last of the tea. "We haven't set one yet," she answered, setting the glass back down.

Janessa sat up on the edge of her seat. "Why not?"

"We've just been trying to enjoy each other. Besides, Geren's been running back and forth to NYC a lot lately. This whole situation took both of us by surprise. I definitely wasn't planning on falling in love, rather less getting married, and I doubt Geren was either."

"Have you met his dad? The great almighty Phoenix Kincaid?"

"Yes, I have." Tempest laughed at Janessa's characterization of her future father-in-law. "He came down last weekend just to check me out."

"And?"

"He's a sweetheart. Just the typical everyday bro man. He just has a lot of money, is all, but he's real cool. He made a point to assure me that I had his stamp of approval. He even offered to send us to a private island in the Caribbean for our honeymoon."

"That's great!" Janessa exclaimed. "Are you going to go?"

"We're not sure. It depends on when we get married because we definitely don't want to fall up in there during hurricane season, like Brandy and them did in *I Still Know What You Did Last Summer*."

"That was the bomb movie!"

"Hell, yeah, it was," Tempest agreed, and they both giggled.

Janessa reached up her hand so Tempest could give her a high five. "My gurl, marrying the son of a multimillionaire. Who would have thought?"

"Not *moi,* that's for damn sure," Tempest chuckled. "Geren and his father are both extremely down-to-earth, though. I'm taking Geren down to Florida next weekend to meet my parents."

"I guess this proves the theory that good things happen when you least expect it."

"I guess so." Tempest sighed. She decided it was time to broach the next topic, since Janessa's frame of mind had improved. "Have you spoken to Dvontè?"

Janessa rolled her eyes in disgust, her mood changing back to negative at the mere mention of his name. "Just once, about a month ago," she answered. "He called to see if I'd come to my senses, as he put it, and wanted to know if I needed any money for an abortion. Dvontè can be so damn cruel at times. He acts like I imagined everything that happened between us."

Tempest's mood drastically changed as well. "Fuck him and the horse he rode in on!"

There was silence at their table for a few moments. The brotha who spoke on his way in decided to speak again on his way out with his carryout bag but they both igged his ass.

As much as Janessa despised Dvontè's attitude, she still cared about him. "Has Geren talked to him at all?" she asked.

"Not to my knowledge," Tempest replied somberly.

"Tempest, I hate the fact that their friendship is strained because of me."

Tempest grabbed Janessa's hand again and noticed it was trembling. The lady behind the counter immediately shot daggers at them again, but Tempest looked at her and shot them back this time, refusing to let go of Janessa's hand because of the hang-ups of others. "None of this is your fault, Janessa. Geren doesn't blame you, and I definitely don't."

Janessa pouted. "But they've been friends for so long."

"Not everyone is meant to be in our lives for a lifetime. Geren and Dvontè started growing apart years before you and I even entered the picture. Geren and I discussed this in detail, and personally, I'm surprised their friendship lasted as long as it did. They're like night and day."

"Well, so are we," Janessa said, thinking about all the times Tempest had warned her not to do something only to have her do it and regret it later.

"Not hardly," Tempest said vehemently. "When it comes right down to it, you and I are a lot alike. And where there are differences, you and I can agree to disagree. There is no room for that in the situation between Geren and Dvontè."

Janessa pushed her plate away. Her appetite was gone. "I'm just going to do the best I can, with or without Dvontè's help. I'm just grateful for you and Geren. I still can't believe you're willing to do so much for me."

"Well, I am. Which brings me to my next question. What about Lamaze? Are you planning to take classes?"

Janessa diverted her eyes to the table in shame. "How can I? I don't have a partner."

Tempest tightened her grasp on Janessa's hand. "You do now!"

# 28

## home sweet home

"Ready?" Geren asked, helping Tempest out of the passenger side of his car. He glanced around at the pedestrians walking past, who were giving them curious looks. Tempest had been bombarding him with questions ever since he showed up at her place, insisting she put on a blindfold and get in the car with him.

"Ready as I'll ever be!" Tempest replied excitedly, messing with the knot on the back of the blindfold with the fingers of her left hand. "The suspense is killing me!"

"Well, we can't have that," Geren teased. He took a deep breath, feeling extremely excited himself, and removed her blindfold in one swift movement.

Tempest's mouth flew open, and for a few seconds, Geren thought she might faint. Then a huge grin overtook her face.

"Geren, what are we doing here?"

He knew she'd already put two and two together but decided to play along. "Why do you think we're here, sweetheart?"

"I haven't a clue," Tempest cooed, blushing uncontrollably. She stared at the three-story brownstone on P Street in Georgetown as if it were the first time she'd ever seen it. Her heart fluttered, her mind rapidly flashing through the happy memories of her youth when her grandparents were still alive.

"No clue, huh?" Geren prodded, still participating in the game.

Tempest lifted her chin to stare at him, gnawing gently on her bottom lip and hesitant to come right out with her assumption. "I see the For Sale sign has been taken down."

Geren chuckled. "So it seems."

"That must mean someone purchased it."

Geren crossed his arms in front of his chest, cupping his elbows and trying to repress the laughter that was building up inside of him. "Yes, someone did."

Tempest couldn't hold back a second longer. She lightly pushed Geren in the chest as they both broke out in giggles. "Are you serious?"

He wrapped his arms around her waist, planting a gentle kiss on her trembling lips. "As serious as it gets."

"You bought this house for me?" Tempest asked, still stunned beyond disbelief.

"No, I bought this house for us." Geren ran his fingers through her freshly washed hair, wondering how fate had stepped in and put them together. He never thought he would know a love so real. "Unless you expect us to maintain separate residences once we're married?"

"Silly ass!" she cackled, burying her head in his muscular chest. "You know what I mean!"

After a moment of tenderness, Tempest withdrew from his

embrace and moved slowly up the front walk, taking baby steps because it was such an overwhelming surprise. When Geren had picked her up, she figured he was taking her out to the country for a romantic picnic or something of that nature. Never in a million years would she have figured on this. "I'm speechless, Geren," she whispered. "I can't find any words to express how I feel."

Geren traced her footsteps and slid his index finger up and down her spine. The gentle breeze carried her pear-scented body spray to his nostrils, making him yearn to make love to her.

"Then don't search for any words, sweetheart." He massaged her arms and kissed her shoulder, left exposed by the pastel pink sundress she was wearing. "Displays of affection are just as appreciated."

Tempest reached for the back of his neck over her shoulder and turned toward him, engaging in a deep, passionate kiss. Less than a year before, she'd given up on finding a decent and loving man. How did she get so damn lucky?

Two children in the yard next door started pointing and giggling at the public display, so Geren stopped the kiss, darting his eyes toward their audience of two. "We better quit. We don't want to corrupt the neighborhood before we even move in."

Tempest gave him one last peck on his sensual lips and then looked back at the house. "Can we go inside?"

"It's our house. We can go wherever we want and do whatever we choose."

"Except make out in the front yard," Tempest added, glancing at the kids and laughing.

Geren shared in the laugh. "Yeah, except that!" He took her hand and led her up the four steps onto the front porch. He reached into his pocket and pulled out a single brass key on a chain that had a picture of a house and the words *The Kincaids* engraved onto it. "Here's the key. Why don't you do the honors?"

Tempest's entire face lit up as she removed the key from Geren's hand and fiddled nervously with the lock. "I haven't been in this house since I was about thirteen years old. This is so amazing."

Geren was tempted to help her get the door unlocked, but she finally managed, and they stepped past the huge mahogany door together. The foyer had gray ceramic tiles, and the living room, dining room, and stairs were covered in lush burgundy carpet.

"It's changed so much!" Tempest exclaimed, taken aback by the renovations the previous owner had made. She eyed the paisley wallpaper in the hallway, speckled with shades of gray and burgundy. "The color scheme, the wallpaper, the carpet. It's all different."

Geren couldn't tell if Tempest was upset or just anxious about the changes. He clamped his hands around her waist, simply because he wanted to feel her warmth. "We can change it all back if you like. Restore it to the way it was when your grandparents lived here."

Tempest freed herself from his grasp and pulled him by the arm toward the kitchen in the rear of the house. "No, I want to create new memories. With you!"

"Then we'll decorate it together," Geren said, bobbing his head and watching Tempest run her fingertips across the new Maytag stove. "Whatever your heart desires, I will fulfill."

Tempest looked at Geren seductively and then leaped into his arms, straddling her legs around his back. He leaned her against the wall and explored her mouth with his thick tongue, letting the mixture of her shampoo and body spray envelop his senses with pure delight.

"I love you so much, Geren," Tempest proclaimed when they finally emerged for air. "You make me so happy."

"This is only the beginning, sweetheart." He let her back down on the floor gently. "You have no idea how badly I want to be your husband."

"You will be," Tempest said with a sanguine smile. "I can't hardly wait."

"Then let's set a date."

"Right now?"

"Right this second, before we look at the rest of the house," Geren demanded.

Tempest chewed her bottom lip, immersed in deep thought. Finally, she said, "What about New Year's Eve? The beginning of a new year; the beginning of a new life."

Geren kneaded her brow. "I think it's perfect. Just like you."

They became entangled in another long, passionate kiss. Tempest reluctantly pulled away from him, heading toward the door in the rear of the kitchen leading to the basement.

"If we keep necking like this, we'll never get to see the rest of the house."

"The house is not going anywhere," Geren protested, following her down the steps. "Besides, we need to christen it properly."

Tempest pretended to ignore his attempt at seduction, even though it was a task. She'd been craving him also, but she wanted to look at the rest of the house. So many memories flooded back to her when she surveyed the basement apartment. Unlike the entry level, it hadn't changed at all, except for new fixtures in the bathroom. "I used to love this old basement. I would play down here for hours. I used to keep a rabbit in that back bedroom," she said, pointing in that direction. "My parents never knew I had him. His name was Floppy, and my grandparents were in collusion with me so I could keep him. My daddy was completely against pets. I never knew why."

"I was blown away with this place when I first had the realtor meet me here," Geren said, checking out the way the sunlight streaming in through the small basement windows was hitting

Tempest's thin dress so he could see the outline of her shapely thighs underneath it. "I told him we just had to have this house, no matter what. There were three other couples interested, so I had to move quickly. I hope you are pleased."

"Are you kidding?" Tempest asked him, a look of astonishment on her face. "I am so shocked. I never expected this, but it has made my decade. No scratch that. It has made my entire life. I can't wait to call my folks down in Florida and tell them this house is back in the family."

"Yes, and this time it's for good."

"Geren, what are we going to do with all this space?" Tempest was suddenly overwhelmed by the fact they would be occupying such a huge home.

"Fill it with happiness and a whole lot of sex."

Tempest giggled and winked at him. "Sounds like a master plan. I was just wondering if you wanted to rent out the basement to cover part of the mortgage?"

Geren looked like he'd been slapped silly. "Tempest, please! I am hardly a man of meager means."

Tempest moved tentatively toward him, noticing his expression had turned cynical. "I didn't mean it that way."

Geren's mood lightened once he glanced into her bedroom eyes up close. "I know you didn't, baby." He placed his arm around her shoulders and drew her close. "Besides, I already paid the asking price in cash."

"Cash!" Tempest exclaimed.

"Yes, that's how I got rid of the other three couples who wanted this place. They got tied up in credit checks for mortgage loans. We have no mortgage. I walked right in and snatched this place up. I just want you to know that I paid for this house, *our house,* with my own money. Not my daddy's. I worked hard for every penny of it."

Tempest was still tongue-tied. "I guess I still have to get used to your money. Old habits die hard. I'm so used to worrying about money matters."

"Well, those days are over." Geren kissed her on the forehead. "I'm full of surprises, and the best are yet to come."

"I bet," Tempest concluded, wondering what other startling discoveries lay in her future.

"I do have a suggestion about the basement."

"What's that, Geren?"

"The upper two floors are more than substantial for the two of us, and it would be a shame to let a perfectly good apartment go to waste."

Tempest was lost. "But you just said you didn't want to rent it out."

"I don't want to *rent* it," Geren clarified.

"Then what do you have in mind?"

"Janessa," Geren blurted out. "Janessa and the baby."

Tempest took two steps back from him so she could take a good look at his face. Was he for real? "You would let them live here?"

"In a heartbeat," Geren answered without hesitation. "I've seen where Janessa lives and the way her parents treat her. That's not a healthy environment for a child."

Tempest totally agreed with him. The fact that Janessa would have to raise her baby under such circumstances had caused Tempest numerous hours of lost sleep. "You don't think she'll get in our way?"

"You don't want her here?"

"Are you crazy? Of course I do." Tempest was really just trying to give him an easy out in case his offer had been an involuntary slip of the tongue. "I'm just trying to be considerate of your needs. You come first in my life; as a husband well should."

*"Husband!* I just love the way that word rolls off your sexy-ass lips." Geren reached around Tempest from behind and palmed both of her breasts, caressing her nipples. "To answer your question, no. I don't think Janessa or the baby will interfere with our lives. After all, the apartment does have a separate entrance."

"You are so wonderful," Tempest whispered, becoming short of breath. The nipple stimulation was making her weak in the knees. "I can't understand how you can be so compassionate and Dvontè is such a— He's such a—"

"Asshole? Imbecile?" Geren said, trying to help her out with a fitting word for him. He hadn't spoken to Dvontè in a couple of months and didn't intend to until Dvontè came to his senses and did the right thing by Janessa.

"All of the above," Tempest concurred.

Geren let go of one of Tempest's breasts and used his free hand to pull the material of her dress up so he could caress her thigh with his fingertips. "Well, if he won't take care of his responsibilities, then I will."

"So when can we move in?" Tempest inquired, trying not to lose herself in ecstasy as Geren darted the tip of his tongue in and out of her ear.

"How about tomorrow?" Geren's voice became raspy as he moved Tempest's panties aside and his fingers found what they'd been roaming for. Once he dipped them inside her wetness, he added, "Hell, we can move in tonight if you want. Just say the word."

"Tomorrow's great!" Tempest succumbed to his fingers, letting her pussy take on a life of its own and maneuver itself around on his inviting hand. "What about Janessa?"

"What about her?" Geren was ready to get all the conversation out of the way so he could make love to his woman in their new home. "Just call her up and ask if she would like a rent-free two-bedroom apartment and all the chocolate macadamia nut cookies she can handle. I plan to do some serious baking, but don't get any clever ideas. You will definitely have to take turns standing over the hot stove. I still expect Chez Tempest to be open twenty-four/seven, too."

They both giggled. "I think I can handle that," Tempest said, welcoming the challenge. "I can handle anything as long as I have you."

Geren moved Tempest toward the steps, never removing his hands from her breasts and from between her legs. "Let's go upstairs and check out the most important room in the house."

"Which room is that?" Tempest chided, already knowing the answer.

"Our bedroom," Geren answered, seductively nibbling the back of her neck.

"Great idea." Tempest startled Geren by pulling his hands off her. She sat down on the steps and pulled him to her, positioning herself so her head was at dick level. She started unzipping his jeans. "But first, I want to create a lasting memory right here on these steps. We might not have a chance to christen the basement once Janessa and the baby move in."

"Good point." Geren chuckled, looking down at her as she drew his dick into her mouth and started milking him. "Damn good point!"

# 29

## chillin' in the new crib

"How about this one?" Janessa asked, holding up a bridal magazine and pointing to a form-fitting red taffeta dress with white flowers on the sleeves and a split all the way up the side.

Tempest glanced at the picture with disdain and picked up another magazine off the sofa to finger through. "You're pulling my leg, right?"

"Dang, that's an ugly dress!" Kensington exclaimed, wondering more and more about Janessa's taste in fashions.

"Forget both of ya'll then," Janessa hissed, rolling her eyes at each of them in turn.

"Janessa, don't cop an attitude. I just want my wedding day to be special." Tempest reached over and teasingly rubbed Janessa on the top of her head. "I'm *definitely* only doing this once."

"True," Kensington quickly agreed. "Everything should be just the way Geren and Tempest want it."

"Tempest, you know I want you to have a perfect wedding, but I should have a little say-so about the bridesmaid dresses." Janessa turned the page and looked at the ones featured. They were much too conservative for her liking. "After all, I do have to wear one of those bad boys."

"Janessa, if you and I could manage to make it through Marquita's wedding in those hoochie dresses, you can make it through mine in *any* dress," Tempest said jokingly.

Kensington threw in her two cents. "I have to wear one, too, and I don't like that one, Janessa."

"Like I said, forget ya'll."

"Give me the book, Janessa." Tempest snatched the magazine out of her hands and turned back to the previous page to look at the dress more closely. "You couldn't get your balloon shape in this dress anyway. You're already showing. In two months, we'll be lucky if you can even waddle down the aisle."

"Whatever, trick!"

Tempest closed up the magazine and threw the entire pile on the floor of the living room. "We'll decide on a dress later. It's almost time for Raoul's game show."

"Oh, word?" Janessa squealed. "Let me go throw some popcorn in the microwave."

"Who is Raoul, and what kind of game show does he have?" Kensington asked, completely lost.

Tempest and Janessa gave each other high fives and shouted in unison, "You'll see!"

Kensington was taken aback. She'd never seen two people so excited about a television show. Then again, her mother would probably have a freakin' seizure if she ever missed a day of *All My Children*.

"Aiight, dang! It must be all that! Ya'll being all secretive and thangs." Kensington got up off the sofa and headed for the stairs. "Let me go check on Sydney before it starts."

"I'm off to get the popcorn," Janessa said, getting up off the sofa, which took a lot of energy. Tempest was right. She was really beginning to look like Shamu.

"Make some Kool-Aid while you're in there," Tempest suggested. "With no fake nails mixed in mine, please. You have to drink one hundred percent juice though, and don't even think about trying to guzzle down some Kool-Aid on the sly. The red tongue will give you away."

"Gurl, sometimes I think you're the one who is pregnant. The way you keep breaking bad with a sistah." Janessa immediately regretted the words the moment they left her lips, but it was too late to take them back.

Tempest glared at her angrily and then realized it was just an honest mistake. Janessa would never intentionally throw her sterility up in her face. They'd moved way beyond that. "I'm just playing with you about the nails, dufus. Stop being so sensitive."

Kensington stopped on the bottom step of the landing and leaned over the banister. "Tempest will probably get pregnant right after the wedding, maybe even on their honeymoon, and then all three of our kids can grow up together."

Janessa and Tempest just stared at each other, both at a loss for words.

"Wouldn't that be cool?" Kensington asked with glee. When she received no response, she added, "I'll be right back. How much time before the show starts?"

"About ten minutes," Janessa replied, still staring at Tempest.

"Okay." Kensington went on up the stairs to check on the baby, leaving Janessa and Tempest alone.

"You alright?" Janessa took Tempest's hand and intertwined their fingers.

"I'm fine." Tempest pulled her hand away, not wanting to be mothered.

"You've never told Kensington, huh?"

"Janessa, it's not exactly something I go around town announcing on a megaphone."

"I know, I know. I just assumed you would have told Kensington by now. You two have become so close."

Tempest walked over to the fireplace and leaned against the mantel. "Yes, we have, but Kensington is just a child. Wise beyond her years and being forced to face up to her mistakes, but still just a child."

Janessa looked at Tempest disapprovingly. "Don't you think you should tell her? She's expecting you to start pushing out babies any second now."

"I'll tell her eventually."

"I'm going in the kitchen." Janessa walked toward the hallway leading to the other side of the house. She glanced back and took one more quick survey of Tempest's facial expression. "You sure you're okay?"

"I'm straight." Once Janessa was out of view, Tempest picked up a photograph of herself and Geren they'd had professionally taken. She had so much to be thankful for. A great man, her dream home, a career that brought her focus and fulfillment, and loved ones who appreciated her efforts. Yes, there was much to be thankful for. "I'm straight," she repeated to herself in a whisper.

"How's the baby?" Tempest asked, startling Kensington in the upstairs guest bedroom.

"Sleeping peacefully." Kensington was leaning over the bassinet, covering up Sydney with a receiving blanket. "I was just looking at her."

Tempest came closer and looked over Kensington's shoulder at the baby. Even at four months, she had a head full of hair. "She's beautiful. Looks just like you."

"You really think so?"

"Without question." Tempest placed her hand on Kensington's right arm and noticed she was trembling slightly. It was obvious she was still learning to deal with the fact that she was a mother at the age of fifteen. "Watch, as she grows older, you'll swear you're looking in a mirror."

"I just hope I can do right by her." Kensington picked up the half-empty bottle of formula out of the bassinet so she could refrigerate it when she went back downstairs. "I'm so scared."

"Don't be," Tempest said, letting her hand slide down Kensington's arm so she could take ahold of her hand. "Geren, Janessa, and I are behind you one hundred percent. So is everyone down at the center."

"Too bad my mother's not," Kensington blurted out angrily.

Tempest could make out a few tears trickling down Kensington's left cheek, even in the dim lighting of the bedroom. "Still giving you a difficult time?"

"That's not even the word for it." She took her eyes off the baby and gazed at Tempest. There had been no more physical abuse. Tempest was sure of that. Apparently Pauline Sparks had taken their talk to heart but she still lashed out at Kensington with nasty comments from time to time. "She says she can't sleep because of Sydney's crying. I try to make her stop."

Tempest tightened her grip on Kensington's hand and rubbed the small of her back with her free hand.

"She says the baby's things take up too much space, and she can barely walk around the apartment. I can't help it if Sydney needs so much stuff."

"It's going to be okay, Kensington," Tempest said, attempting to sound comforting. "Everything will work itself out."

"What am I going to do?" Kensington let go of Tempest's hand and wiped her eyes with the sleeve of her long-sleeved T-shirt. "I can't keep up with my schoolwork. It's impossible. The baby stays up half the night, and I'm always falling asleep in class. Sometimes I wish—"

"Sometimes you wish what?"

"Sometimes I wish I'd explored other options."

"Like adoption?" Tempest asked, even though the answer was clear.

"Yes," Kensington responded sullenly. "Like adoption."

"We can still arrange that, if you like."

"Really? It's not too late?"

"It's never too late. You never have to feel trapped Kensington. You always have choices."

"But wouldn't that make me evil? Giving her up like that?"

"What you would be doing is ensuring Sydney had a stable home and secure future."

"But to hand her over to a couple of complete strangers like that? I'm not sure I could go through with it."

"All of the couples are thoroughly screened. Their backgrounds and homes are gone over with a fine-toothed comb."

"What if the fine-toothed comb misses a few hairs?"

Tempest didn't have a feasible answer, so she didn't attempt to give one.

"Seriously, Tempest," Kensington prodded. "What if they turn out to be maniacs or child beaters or drug addicts on the downlow?"

Tempest diverted her eyes down to Sydney, still sleeping soundly in the crib.

"Can you assure me that wouldn't happen? Huh? Can you?"

"No, I can't," Tempest finally responded. "There are never any guarantees in life, Kensington."

"Now, it would be different if it were you and Geren." Tempest was the one who started trembling then. She realized that Janessa was right. She would have to tell Kensington the horrible truth at some point. "I know you guys are going to be the perfect parents once you start having children. Heck, too bad you can't adopt me." Kensington chuckled.

That comment took Tempest off guard and left her speechless for a moment.

Kensington noticed that the baby was stirring a little in the bassinet. "Come on, let's go back out before we wake the baby."

"We'll discuss this further later on when we can sit down and have a real heart-to-heart," Tempest replied.

Kensington smiled at her. "As far as I'm concerned, every conversation we have is a heart-to-heart."

Tempest returned the smile. "I feel the same way."

"The show's coming on!" Janessa shouted up the stairwell. "Hurry up!"

"We're coming," Tempest said, as she and Kensington descended the stairs.

They sat back down on the sofa next to Janessa and took turns grabbing handfuls of popcorn. Tempest picked up one of the glasses of cherry Kool-Aid Janessa had on a bamboo serving tray and did a close inspection for loose nail fragments. Janessa glanced over at her and rolled her eyes, knowing Tempest was acting stupid as usual.

"What is this mess?" Kensington asked as Raoul suddenly appeared on the screen in a pair of red, white, and blue bikini briefs.

*"Raoul's Midget Gladiators,"* Janessa replied. "It's the bomb!"

"Say what?" Kensington couldn't believe her eyes or ears as dozens of midgets flashed across the television in the background while Raoul explained the activities for the evening: midget mud wrestling, midget wall climbing, and midget boxing.

"Hello, ladies, what's up?" Geren asked, walking in the front door and spotting the three of them propped up on the living room sofa.

"Shhhhhhh, baby!" Tempest yelled out excitedly. *"Raoul's Midget Gladiators* just came on."

"Great, I'm just in time!" Geren threw his coat on the banister and rushed over to grab a seat in his recliner. Raoul's show was his favorite. In fact, he and Raoul had become good friends. Geren was even advising him on his investment portfolio. "Janessa, can you pass the popcorn, please?"

# 30

## beginnings

"Janessa, I need to see Geren. Go get him for me," Tempest demanded.

Janessa straightened Tempest's ivory veil. She was almost in tears; she'd never seen Tempest look so stunning. "You'll see him in a few minutes when you walk down that aisle. You look so beautiful. Makes me want to start boo-hooing."

Tempest took Janessa's hand, intertwining their fingers. "You better not start crying, because then I'll start, and there'll be mascara everywhere."

Janessa started giggling. "Well, we wouldn't want that."

Tempest looked Janessa square in the eyes. "I really need to talk to Geren *before* the wedding."

"Tempest, are you crazy?" Janessa protested. "It's bad luck for him to see you in that dress."

Tempest sat down on the vanity stool in the choir makeshift

dressing room. "I'm not leaving this room until I talk to him."

Janessa had an eerie feeling overcome her. "Uh-oh, you're not getting cold feet are you?"

"No, of course not," Tempest cackled. "I just need to ask him something important."

"Whew, you scared me for a second!" Janessa exhaled the breath she'd been holding in. "I couldn't picture you having second thoughts about marrying Mr. Wonderful."

Tempest blushed. "He is wonderful, isn't he?"

"I don't even need to tell you. He's your man, not mine."

"I would never have second thoughts about Geren. I love him with all of my heart."

"Then ask him the question *after* the ceremony," Janessa suggested.

Tempest stood up and grabbed Janessa by the arm. "No, get him for me, please," she whined. "I'll hide behind something so he won't see my dress, but I need to see him. I need to be able to look into his eyes."

"How come?"

"So I'll know he's being honest about his answer."

"His answer to what?"

Tempest yanked on Janessa's arm, pressuring her toward the door. "I'll explain it to you later. Just hurry up and go get him. I don't want to keep everyone waiting for a long time."

Janessa wanted to refuse, but she knew how stubborn Tempest could be, so she caved in. "This is one of the most convoluting stunts you've ever pulled, but I'll go get him if it will get you down the aisle."

Tempest gave Janessa a huge hug. "Thanks, sis!"

A couple of minutes expired before there was a knock at the slightly ajar door. "Tempest, are you in here?" Geren asked, inching his way into the room.

"Yes, hey, baby," Tempest answered. She was strategically positioned in a closet reserved for choir robes. She could see him, but he couldn't see her.

"Why are you in the closet?" he inquired after targeting where her voice was coming from.

"Because you can't see my dress!"

Geren shook his head. He'd tried not to panic when Janessa came speed-walking into the sanctuary to get him. Everyone asked him what the problem was as he made his way up the aisle. People always tend to assume the worst. He was hoping they were wrong. "What's this all about, sweetheart? Janessa said you wanted to ask me something."

"I do."

Geren flashed his cinematic smile, and Tempest almost melted into the wood of the closet interior. She was so in love with him. "I'm glad to hear you speak those two simple words, but you're speaking them in the wrong place. Let's get hitched so we can start the honeymoon. I bought some new body oil at the Pleasure Palace I want to rub all over your body."

Tempest wanted to dash out of the closet and tongue-whip his mouth, but she had to keep to the task at hand. "Geren, I need you to do something for me. Something for us."

"I'd do anything for you," he said, idly playing with the wedding band in his pocket. He let the ring bearer carry a costume one. The real ring was on his person and he couldn't wait to place it on her finger. "Just name your request."

Tempest decided the best way to say it was to blurt it out before she lost her nerve. "I know we decided we would spend the first couple years of our marriage making love morning, noon, and night and traveling the world but—"

"But what?" he asked, sensing hesitancy in her voice.

"I know we agreed to adopt a baby in about three years, but—"

"Just come on out with it, sweetheart! Nothing's going to change my love for you." Tempest had to search for her next breath. "Tempest? You there?"

"I want to adopt Kensington's baby! I want to make Sydney ours!"

Geren had to take a step back and lean against the door. "Say what?"

Tempest could see the shock on his face. "Please don't be angry with me. I'll understand if you say no." She waited for him to comment, but he didn't. He just looked dazed and confused. "I'm marrying you regardless, but I wanted to ask you before the wedding, so you wouldn't think I purposely waited until after the ink dried on the wedding certificate to throw this on you."

Geren held his forehead and messed with his black bow tie, like it was strangling him. "I'm not upset in the least, but what about Kensington? Have you even discussed this idea with her?"

"In a roundabout sort of way," Tempest answered. "I think she'll be happy with the arrangement. She's so young, and she really wants a chance to get a high school education. She hasn't even really begun to live. I know how trapped she feels. I was there, remember? This is the perfect solution."

Geren took a few steps toward the closet. He felt they really needed to discuss the matter face to face, but he reluctantly retreated. "It's not that I exactly have a problem with your suggestion, but I was just hoping things wouldn't get so complicated. In a regular adoption, the natural parents wouldn't be involved with us in any manner. You and Kensington are so close. Does that mean she'll still be coming over for dinner and staying over at the crib some weekends?"

"I haven't thought all of that through yet," Tempest admitted.

"What if she gets attached to Sydney and wants her back? Where does that leave us?"

Tempest and Geren stared at Janessa, confused by her behavior. There she stood glassy-eyed, holding the remains of a gold balloon in one hand and her flute of apple juice in the other.

"It burst!" Janessa screamed over the music.

Tempest looked down at the balloon, wondering if Janessa had lost her mind. "So what? We'll get you another one."

Janessa frowned and threw her apple juice all over the front of Tempest's dress. "Not the balloon, dufus! My water broke, dammit!"

Realization dawned on both Geren and Tempest after they spotted the puddle of clear liquid surrounding Janessa's feet.

"Oh, shit!" Geren shouted at the top of his lungs. The music halted while people speculated about whether or not the marital problems had started before the reception even jumped off good.

"Get the limo!" Tempest exclaimed, pushing people out of the way to make a clear path to the door. "We're having a baby!"

Geren picked up Janessa and carried her out to the car. His father carried Mrs. Porter, who had fainted at the news.

The limousine with "Just Married" on the trunk pulled off from the hotel entrance with a screech, headed to the hospital so Tempest could do her Lamaze coaching in her wedding dress.

# 31

## startin' over

### eight months later

"Janessa, are you completely sure about this?" Tempest asked, seemingly more nervous and agitated by the current situation than anyone else. She was pacing the floor in Janessa's basement apartment and biting her nails. "If you have any doubts whatsoever, you shouldn't go through with it."

Janessa struggled to get Brendan's suede boot onto his left foot. He was sitting up on the couch, smiling and cooing, obviously amused with the hard time she was having. He looked so much like his father that it was downright scary sometimes.

"I'm not *positive* this is the right move, Tempest," Janessa replied in a near whisper, not even glancing in Tempest's direction. "But like you've told me buku times, there can be no progress without discussion."

"Hmph, true," Tempest reluctantly admitted. She was still hoping Janessa would change her mind at the last minute, so she could have the honor of telling Dvontè to fuck off before slamming the door in his face.

"Don't get me wrong. I was just as shocked as you, more even, when Dvontè called here out of the blue."

Tempest stopped pacing, abandoned the idea of gnawing her nails, and opted to place her hands on her hips instead. "What do you think he wants?"

"How should I know? Do I look like a psychic?" Janessa asked with a tinge of sarcasm in her voice.

"No, actually you look like a fool," Tempest snapped back at her. Ever since Dvontè had called a few days before, Tempest had desperately tried to keep her composure, but enough was enough. "How in the world could you even agree to see him, even for five seconds? Where was he during the pregnancy? Where has he been for the past eight months since Brendan was born?"

Janessa sucked in air to prevent herself from going off on Tempest. "Look, Tempest, I really don't need this crap from you today. Aiight? I'm stressed enough as it is."

"Whatever. It's your life."

Tempest walked over to the playpen and wiped formula off Sydney's mouth with a bib. She was so elated that Kensington had allowed Geren and her to adopt the baby girl. Tempest had her already lengthy hair in small cornrows and had requested the doctor pierce Sydney's ears during her last immunization appointment. Tempest loved the way the diamond studs brought out the hazel in the baby's eyes.

"Dvontè *claims* he just wants to see Brendan and talk. What harm can come from that?"

"None, I suppose," Tempest replied sullenly. If you can't beat them, join them, so she decided to get with the program. It appeared Janessa was hell-bent on seeing him. "You sure you don't mind Sydney tagging along with you guys?"

Janessa had succeeded with the shoe task and had moved on to stuffing Brendan's short arms into a fleece Dallas Cowboys jacket. "Not at all. The more the merrier. At least he can't try to get in my pants with two babies in tow."

Tempest swung around and glared at Janessa like she had lost her damn mind. "Are you saying you would mess around with him again?"

"I'm not saying anything of the sort!" Janessa stated angrily, raising her voice a notch. "I just mean that he won't *try* anything with them around."

"I wouldn't be so sure about all of that." Tempest hoped Janessa wouldn't hop back in the sack with Dvontè at the drop of a dime. She took Sydney out of the playpen, walked across the room, and sat her down beside Brendan on the couch. The two babies immediately started giggling and smiling at each other. "We are talking about Dvontè, after all."

Janessa really didn't want to get into a full-blown altercation with Tempest. She was tense enough, so she decided to change the subject. "The kids sure love playing together."

"Aren't they the cutest things?" Tempest asked, grinning from ear to ear herself at the scene. "Oh, by the way, Kensington said to tell you hello. She called yesterday."

Janessa left the babies with Tempest and went into her bedroom to get a pair of athletic shoes to slip on. She shouted back out into the living room. "How does she like the boarding school in Connecticut?"

"Well, needless to say, it's quite an adjustment for her," Tempest replied. Geren and Tempest had convinced Pauline to let Kensington attend boarding school. Pauline eagerly agreed as long as Tempest and Geren were footing all of the bills. It gave

Kensington a chance to flourish academically and gave Pauline a chance to finally grow up herself. "She said that there are less than ten African-American girls in the entire school."

"Really? That's wild!"

"Yes, it is, and of course she misses *boys*. Hopefully, going to an all-female school will help her to concentrate on her studies and not get into any more sticky situations."

"Oh, I'm sure Kensington has learned her lesson," Janessa said, prancing back into the room. Tempest couldn't help but notice that Janessa had put on some eyeliner and lipstick while she was back in the bedroom, but she decided not to take issue with it. "I know I have. No more babies for me until I'm married and have a successful career."

"You go, girl, with your making-straight-A's-in-college self!" Tempest exclaimed, getting up from the couch to give Janessa a high five. Janessa had started Howard a couple of months before and was acing everything, just like Tempest knew she would. "All in all, I think Kensington will be happy there. She seems to like her roommate a lot. She's from Boston."

"That's cool. What's even cooler is the way you and Geren keep looking out for Kensington, and me, for that matter. We both owe our lives to you."

Tempest could feel her eyes filling up with tears. She dabbed at them, praying a full stream wouldn't start. "Aw, hell, don't make me cry up in here."

Janessa snickered at her. "You know you're my shero."

Tempest gave Janessa a bear hug and whispered in her ear, "I love you, Janessa. You're the best friend anyone could ever ask for."

"Love you, too," Janessa whispered back in Tempest's ear.

Tempest broke away from the hug and went to scoop Sydney up off the couch. "Let's get the kids upstairs. Where are you going anyway?"

"Probably to the zoo and to grab a bite to eat."

"The zoo?" Tempest started heading up the steps while Janessa picked Brendan up and followed her. "In that case, we better bundle the kids up better. It's kind of chilly outside."

"Okay," Janessa agreed, grabbing a baseball cap and glove set off a coat tree before going upstairs.

Geren was waiting for them at the top of the stairs. "Did you change her mind?" he asked Tempest while Janessa was still out of earshot.

Tempest shook her head. "She's going through with it."

Geren sighed in dismay. "That's too bad. I just hope Dvontè has changed."

Tempest smacked her lips. "You and me both hope so."

No sooner had Janessa made it to the top of the stairs with Brendan than the doorbell rang. The three adults just stared at each other, wondering who was going to answer.

"I'll be in my study," Geren said, stomping off down the hall and taking himself out of the equation. He had no interest in even laying eyes on Dvontè. Maybe in time they could become friends again, if Dvontè was planning on acting responsibly, but today was not the day for a reunion.

Tempest rolled her eyes at Janessa. "Well, don't look at me. Give me Brendan, and I'll take the babies in the living room."

Janessa handed Brendan over to Tempest and then turned toward the door. She was so nervous at that point, her teeth were chattering. "Hello, Dvontè," she blurted out, overwhelmed by both positive and negative memories of him the second she opened the door.

"Hey, Janessa." Dvontè was equally apprehensive. He couldn't help but grin when he noticed how much her appearance had changed. She had her hair pinned up in a bun and was wearing a pair of glasses that made her look sophisticated—a far cry from the hoochie he used to kick it with back in the day. "You look different."

"Is that good or bad?" Janessa asked brazenly.

"It's definitely a good thing!" Dvontè exclaimed. He was startled when Tempest suddenly appeared behind her, looking him up and down. He knew he was hardly her favorite person. "Hello, Tempest!"

"Hey," Tempest said nastily. "Janessa, you need me to do anything else? If not, I'm going to go in the kitchen and start on the dishes."

"No, I'm fine," Janessa replied.

Tempest wasted no time hauling ass in the other direction. She wasn't quite ready to deal with Dvontè either.

Dvontè followed Janessa into the living room and almost succumbed to tears when he noticed the babies sitting on the couch. The little boy in the baseball cap looked just like him. It was almost as if he had spit him out. He instantly knew there was no denying the child was his.

He went over and picked Brendan up off the couch, "Can I hold him?" he inquired, having already gathered him up into his arms.

"Sure, you can carry him to the car," Janessa replied, picking Sydney up. "We better get a move on if we want to visit the monkey and reptile houses. They close the animal buildings earlier than the rest of the zoo."

"Great! Let's hit the road then!" Dvontè exclaimed, beginning to feel a little like a parent after about thirty seconds. He was excited about spending time with his child. He was also hoping to talk Janessa into giving him another chance. Much to his own surprise, he was ready to become a committed and responsible man. "Maybe after we leave the zoo, we can take a ride out to Virginia."

"Sounds like a winner," Janessa replied, prodding him toward the door. She was trying to get him out of the house before Geren became overwhelmed by the mere thought of him being there and confronted him.

Tempest watched from the kitchen window as Janessa and Dvontè strapped the infant seats into his car and put the double stroller in the trunk. She couldn't help but notice the huge grin on Janessa's face as they pulled off down the street. Maybe there was a chance for things to work out for Janessa and Dvontè after all. "Stranger things have happened," Tempest whispered to herself, picking up another breakfast plate to wash.

Geren walked back into the kitchen and sat down at the glass-topped table. He picked up the newspaper and pretended to be reading, but his eyes were really glued to Tempest's ass. The way it swayed back and forth while she scrubbed the pots and pans gave him an instant hard-on.

"I think it's great that Dvontè is showing some interest in the baby," Tempest said with a grin. She couldn't help but carry an ounce of hope that Janessa and Dvontè would work things out. "You know, everyone might end up having a happy ending after all."

"I wouldn't read too much into it if I were you, darling," Geren replied. "Dvontè still has a whole lot of growing up to do."

Tempest turned the faucet off and swung around to face him. "Why are you always so hard on Dvontè? It took a lot of ego swallowing for him to even show up here. At least he's trying."

Geren wanted to debate the topic but decided he would rather make better use of their time alone together. He wondered if this was the same Tempest that had talked trash about Dvontè the night before, calling him every foul name in the book while he was trying to get some sleep.

Tempest started drying the dishes and putting them away. Geren neatly folded the paper and went over to help. He took the

3
333333

3

towel away from her and dried the dishes as she handed them to him.

"You notice anything strange?" he asked, licking his lips.

"Strange like what?"

"We're alone."

"So it seems." Tempest giggled, beginning to read his mind. "You aren't afraid I might take advantage of you, are you?"

"Afraid? Hell, naw!" They both chuckled. "In fact, I'm praying like all hell you will molest my ass something terrible."

Tempest put the salad bowl she was holding back into the dish drainer. "Is that right?" she asked, caressing Geren's dick with her right hand.

He threw the towel down on the counter. "That's right!" He palmed one of her breasts and then suckled on her bottom lip. "We never officially christened this house. Just our bedroom and the basement steps. Don't you think it's about time we took care of the rest of the house?"

"What do you have in mind?" Tempest stuck her tongue into his left ear and then nibbled on his earlobe.

"I say we get busy in every room. Make some freaky memories to reminisce about in our old age. So that when we're sitting on the front porch with the grandkids on our laps, we can look at each other and play them back in our minds."

Tempest laughed. "Why, Mr. Kincaid, I love that idea!"

"Why, Mrs. Kincaid, what hard nipples you have!" Geren proclaimed, unbuttoning the front of her cotton oxford shirt and letting it fall down off her shoulders so he could get a frontal view of her breasts.

She started to unbuckle his khaki trousers. "So what room do you want to get freaky in first?"

"I vote for the family room. I can think of a few kinky things I want to do to you with the Ping-Pong paddles."

"Oh, my!" Tempest exclaimed. "Sounds promising!"

"It is," Geren assured her, taking one of her areolas into his mouth. "Very promising!"

"In that case," Tempest said, pulling away and running through the kitchen to the family room in the rear of the house. "Last one on the Ping-Pong table is a rotten egg!"